Divided Together 2084

by

Bruce Leiter

W & B Publishers
USA

W & B Publishers

For information:
W & B Publishers
9001 Ridge Hill Street
Kernersville, NC 27284

www.a-argusbooks.com

ISBN:9781635540482

:

This is a work of *fiction.* All of the characters, organizations and events portrayed in this novel are either products of the author's imagination or used fictitiously

Book Cover designed by Dubya

Printed in the United States of America

Also by the author:

Doubtbusters! God Is My Shrink! (a postmodern *Mere Christianity*)

Be Bolder Growin' Older (a devotional Bible study)

Pray and Play: Dealing With a Fun-Loving Culture
(a devotional Bible study)

Chapter One

New starts

Great Peninsula Nation's capital city, New Tehran, August, A.D. 2084

A petite female jogger dressed in a short-sleeved shirt and short jogging pants took off her white scarf and sighed. She blinked as dust from the edge of the school parking lot got in her eyes. She hoped that she and her athletic clothes were out of the C-POV's vast view.

Despite the sultry heat of the late-summer evening and her familiarity with the palm-lined path ahead of her, she shivered as she paused. Since darkness hid a tall figure on the path's edge, she wasn't aware of the reason she had shuddered.

Her mind condemned the cultural norms that kept her from jogging in the daylight, the way reasonable people did in the States. She was also irritated at the daytime heat that prevented her from doing her favorite activity while the hot sun shone.

The woman's run was at the New Tehran city limits on a moonless evening with a hint of the sunset's afterglow still in the sky. That well-trodden walkway was between a subdivision and a school in a palm grove on the edge of the capital city.

The black-clad apparition felt a surge of predator adrenaline, emerged from the shadows, and asked, "Ma'am, could you help me with my backpack? Its strap broke." She hesitated because of the recent news about abducted women. However, since the dim light from the school parking lot revealed a seemingly-genuine smile, she bent over to inspect his broken backpack. Then, her body crumpled to the dust.

Filled with excitement, he lugged her toward the elementary school parking lot thirty meters away, where he had parked his old fusion Ford. Gratified with his catch, the evil fisherman took his prize fish on gravel roads to his dungeon destination.

* * *

One evening Farhan ate his evening meal of steak, potatoes, and vegetables in front of his almost-extinct, fusion, 4-D TV. He ate alone in his third-floor, one-bedroom apartment cluttered with moving boxes and newspapers. During dinner, he watched English-Muslim versions of *Wheel of Allah's Rule* and *Jeopardy*.

Then, he read in the *New Tehran Times* on his eyeglass computer, "The Committee for the Prevention of Vice and the Promotion of Virtue (C-POV) last evening arrested a male mascot dressed like a puppet-female for the downtown Alevi-Muslim celebration. The charge was 'not wearing a veil or a scarf.'"

Then, he almost jumped out of his recliner when he read an article about a female Muslim. Her veiled likeness accompanied a feature article about her recommitment to Islam in her teens. The reporter quoted her as saying, "Our family emigrated from Turkey to the Great Peninsula Nation when I was sixteen years old. When I was a nineteen-year-old GPNU student, I compared Christian and Muslim beliefs. I felt that Islam completed Christian ideas. However, I decided to become a Sunni Muslim, even though my family was Alevi Muslim and my best university friend was a Christian."

Farhan felt a surge of eager interest when he discovered that the woman in the article, Akilah Jamal, was also a criminology professor at GPNU. *It's amazing that I read about a college colleague in the newspaper this soon after moving here.*

He then composed a World-Web-mail holo-letter to the editor answering Akilah's claims about Christian and Muslim beliefs. He also looked up her number in the university directory online and called her, "Hello, Dr. Jamal. This is Farhan Issah, your new colleague in the criminology department. I saw the newspaper article about you and would like to get together with you for lunch tomorrow. Are you available?"

Akilah sat up straight and thought, *This guy seems to be really aggressive. Since he is a colleague, I'll play along to see where his call leads.* As a result, a chuckle came from Akilah as she said, "Well, I'm a widow and would be willing to meet with you. However, won't your wife object?"

Farhan said with a slight smirk, "I'm a widower. As a result, I'm positive she won't care. After all, we wouldn't be on a date, since we would be two university professors getting together for lunch in a large city. We're not very likely to be victims of gossip here. Besides, I only want to ask you about the newspaper article, your teaching career, and your interests."

Akilah relaxed her tense muscles.

* * *

Later that evening, when Farhan was about to go to bed, muffled hallway sounds diverted his attention. When he looked out of his door, he caught a fleeting glimpse of his next-door neighbor clattering down the staircase under the 3-D laser exit sign.

* * *

She awoke with a start in a dark, concrete-block room; felt shear, paralyzing panic surge through her whole body; and wriggled in vain against her captor's duct-tape. However, she managed to say with a quivering, muffled voice at the dim outline of a man, "Why did you kidnap me?"

In the darkness, the perpetrator with a bandana-covered face felt his own adrenaline increase, jumped high, clicked his heels, chuckled a fiendish sound, pranced around her, and mouthed his silent, "You're mine!" He relished his predatory prize like a hump-less camel sizing up its first victory over a young alligator in the Everwaters. His elation increased astronomically when the women were awake to react with horror to his advances.

In response, the brown, black-eyed beauty jerked her limbs against the abundant bonds without success. Then, she fainted.

* * *

Akilah—a woman wearing a gray veil and matching ankle-length dress buttoned up to her neck—entered the northwest New Tehran bistro, squinted because of the comparatively-dark restaurant, and spied Farhan.

As he saw her, he gathered up his courage because this meeting was his first one-on-one time with a woman since his wife died. He then finger-waved to her from a booth in the back.

Tall, handsome Farhan, dressed in a light-blue business suit, stood as Akilah approached. After they settled opposite each other, he began with a hint of a smile, "May I call you by your first name?"

She avoided eye-contact, hesitated, but then said with raised eyebrows, "Yes, you may."

"I saw the *Times* article and had some questions, Akilah. I'm curious. Why did your family move from Turkey to the GPN?"

A tall, purple-scarfed-and-robed waitress interrupted the barely-begun conversation for their orders.

Akilah felt at ease with Farhan because of his pleasant smile. "May I call you 'Farhan'?" She still stared at the table but proceeded hesitantly with his nod, "My family was made up of Turkish Alevi Muslims. My grandparents moved from Illkhitchi in Anatolia to Istanbul early in this century, because my grandfather could not find work in his hometown.

"However, my parents' four friends died in a 2056 Istanbul massacre of thirty-three Alevis, when Turkish Sunnis, fresh from Friday mosque-prayers, burned down the

Madimak Hotel. Those Alevis were in town to celebrate a festival, but a small minority of Muslims murdered them, instead. Allah (all praise to him) will judge those Sunnis.

"Then, after some Sunnis' drive-by shooting of several Alevis in 2061 and because my parents feared for our family's safety, they decided to immigrate to the GPN that same year, when I was sixteen."

She stole a furtive glance at the man across from her and asked, "Why are you smiling, Farhan?"

"You sound like a professor. Your family history interests me. How did you learn to speak such good English? You must have spoken Turkish before you came here."

Akilah suddenly relaxed and leaned against the booth's firm back support, still studying the table's texture. She felt that Farhan was asking a lot of questions but that it was somehow okay. He seemed sincere. "Yes, I did in our family. However, I had an excellent teacher originally from England during my fourth and fifth years in school, who expected us to speak and write English rather than Turkish during class. Then, when I attended university here, I easily picked up more English from my fellow students, especially during my time with my Christian friend at GPNU."

Farhan's usual curiosity surged as he warmed up like a hot New Tehran afternoon to this female professor, "I've also noticed that people use only English here without Arabic words, except for Muslim names. Why do they speak only English?"

Since Akilah realized that Farhan was a friendly, curious man interested in life, she said, "I guess that the States' culture has influenced us with their melting pot that teaches us we need to be English speakers and writers in order to communicate with them."

Farhan's back leaned against the firm support of the booth as he grinned more broadly. "What do you do in your spare time?"

Akilah's remaining reserve melted away as she leaned toward this square-chinned man, "I enjoy solving word puzzles on TV's *Wheel of Allah's Rule*, answering Muslim and American trivia on *Jeopardy*, reading murder mysteries and nonfiction books, watching TV crime dramas, fixing jigsaw puzzles, playing scrabble online, and being a criminology consultant for the New Tehran police."

Farhan's jaw dropped and his eyes widened, "That's amazing! I also enjoy playing along with those TV shows, reading mysteries, watching TV crime dramas, and fixing puzzles. However, I also enjoy sports. May I ask how you became a professor of both criminology and Islamic studies?"

Akilah felt completely at ease with Farhan, as she finally made full eye contact with him and answered with a slight smile, "As you read in the *Times* article, I consciously decided to become a Sunni Muslim in my teens. In addition, I was fascinated with TV crime dramas. The natural result was my double major in both areas at GPNU, resulting in my dual doctor of philosophy degree. Then, after I graduated six years ago, GPNU broke through a barrier of sorts by hiring me to teach both subjects."

Farhan asked her, "May I ask why you changed to be a Sunni rather than remaining an Alevi Muslim like your family? By the way, what is an Alevi Muslim?"

"Well, Sunnis follow the traditions in the centuries following Muhammad that Muslims should pray together five times a day, go on a Hajj trip back to Mecca once a lifetime, and follow the Ramadan month of fasting. The Alevis don't follow any of those traditions but believe that their religion is much more a matter of an inner life of devotion to Allah. As a result, Alevi women are modestly dressed but without head coverings.

"By changing to be a Sunni, I combined the inner and outer aspects of both Muslim sects. That is the reason I was able to meet you alone at all, Farhan. My Alevi past has enabled me to treat men as equals, since Alevis believe in full respect among all people." A tiny grin crept across Akilah's face.

Akilah's curiosity then kicked into high glide, "What about you? What is it like to be a Christian leaving your homeland and living in a predominantly-Muslim land?"

Farhan felt some discomfort like a waterless duck about sharing his decade-long experience. However, he decided to answer Akilah because of her openness and seemingly-genuine interest, "I found it hard leaving my family and friends in our small Indiana town after going to a nearby college and then moving out of the country. After Trish died, however, I needed a change of pace. I'm thankful for the W-W-Web to keep in touch with my family and friends back home."

Akilah decided to take a big chance and ask a personal question because of Farhan's curiosity about her life. Thus, she asked in a muted tone, "How did you become a widower, Farhan?"

Chapter Two

Two past losses and a new challenge

For a moment, Akilah regretted asking Farhan such a personal inquiry, since his eyes narrowed and a tear crept down his face. However, she waited a few silent moments. Then she mustered up her courage, because of his questions, to say with her voice barely above a whisper, "Farhan, I asked you how you became a widower."

He re-focused on Akilah as his eyes opened wide, "My wife, Trish, whom I met in high school and married after our graduation from our undergraduate years, came down with an aggressive breast cancer shortly after we entered graduate school. She died four years later, just as we were both supposed to graduate with our Ph.D. degrees. I've had to make major adjustments, especially cooking for myself. May I ask how you became a widow, Akilah?"

Akilah sighed with the fearful memory, "My husband, whom I met at GPNU, died three years ago in a hover-cycle accident when a camel-hauling hover-truck hit him after running a red laser-light here in New Tehran."

"A huge shock!"

Akilah and Farhan sat for a while in sympathetic silence as tears crept down their faces.

* * *

Wiping a tear away, Farhan sliced the silence like meat with a laser knife, "Akilah, the *Times* article said you believe that Islam's ideas 'complete Christian beliefs.' Sometimes I'm just too curious, a fault of mine. May I ask what you meant by that comment, if you made it?"

Because Akilah felt temporary relief from her emotional burden because of their similar experiences, she said, "Yes, when I was a teenager, I felt that Muslim beliefs were built on Christian beliefs but went a few steps further than Christianity did."

Farhan felt a touch of fear but mustered up his courage as he said, "I see. Don't be shocked if my holo-letter to the *Times* editor appears there answering your ideas."

He then sought to ease her possible negative reaction to his disagreement with her ideas by saying, "As far as I'm concerned, you can believe anything you want to. I will never try to change your or anyone else's opinions.

"Since I was raised a Christian, I accept the basic belief system of Jesus' followers. Based on my many discussions with Muslims at college, my understanding is that they and Christians worship and serve different Gods."

Akilah felt her ultra-holo-watch twitch for a number of seconds, realized that she had an impending appointment, leaned forward, and pursed her lips as she responded just above a whisper, "I find your thoughts stimulating and worth discussing, but a surprising thought just popped into my mind. The police and I have a very difficult case about the disappearances of at least five women. A report about a sixth one came in this morning. This idea is very sudden, Farhan, but would you be willing to go along with me this afternoon to be part of the investigation in an advisory capacity?"

Farhan's heart leaped as he leaned forward with eager, rapid words, "I read about that case in the paper. I would feel greatly honored, Akilah. It sounds like a challenge. I'm always interested in solving mysteries and seeking justice."

Outside on the sidewalk, Akilah used her ultra-holo-watch to set up a brief interview of both of them with the police detective in charge. Their two images appeared on the First Police Detective's holo-watch at the police station, while his image appeared above Akilah's watch. After she introduced them, he asked Farhan, "So you're the new assistant criminology professor at GPNU?"

"Yes, I got my doctor of philosophy degree in criminology at Purdue University in the States. After my wife died from cancer that same year, I needed a fresh start."

"That's a very good research university. My sympathy for your loss. Welcome aboard as part of our team, Dr. Issah."

Then, Farhan and she rode to the police station in his old, fusion-fueled zip-mobile. The rest of the life-protection task force (LPTF) floated to the New Tehran police station as their vehicles sliced through the August 2084 heat and humidity.

First Detective Fahyim Srour convened the meeting with his head held high, "We have a new member of our team! Issah, please introduce yourself."

Farhan said, "I am Dr. Farhan Issah, a new, full-time GPNU assistant criminology professor. Dr. Jamal asked me to help with your investigation of women's disappearances."

Two-meter-tall Fahyim Srour thought, *I'd better keep an eye on this stranger*, but said, "We can use all of the minds we can get to catch our slippery perp. Gentlemen and lady, we officially now have six disappearances of women and eight of us to solve them. Now that we have a pattern of abductions, our first order of action is to investigate the apparent crime scenes, talk to their families and friends, and seek any possible witnesses. It appears that this perp likes to abduct women in deserted public places after sunset. We've announced the danger to the New Tehran public and requested their assistance. Any questions?"

He peered around the life-protection task force circle. To his right was tall, lean Second Detective Abasi Huda. To Huda's right was heavy-set, short Third Detective Basim Daher. The next one was bearded Fourth Detective Fayiz Maloof. Friendly First Policeman Ziya Touma and frowning Second Policeman Mamduh Ghanem were next in order. Next was Akilah Jamal, the only Muslim woman ever hired to help the police force solve crimes. Finally, newbie Farhan Issah sat on Srour's left hand.

Rigid, erect First Detective Srour, who felt at ease as their leader, gave orders to his life-protection task force in rapid-fire succession as he looked from left to right. "Jamal and Issah, ask around GPNU for people who knew the two missing women students and try to discover any relevant information. Touma and Ghanem, canvas in the neighborhoods of the last places to which the victims probably went for any witnesses. Maloof and Daher, interview the families of the victims. Huda and I will remain here and try to piece together the victims' lives to find out what they might have in common. Let's get to it, gentlemen and lady."

They felt great urgency because the safety of at least six women was at stake. As a result, they scurried out of the squad room with clenched fists like boxers in the old days leaving their corners to slug each other.

Chapter Three

Fellow university professors

Akilah and Farhan removed their sandals and knocked on the door of a missing Great Peninsula Nation University woman's dorm room Sunday afternoon. Her roommate answered the door and ushered them in. While the scarfed, squat student sat on her single bed with her navy-blue robe covering her crossed legs and bare feet in a well-kept dorm room, Akilah asked her, "How well did you know the missing student?"

While she avoided eye-contact in agreement with GPN-Sunni custom, she said in a barely-audible voice, "We've been roommates for two years. I know her quite well."

Feeling encouraged by the student's response, Akilah said, "Did you ever hear her talk about leaving the university?"

The young woman warmed up with a stronger voice, since she enjoyed talking about her friend and roommate, "Never. She's happy as a GPNU student. It's a total mystery to me why she vanished a month ago."

Encouraged by the auspicious beginning to their interview, Farhan asked, "What do you know about her last day here?"

As her eyes studied the worn parquet floor, she spit out her words with a tight face, "She went to her classes as usual and then told me that she wanted to shop in the mall for a new purse.... That conversation was our last one. We women students are scared stiff that a madman may grab any one of us!"

Frowning Akilah shuddered and said, "I share your fear. It's a very scary time for New Tehran women. Thank you for your time. Here's my card. Call me if you think of anything else."

* * *

Akilah Jamal made eye contact with her thirty-three robed students and began her first Saturday class of the new semester in late August. As students moved their eyeballs swiftly on virtual keyboards with their eyeglass computers, she began, "This Islamic Studies 101 course will deal with Muslim beliefs and practices. First, it will trace the roots of Islam's presence in the New World.

"Revisionist historians in the United States and Europe endorse the fanciful fiction that Christians won several battles in Europe from A.D. 700 to 1492. However, their selective memories and sources are biased and wrong."

Akilah paused to let her point sink in and then continued, "For example, during the Battle of Tours in the present-day country of France, Umayadd Muslims, originally from Syria as part of the Ottoman Empire, the fifth largest empire in the history of the world, attacked Tours. The Christian Franks under Charles Martel in October, A.D. 732, defended it. The Umayadd cavalry challenged his well-experienced infantry, an obstacle between them and the town of Tours. Charles Martel arrayed his troops in a large square of battle-tested soldiers as an inner circle protected their general. They hid in cowardly fashion among the trees on high ground. Charles Martel's troops achieved a temporary victory by attacking and killing a number of Muslims, including the Muslim general.

"Then, when the Christian army approached the Muslims' tents to retrieve the spoils of war, accurate Muslim scholars tell us that cavalry soldiers, hiding in the nearby woods, ambushed and overwhelmed the Christians. Then, they won the cities of Tours and Portier. They eventually conquered the rest of that country, known today as France.

"The revisionists would have you believe that Charles Martel won the Battle of Tours, but their claim is less than a half-truth.

"The Shi'ite descendants of the Umayyads established the Great River Nation to our north and west in the first decade of the 1500s. Their migration and settlement of the land along both banks of the great river that bisects our American continent were the reasons that the English and other Europeans named their country the Divided States of America or the DSA

"Furthermore, those same historians' wishful thinking would try to convince you that the Christians gradually took over the Iberian Peninsula from the Muslims, to control the Muslim nation of Al-Andulus, now known as Spain, between the Mediterranean Sea and the Atlantic Ocean from A.D. 700 to January, 1492.

"In fact, just the opposite occurred. Sunni Berber Muslims from North Africa crossed the Mediterranean Sea at Gibraltar and conquered Granada in the southern part of the peninsula in the A.D. 700s and gradually spread their rule and influence northward during the next seven hundred years to complete their conquest of all of that peninsula in January, A.D. 1492. As a result, beginning in that same year, they explored the New World wanting to conquer India.

"The revisionists would also have you believe, instead, that Christians—under some Italian man named Christopher Columbus—actually discovered the New World for Spain.

"Instead, Sunni Muslims traveled from that peninsula in Europe to this large peninsula between the Atlantic Ocean and the Gulf of Mexico. Later, Christians reconquered their former European lands during World War 1—then called the Great War—as they also conquered the German war machine. As a result, they restored the names of the present-day countries of France and Spain.

"Moreover, during the 1930s as well as the 1990s, many Alevi Muslims immigrated because of Sunni persecution in Turkey to our land. They brought with them Ataturk's

Turkish ideas of secular political and justice systems that our country put into place in the 1990s. However, our government imitated the efficiency of the Divided States rather than the inefficient Turkish justice system.

"As the twentieth century proceeded, many more Alevi Muslims populated our nation because of a Sunni massacre of Alevis and other violent acts in Turkey. You see one of the descendents of the mid-1990s immigrants before you today.

"Meanwhile, just seventy-two years ago, the Divided States used a minor offense as a pretext to invade and conquer the Great River Nation in the War of 2012 to become the United States. A large number of GRN Shi'ite refugees flooded our Great Peninsula Nation, found good jobs, and gained a majority in Parliament in A.D. 2070. Then, they reinstituted Sharia law along with the requirement that women wear robes and head-coverings to maintain their modesty. They also started the Committee for the Promotion of Virtue and the Prevention of Vice (C-POV) and changed the name of this city from New Istanbul to New Tehran.

"Any questions?"

* * *

Akilah exited a Great Peninsula Nation University classroom building with a satisfied feeling that her classes had gone well. Then, she rode her fusion hover-cycle on palm-tree-lined streets to her condo complex after her full day of teaching two classes each of criminology and Islamic studies. As she parked her Harley David & Sons hover-cycle on her condo parking lot, she glanced at two camels standing guard.

In her super-air-conditioned condo that evening in the hot late August of 2084, she ate her supper of salad, lamb, beans, and brown rice in front of the TV, while playing along with the English-Muslim versions of *Wheel of Allah's Rule* and *Jeopardy*. Then, she read the newspaper and solved its puzzles. She also prepared her lectures for her four Monday classes as she watched a couple of crime dramas.

However, as her evening began, the noise of a hover-van's loud engine in her condo parking lot made her peek out of her front window as it pulled away. She recognized her black-robed neighbor who lived across from her on their private drive.

* * *

That same Saturday evening as the sun was setting and as Farhan approached his apartment door, his fully-bearded next-door neighbor came out of his apartment door. Farhan smiled and said to him, "Muhammad, are you going out for a night on the town?"

The fully-bearded Muhammad Ibrahim looked down and mumbled, "I'm visiting my mother across town."

Chapter Four

Frustrated investigators and a successful perp

The life-protection task force assembled as a glum group in the New Tehran police station squad room at 3:00 P.M. on Tuesday afternoon. All of the investigators sat on outlined, transparent, air-cushioned office chairs. First Detective Fahyim Srour said, "Let's discover what all of you have learned, if anything, about the missing women. Jamal and Issah, what did you learn at GPNU?"

Akilah's frustration showed with an uncharacteristic frown as she said, "The two missing students were both well-adjusted and happy at the university and had never talked about leaving GPNU or changing schools. Their boyfriends, roommates, and other friends were completely shocked when they disappeared."

"Touma and Ghanem, what did you discover in the possible crime scenes?"

Second Policeman Ghanem with a more-exaggerated frown than usual and a shake of his turbaned head volunteered, "We came up empty, boss. We could find zero witnesses at any of the places where the victims were supposed to be when they disappeared. One person thought he saw an unfamiliar, older zip-car in the darkness on a side street near the mall the night of one woman's disappearance but couldn't remember anything about it."

First Detective Srour replied with a scowl, "Many witnesses are unreliable by being poor observers. Maloof and Daher, I hope that you came up with some tangible leads to work on."

Fourth Detective Maloof said with a serious look, "We interviewed all of the families. The missing women had no disgruntled boyfriends or husbands. They all seemed to be quite well-adjusted young women. None of them had reported anyone following them. No one could think of anyone who even disliked them. Everyone was devastated at their disappearances. It's frustrating to come up with a big fat zero!"

Srour thought to himself, *Interesting.* He then prompted Huda to report on their attempts to discover some clues to connect the five women. Second Detective Huda walked to the holo-white board and walked among the women's holo-pictures, "We now apparently have a sixth victim, but we investigated the first five and came up with a big zero. The women have very few characteristics in common except that they are all in their twenties and are all short with lean bodies. Two are from well-to-do families, one is from the poorer part of town, and the others are university students. They appear to be victims of opportunity, not carefully-planned abductions of highly-stalked victims."

Srour hung his head and concluded the meeting, "Let's investigate the sixth disappearance to see if we can discover any clues in this baffling case."

Assertive Akilah piped up, "What should Issah and I do about this new victim, who isn't a GPNU student?"

"Why don't you wait to see what the other members of our team discover? We will meet again on Tuesday in four weeks. If you discover any relevant evidence, mind-text me right away."

* * *

As Akilah and Farhan walked down the steps of the police station after the LPTF meeting, they looked at each other with wide eyes. Akilah voiced their thoughts, "Let's examine all of the places where the victims were supposed to be when they disappeared."

Farhan nodded and said with a half-smile, "Akilah, I'm relieved that we're going to investigate the women's disappearances instead of sitting on our hands." When Akilah looked at him with pinched lips and creased brow through her veil, he explained, "That expression is a United States phrase that means 'doing nothing.'"

Akilah drove her clear-plastic, bubble hover-cycle. Farhan, behind her, gripped the cycle's seat with white knuckles, thinking that they had better use his zip-car from now on. They visited the New Tehran Aquarium, Symphony Hall, Muslim Museum, a palm grove on the city's outskirts, and the Muslim Mall.

At the last place, Akilah suggested with little hope in her heart, "Farhan, you can start at the far end of the parking lot to examine it thoroughly, and I'll start at this end. We can meet in the middle. Maybe we will find some evidence of a scuffle between the perp and the victim."

After they scoured the parking lots on all four sides of the mall, Farhan declared, "I found nothing except some white threads on the north side. I collected them with my latex gloves in a sterile evidence bag. I wish this mall had installed 4-D, parking-lot, security cameras. In that way, the GPN is far behind the USA and the rest of developed world."

At the aquarium, symphony hall, museum, and eighteen-acre palm grove, they found only multiple footprints in the last location. Akilah said, "This footpath is useless in providing meaningful clues, since those footprints could have been from anyone at anytime.

In the school parking lot at the end of their fruitless search, Farhan said, "Until we find the women's bodies, I'm afraid this investigation is futile. Let's stop at that little cafe on the way home to brainstorm."

* * *

After sunset that same evening, a shadowy figure, dressed in a flowing, black robe, thought, *Now's my chance to go fishing. That woman looks a lot like a challenging marlin.* He exited an old fusion car in the Muslim Mall parking lot. At the same time the stores closed, a scarfed, dark-haired woman approached her new hydrogen zip-Chevy after an hour of shopping. He smiled and asked her, “Could I please have a ride? My car won’t start.”

She said, “No, of course not! You might be that monster!” After she lurched away from him to enter her car, he grabbed her from behind and put a monogrammed handkerchief over her mouth. She jerked and jerked against his iron grip but then went limp. He experienced the joy of a hunter with his first kill, even though she was his seventh victim, as he carried her to his vehicle.

Chapter Five

Friendly and forced disagreements

At a table halfway to the back of the eating establishment over New World coffee for Farhan and Old World tea for Akilah, she felt forlorn like a lover losing her love as she began, "This criminal is very smart. He only kidnaps his victims in deserted public places where and when no one will observe him."

Frustrated Farhan said, "Our country better catch up with the rest of the technological world, where 4-D cameras are everywhere like a Big Brother watching out for the people's safety. I sincerely hope that those tiny, white filaments from the mall parking lot will yield useful information. We also need an organization like the USA's Super-FBI Behavioral Analysis Unit to profile and help us catch the perpetrator."

"That is true." Akilah's words sounded more confident than she felt, "However, we will catch this vicious fiend eventually."

With some hesitancy, Akilah plunged into their discussion about their differing beliefs, "Farhan, I have been thinking about...a comment that you made when we talked last time....I remember your saying that you believe the Muslim Allah and the Christian God are different Gods....What did you mean?"

Farhan remembered similar discussions with Muslim friends in the past, but he wanted to put her at ease again, "Again, you can believe what you want to, and I will never argue with you or try to change your beliefs." At that very moment, the restaurant's security cameras turned away from them.

He continued with his voice just above a whisper, "However, I'll explain my comment about the Muslim and Christian Gods. The church based the traditional Christian belief about God on the whole Bible, which we believe is God's Word in all of its faithful translations and copies as well as its original manuscripts. We believe that the amazing God of the Old and New Testaments is only one God revealed as three Persons: the Father, Jesus Christ, and the Holy Spirit."

"I always thought that you believe in three Gods, not one."

Akilah's misconception encouraged Farhan to continue, "No, we believe that God is mysterious as only one God revealed as three Persons, based on many Bible passages but most clearly on Prophet John's book about Jesus' life.

"However, I know that followers of Jesus and Muslims all believe in a God of justice who is the just Judge of all humans' rebellion. Isn't that so, Akilah?"

"Yes, we do. That belief motivates me to overcome the extreme evil perpetrated by criminals, especially serial-killers." **(Read more of their discussion on pages 226-227.)**

"I have the same incentive to protect all human life from predators of all kinds, but the natures of our Gods and the ways we can receive his mercy instead of his justice are very different." As Akilah nodded, Farhan said, "However, that last topic is for another discussion, since it's getting late."

Akilah said, "Yes, we'd better get home. Why don't we get together again at noon two weeks from today and plot our next moves?"

"Good plan."

* * *

The dark, concrete-block basement came slowly into focus for a brunette woman. She was in full panic mode as she writhed against the plentiful duct-tape on her mouth, wrists, and ankles.

A tall, dark form bounced and pranced around the edge of the dungeon. As he came into the woman's view, she gave out a muffled shriek and fainted. Her disappointed captor thought, *Typical of many weak women! What a pitiful gender!*

The perpetrator returned to the dungeon every night to bring food and water to the dark-complexioned woman chained to a cot in a separate room. She cried and begged to no avail with muffled sounds for her release. In reply, the perp just mouthed his stock, silent statement, "You're mine."

Eventually, he carried her squirming body into the main dungeon. He then secured her with thick ropes to a table, tied her legs in stirrups like a woman on a hospital birthing table, and used his weapon to violate her over and over again.

On other occasions, the perpetrator beat her to a helpless pulp barely short of death.

During his extreme physical and sexual abuse of his victim, he never uttered a word but galloped around his basement torture chamber as a prelude to her helpless pummeling and abuse.

After a month, he grew tired of her. Then he stabbed her, cut her into pieces with his butcher knife, disposed of her inside a body bag in his secret body dump with the other six bodies, and went out hunting for another victim.

Chapter Six

Aggressors in attack mode

One Wednesday morning, loud snorts, hisses, and grunts in the parking lot of Akilah's condo building drew her to the front window facing the paved space. She gasped as she observed the male, hump-less, jet-propelled camel at the far edge bouncing around a foot above the ground. The camel defended its floating female a few feet behind it. The male spit its vomit with amazing accuracy at the eyes of a "teenage," six-foot, snub-nosed alligator. The reptile had slithered out of the nearby, shallow water that emptied into the Everwaters and then the Atlantic.

Akilah grimaced as she thought to herself, *That ominous alligator probably wants to sun itself on the warm pavement and puncture a few vehicles' frames with its sharp teeth, while mistaking them for enemies. However, I certainly don't want it biting my hover-cycle!*

The camel then hover-circled the menace and again spit its toxic vomit into the reptile's eyes. It kicked and bit the alligator's broad snout as it swooped down at it. Finally, the male hero plopped on top of it until the reptile wriggled out from under it and slithered back into the swamp.

* * *

That same morning, Akilah began her two Islamic Studies 101 classes by describing the camel-alligator confrontation and then asked, "Why do you suppose we have so many camels here in the GPN, when they usually live only in arid, desert places?" No one answered.

"I'll tell you why. The first Muslim explorers, who came to this peninsula from the Al-Andalus peninsula (now Spain) in A.D. 1492 trying to find India, naturally brought camels with them. They were the one-hump variety originally from the African Sahara. However, when those early, intrepid explorers discovered alligators here, they decided that having camels around would be a way to counteract that prehistoric menace.

"As a result, during the last six centuries, GPN Muslims have bred and power-equipped camels to fight alligators as their enemies. Of course, the males naturally fight each other in breeding season, especially with a female nearby. They also fight our alligators and provide us with sports competition the way they do in Turkey.

"However, in a land with plentiful, fresh water, camels gradually lost their unneeded humps. Other camels' handy humps contain fat that they convert into water between infrequent, thirty-gallon gulps in dry, desert lands. In addition, humans can ride flat camels more easily than the one- or two-hump varieties. More recently, humans have fitted camels for more speed.

"Now, where did we leave off Monday? Oh, yes, I remember."

* * *

The following Friday afternoon after Farhan had gone to his church in the morning, he noticed an ad in the *Times* for a camel-wrestling event. He also read with great interest a front-page article with the headlines "Great fear grips New Tehran" and "Odd-couple crime-fighters on the job" about Akilah and him.

After a cross-town trip to witness camel combat, he exited his zip-car and paid the four-lira admission fee on the edge of a field inside a crude, wooden fence, where a crowd had gathered. After he had set up his lawn chair in the middle of the spectators, two men floated three camels to the center of the open space, while onlookers speculated about the outcome.

The announcer shouted in a deep, base voice, "Our show demonstrates the authentic Turkish camel-wrestling that has been practiced for at least three millennia but now with up-to-date fusion propulsion. Today, our first match pits two camel combatants named after USA President Joe Smith and Ukrainian President Giorgi Levanshov, similar to the way Turks name their camels. On with the show!"

Farhan thought, *This camel combat looks as though it might be fun!*

The two handlers freed the two large male jet-pack-wearing camels, hovering just above the ground and dressed in elaborate, multicolored saddles. They then faced off in an attempt to win the roped female, which looked on with a hint of a smile. Levanshov was the first attacker when its right leg lunged at Smith's left leg. Smith backed away to avoid a Levanshov takedown. Levanshov then spit its toxic vomit at Smith, which again backed away and unleashed its own vomit. Levanshov attacked again by biting Smith on its nose and kicking its chest. It again used its right leg in an attempt to lock Smith's left leg and topple it.

This time, Smith turned and fled the arena in Farhan's direction. He thought, *Oh, no! I'd better scurry sideways fast! Protect my life, dear God!* Smith trampled the wooden fence flat, as Levanshov galloped after it. Spectators' quick, sideway moves prevented any human injuries. Smith raced toward the gravel road with Levanshov, the handlers, and the camels' owners in fast pursuit. *Thank you, Father!*

Because of Farhan's narrow escape, he thought, *I've seen enough camel combat for one day and possibly for a lifetime.* Therefore, he returned to his comparatively-safe apartment.

* * *

Night had come on a Sunday night in October when a burqa-covered mosque secretary—after a long work day straightening out the mosque's business—emerged from a large, turreted Sunni mosque. After peeking out of the door to see if anyone lurked in the parking lot and seeing no one, she walked to the far edge of the parking lot, where employees parked. As she approached her small Ford on the poorly-lit edge far from parking-lot lights, a long, murky shadow glided toward her from behind a palm. She stopped and stood stock-still and silent.

The ghost said, "I locked my keys and laser-phone in my old hover-car down the street. Could you please help me by calling the police?" She turned and dialed 2-1-1. Then, before she completed her call, the apparition moved like a swift, slithery snake and ripped her burqa off. Her deep darkness ensued.

Chapter Seven

Progress?

When Farhan and Akilah met the following Tuesday noon over lunch, she asked him, "I've wanted to ask you, Farhan, why do you have a Muslim name, even though you are a Christian from the States?"

"Well, my parents and I were nominal Muslim immigrants from Jordan. However, when I was a high school student, I decided to investigate different religions for myself the way you did. My parents said they would support whatever decision I would make. I found out that the Bible makes amazing claims about God and especially about Jesus. Therefore, I began reading that book to find out more. As a result, I found out that the Bible has many prophets' words that Jesus' life fulfilled

"When I attended Purdue University, my final decision came down to Jesus' claims to be fully God along with his heavenly Father and the Holy Spirit.

"I also found out that in many discussions with Muslims that they deny Jesus' definite death and his real resurrection.

"On the other hand, I discovered that eyewitness Prophet John quotes Jesus in John 14:6 as saying, 'I am the way and the truth and the life. No one comes to the Father except through me.' I concluded from his statements that only a God-man can claim to be such an exclusive Pathway to God, mainly because he says, 'I am,' an obvious claim that he is the God of Moses' burning bush, who says that his name is 'I AM THAT I AM' and therefore is the faithful God in Exodus three and four.

"Furthermore, when I investigated the Bible, I discovered in the book of that same Prophet John that he claims to see Jesus die and the Roman soldier stab him to make sure he is dead. He also sees water and blood come out of Jesus' stab-wound, a sure sign that Jesus is really dead, since the plasma had already separated from the red blood cells."

Farhan's description of how he became a Christian surprised Akilah, but she smiled her little grin and said, "Obviously, I disagree with your conclusions, Farhan, because I believe that Jesus was a great prophet—nothing more.

"However, last time you were going to tell me why you think that the Bible is identical with the Original Manuscripts instead of being corrupted over time. How can you make that statement when it has been about 3,500 years since Prophet Moses (peace to him) began writing the First Five Books?"

Farhan felt pressure that God was his baseball Manager putting him at the plate with the game on the line. He said a prayer to hit a home run. Then, he said, "The main reason is that your Qur'an claims that Allah protects your holy book from changing. Thus, since the Qur'an recognizes God's words in the Bible as well, God must have also preserved his words there from becoming corrupt over time. I also believe that God took care of the Bible as you do the Qur'an."

Farhan's reasoning made Akilah feel as anxious as a tightrope walker. She shifted from side to side and said, "Okay, okay, professor. Yes, you are right that we believe Allah (give him all the praise) preserves the Qur'an. I still disagree with you, but you've given me some food for thought." **(Read Farhan's other four reasons on pages 228-232)**

She preferred to talk about the missing-women case, since Farhan's reasoning unsettled her confidence in her beliefs a little bit. As a result, she said, "Now, let's get down to the case at hand. Another woman, a Sunni mosque secretary—this time middle-aged—has been missing since Sunday night. Do you have any thoughts about the kidnapper of those seven women?"

Farhan frowned, scratched his head, and put his hands to his face, "I think that the perp has to be an organized, thrill-seeking, mother-hating serial-murderer. When he no longer gets a high out of keeping, violating, pummeling, and terrorizing his mother-substitutes, he disposes of them to keep them from identifying him. He must have at least one secret body dump somewhere in the area, but where?"

"I tend to agree with you, Farhan. How could we possibly find that place in or near the large city of New Tehran?"

Farhan guessed, "Maybe, we have to wait for someone to find it for us. I have been praying for that discovery to happen."

Then, a couple arose in a booth closer to the restaurant's front, looked in their direction, and walked toward them. They stopped at Farhan and Akilah's booth, and the short, purple-robed man said, "Aren't you two the consultants who are working on the missing-women case?"

Akilah said, "Yes, we are."

The brown-robed and scarfed woman said with lowered eyes, "We're scared stiff. Please find that madman and put him out of commission!"

Farhan said, "Our task force is investigating those disappearances, but the perpetrator is hard to catch. We'll do our best."

* * *

She awoke with her eyes focusing off and on. She still wore her blue burqa with her matching robe. His masked face leaned over her torso as she said through the mouth-muffler, "Remove my duct-tape, and I'll be good. I won't yell."

He thought, *What could it hurt? I'm stronger than she is and have my weapons.* His surprising, overconfident response was to remove her restraints. "Would you like to go for a walk?" he asked, as he picked up his butcher knife.

They walked around the dingy dungeon until he brandished his weapons to make her lie down in her anteroom bed. She thought that she had to get on his good side. Therefore, she smiled at him as she lay down and accepted his padlocked chains.

Chapter Eight

Routine events

On the following Sunday afternoon, Akilah rode her hover-cycle to Harley David & Sons' Camel & Cycle Sales & Service—"Harley's Place," for short—to get it serviced. She floated her cycle into the wide parking lot near the two elevated camel and hover-cycle up-ramps to the New Tehran traffic laser-lanes reserved for that curious mix of vehicles.

A large sign at the north edge of the parking lot announced Harley's Place to the expressway traffic. The sign was a large badge with the words "camel" and "cycle" above and below a long banner proclaiming "Harley David 'n Sons." A large GPN red, white, and black flag flew from another high pole.

The parking lot had a wooden platform on concrete stilts hanging out from its edge over the lower terrain to the west.

Those two east-west laser-lanes, which were all suspended three meters above the ground, were parallel to the four car-and-truck lanes, one on either side. Since all of the vehicles moved vertically as well as horizontally, they could avoid accidents, which were so rare that they always made big news, even fender-benders. In fact, the newer models floated with automatic, safe ease without a driver's assistance.

Furthermore, a large, five-peak tent contained new fusion hover-cycles and nuclear zip-cycles in one half as well as jet-pack camels in the other half—all for sale. The building had large, square, twenty-five-windowed, lookout towers on two of its four corners with a smaller, sixteen-windowed one on another corner. A little grassy ridge to the north and a palm grove to the west stood between the parking lot and the traffic onramps.

The salesperson who greeted Akilah in the parking lot tried to sell her on trading in her older fusion hover-cycle for a new hydrogen-powered zip-cycle. However, when he discovered that she was satisfied with the one she had, she took it to the service department.

She speculated aloud to the service attendant, "I've often wondered why your owner built that deck out from the side of the parking lot. Is it an observation platform of some kind?"

The short young man, one of Harley David's sons, replied with a high-pitched voice, "That's the performance platform, where musical groups entertain people during concerts. Our customers are the audience sitting on their suspended hover-chairs in the parking lot."

Akilah replied with her subtle grin, "I'm sure they play Beethoven and Mozart." The young man laughed.

She also asked another young man named Ahmad, who took her payment for the fusion-fuel change and checkup, "Why does your building have lookout towers on three corners? They look like prison gun-towers."

He stopped filling out her bill and said, "I've often wondered about those towers too. No one has asked your question before. I'll try to find out for you before your next visit."

Akilah finished her other errands of grocery shopping, eating lunch, and mall wandering. Then, she decided to go to a 5-D movie matinee entitled *A Murder Mystery* at the mall theater.

* * *

The following Wednesday afternoon, Professor Farhan Issah began his Criminology 301 class, "Today we will learn about the subject you've all been waiting for, serial murderers."

His students sat up straight and leaned forward.

He and his twenty students exchanged information after he asked, "What do you know about serial killers?"

"They're men." "It's true that about 90% of known killers are male, but a few have been females."

"They're mentally deranged." "It's true that some are psychopaths, but many are part of the general population leading seemingly-normal lives with their families. Only a few are legally insane."

"There have been many serial killers." "That's a misconception. Experts know that serial killers make up less than one percent of the population in the United States. We have even fewer here in the GPN. However, a large number of murders may be serial but not classified as such because the police have found no connection between them."

"Serial killers have 'signatures,' special actions that distinguish their work from others." "A signature happens in only a small percentage of serial killings."

"All serial killers hate their dominating mothers." "Many do, but serial killers have many motives for killing repeatedly."

"Their childhood homes had alcohol and substance abuse." "About 70% did."

"Many of them experienced psychological and sexual abuse." "Yes, you're right."

"Many of them have fantasies about dominating and violating others." "True."

"The USA government defines serial murders as at least three related killings." "Excellent!"

"They prefer erotic activities like observing pornography." "Many do."

"When they were young, they acted out their fantasies on small animals." "99% did."

"A large majority came from dysfunctional families with an often-violent, dominant, inconsistent mother but without a father." "Absolutely."

"Many had physical injuries, especially head injuries." "Correct."

"Many serial killers also were obsessed with setting fires when they were younger." "Right!"

"Many have a history of attempted suicide." "Right on."

"A majority wet their beds past the age of twelve." "Yes, 57% do.

"However, these characteristics describe only those we know about. Furthermore, a number of well-adjusted adults shared many of the same experiences when they were young but, instead, became productive members of society. Even in A.D. 2084, we still don't know what causes the serial killer to murder, while at the same time many other people share similar upbringings but don't. It's not mental illness all the time.

"Notice also in our list of characteristics that one must never generalize about any group of people, even serial killers. All groups have some exceptions who don't fit a general observation. We must always treat people as individuals, not as a part of any group.

"Moreover, always remember that we can understand why serial-killers murder other people, while we must never excuse their actions and need to bring them to justice to protect the public.

"Great! I see that most of you read the assigned chapter and watch TV's justice drama *Criminal Minds GPN*," said smiling Farhan.

* * *

The next time the perpetrator visited his latest victim in his basement dungeon, she grinned and managed to mouth, "Can you unchain me again, please?" As he brandished his huge butcher knife, she stretched and walked up and down, while he admired her curves.

When he left to visit the small kitchen next to the dungeon door in order to get food and water for his victim, she ran to a large air vent and tried to climb into it. As her legs were disappearing, the shadowy perp grasped her feet and yanked her out of the vent. Then, scowling, he restrained her in the main dungeon. *She won't defy me again!* Her muffled screams ended with a few swift, butcher-knife swings.

Chapter Nine

A January visit

After a spring, summer, and early fall in 2084—during which the serial murderer kidnapped, abused, and disposed of seven women—the serial murderer's six-month cooling-off period ensued. For Akilah and Farhan, the busyness of teaching full-time with the routine of grading papers, tests, and final exams took their full attention. Meanwhile, the life-protection task force busied themselves with other pursuits.

However, on Thursday morning, January 2, 2085, the following text message came to the life-protection task force members: URGENT! COME TO STATION THIS AFT AT THREE. All of them arrived at the New Tehran police station at the appointed hour.

***

The police station and courthouse were both on the north side of the city square at the center of New Tehran. The national capitol building, where the president worked and the national parliament met, was on the south side. Various shops and restaurants were on the east and west sides.

On its front, the old, three-story courthouse—rebuilt way back in 2010—had a long, building-wide staircase leading to a colonnade of Corinthian pillars, through which visitors entered.

A palm park in the city square's center with multicolored playground equipment along with benches facing the children's play area completed the scene.

In the police station squad room, First Detective Fahyim Srour began with a sense of urgency, "We have an important visit coming on January 30, as some of you know. The United States President Joe Smith will make a state visit to our president and parliament in New Tehran that day and stay for two more days.

"However, our security division has discovered increased World-Wide Web chatter with many veiled threats against his life. Since we as a task force are in the business of protecting human life, we need to brainstorm ways to protect the USA president while he is here. Do you have any ideas about how we can thwart any possible assassination attempt?"

Farhan felt some nostalgic, patriotic pangs from his childhood as he asked, "Can we trace the perps who are making the threats?"

Srour frowned, "Unfortunately not. They use many super-servers all over the world to hide their locations and identities."

Farhan grinned and thought, *Why would he come here—to pet the camels?* However, he asked, "Why is he coming this time of year—to escape the frigid north in both the weather and USA politics? We have such difficult weather this time of year, you know. I think that President Smith wants to golf here, as he has everywhere else."

Everyone shared his grin.

Srour said, "Everyone, please brainstorm between now and next Tuesday, when we'll meet again to discuss our tentative plans to protect Mr. Smith. At that same time, we will meet with two USA Secret Service people."

* * *

"These men are United States Secret Service Agents Eric Hansen and Joe Sleet, two of the people assigned to protect the USA president," Srour began. Then, he asked them, "How may we help you protect your president's life, gentlemen?"

Joe spoke up, "Well, you know New Tehran and your people much better than we do. What ideas do you have?"

Second Detective Huda, feeling puzzled, said, "It would be helpful if we knew what his schedule is going to be."

As Eric handed out half-slips of paper to each task force member, he said, "Here is a list of the president's planned appearances."

They took a moment to read the itinerary. Then, Fourth Detective Maloof leaned forward with an excited feeling like a boy with a new toy and ventured, "I think that we could have a look-alike ride in a limousine from the airport backed up by a police escort. At the same time, a plain, ordinary car could take the president to our capitol building by way of a back road for his speech to parliament."

Srour said, "That's a very good idea, Maloof."

Farhan's face frowned, reflecting his skepticism, as he said, "I see that he will speak on his second day to an out-door crowd in the city square. Is that plan wise, considering the danger of snipers on rooftops and assassins in such a crowd? Why not schedule the speech in the Parliament chamber?"

Joe answered, "Both presidents want more exposure for their messages than they would have in the Parliament room. Our group and yours should be enough people to pre-vent any attempts then."

Srour eagerly jumped in, "So you want us to join you in observing the crowd at that event?"

Eric narrowed his eyebrows and said, "We need all the help we can get."

Akilah shared Farhan's misgivings, hesitated to speak up, but remarked, "I see that on his third day here, he plans to golf that afternoon at the golf course near the zip-port be-fore he leaves in his Air Force Fifteen. How can we help you protect President Smith on the golf course with so many open opportunities for terrorist assassins to kill him?"

Joe said with a slight grin, "We are well-practiced in protecting him on golf courses with atomic golf balls flying in all directions, but we could use a few more pairs of eyes there."

Srour nodded, glanced at his team, and said, "We'd be happy to help you any way we can."

Third Detective Daher said, "I like Maloof's idea for the president's whole stay. We could switch cars for each trip. That plan will keep possible terrorist assassins guessing." His sense of humor showed itself as he said with a smirk, "Perhaps, the president would like to ride an unassisted hydrogen-propelled camel for one trip and a hover-cycle for another one."

Farhan joined in, "One other trip could also be on a zip-bicycle."

Everyone laughed.

* * *

On Friday afternoon, January 30, after nuclear-powered Air Force Fifteen completed the fifteen-minute flight from the District of Columbia, the ruse and speech came off without a hitch.

The next day, the life-protection task force gathered at noon to infiltrate the gathering crowd. Even though Farhan felt uncomfortable in a sky-blue robe and turban, he found a spot between the courthouse and the police station facing south toward the city hall across the city square, where carpenters had constructed for both presidents' speeches a platform and a podium facing north.

Hoping that no assassins would show up, Akilah faced the city hall and positioned herself between the children's red slide and chartreuse merry-go- round.

A sea of colorful turbans, robes, burqas, and scarves, including possible destructive hurricanes, went from low to high tide until 1:00 P.M. At that exact moment, the two presidents, accompanied by parliamentary dignitaries, walked down the steps of the city hall and climbed onto the platform.

Farhan surveyed the crowd near him in front of the courthouse and police station. He centimetered back and forth on the sidewalk.

One man's tiny, jerky, right-arm movements with his hand in his right robe pocket attracted Farhan's attention. The average-size man, dressed in dark-red turban and robe, twitched as he removed a nine-millimeter fusion-gun from his pocket. Farhan ran at him and tackled him on the court-house sidewalk. Dazed by their concrete-encounter, they sprawled. Farhan leaped to his feet, grabbed the gun, and commanded, "Raise your hands!"

However, the apparent assassin fled through the crowd with Farhan, some LPTF members, and the Secret Service in pursuit. The fastest detective, Maloof, caught up with the attempted killer and tackled him on the sidewalk a block from the city square. The black-suited Secret Service arrest-ed him and put him in police-station custody for questioning.

At the same time, Akilah thought to herself, *Oh, no! There's a suicide bomber!* She saw a woman dressed in full, black burqa and robe approach the presidents' platform. She held a remote button for a probable bomb strapped inside her robe. Akilah rushed at her from behind, grabbed her and her remote, and turned her over to policemen Touma and Ghanem, who were nearby. They uncovered the scatter-laser-bomb strapped to the assassin's waist.

Then, aside from those distractions, the presidents' speeches came off without further interruptions.

* * *

Short GPN President Zafar Ghazi and lanky Prime Minister Tawil Khatib—sometimes nicknamed in impolite circles as the government's "Mutt and Jeff"—said in unison, "Tough shot, Mr. President!" Pres. Smith had hooked the fusion-ball out of bounds into the trees on the third fairway. The USA president then hit a much-straighter, provisional drive. They all walked toward their golf balls only seven hundred and fifty yards, more or less a third of the way to the green.

Farhan, still feeling relieved about his previous terrorist tackle, had posted himself on the left out-of-bounds line, where President Smith's first fusion golf ball ended up. Then, he saw the dim outline of a man who was eight meters high on the fourth, sturdy limb of an oak tree among the palms.

Farhan thought, *I'd better stop him before the President arrives looking for his ball!* He hustled behind the would-be assassin, pulled out his police-issued laser-revolver, and shouted at the form, "Get down or I will fire." The man turned around, pulled out his powerful hydrogen-gun, and pointed it at Farhan.

Farhan shot the man's left leg as the potential murderer's shot gutted a nearby palm. The man slumped and fell like a bag of camel manure to the fern-cushioned floor of the palm fringe. The USA Secret Service arrived to take the unconscious, would-be assassin into custody.

Chapter Ten

Making informal connections

The two GPNU professors continued to meet every fourth Tuesday at noon for lunch. During one lunch in mid-February, 2085, when they met in a booth at the very back of the restaurant away from other diners, Akilah said, "It's been frustrating not having any bodies and therefore no further evidence to go on."

Farhan winced, "Yeah, what is it that we're missing?"

"I wish I knew. The murderer must have cooled off by now...."

After the server brought their chicken sandwiches and lentil soup, Akilah felt comfortable plunging into a discussion of their differing beliefs, since no anger was involved. She said, "I've always wondered, Farhan, how followers of Jesus can possibly believe that Jesus is the Son of God. The Qur'an clearly says that Allah (may he receive all of our praise) can't have a son or any children because he's one God, not two or more persons."

Farhan also plunged, just above a whisper, into the depths of his dearly-held ideas about God, "I'm glad that you mentioned Jesus, Akilah. I'm also happy that we agree that God is only one God. I believe that Jesus has always been God. However, he joined humanity by way of a miraculous birth through Mary without a human father. Muslims also believe in Jesus' virgin birth, don't they?"

"That's right. However, we believe that when he was born, he was human, not divine, like other miraculous births in the Qur'an. How can you believe that Jesus was divine while he lived on earth?"

After Farhan shot an arrow-prayer to his Target, God, he spoke just above a whisper, "Um,...well, I believe that the Bible is correct in saying in the first chapter of Genesis that God made humans like him in some ways. We certainly aren't all-powerful, everywhere-present, all-knowing, and eternal the way he is; but we can love people in a way somewhat similar to his love, for example.

"Therefore, since God made us like him and since he is the all-powerful Creator, I believe that he easily joined the second Person of God to a perfect unborn baby's body to make Jesus, his Son. He can also re-create us Christians to be his adopted sons and daughters."

Farhan felt his confidence grow as he added, "God changed me from a complete unbeliever to be his follower. Thus, I believe that the God-man, Jesus, gained my rescue from my spiritually-dead condition when he died on the Romans' torture tree and when he came alive triumphantly from death to give his followers eternal life. He continues to change my life for the better."

Akilah flashed her slight smile, "Well, I'm not convinced, professor, but we'd better get back to our eternal papers and tests."

They both laughed as they rose to leave the bistro.

That night as Akilah entered her condo building after parking her fusion-cycle, her neighbor across the hall came out of his door and almost bumped into her in his hurry to leave.

* * *

Instead of meeting formally at the police station while the killer went on hiatus during the winter and spring of 2084-85, the task force took turns inviting the rest of the members to their homes for a monthly social time that they hoped would produce the closeness that might be needed to solve the baffling missing-women case.

During the fourth week of February, Second Policeman Mamduh Ghanem welcomed the crew to his humble, two-bedroom apartment on the north side of New Tehran. They all removed their sandals and placed them in the floating hall sandal-stand. All of them except Farhan sat cross-legged in Mamduh's tight living room with their robes covering their feet. Instead, he wore a short-sleeved shirt and slacks with a light-blue jacket.

As they drank mugs of tea, coffee, and water, Akilah's curiosity arose as she asked Mamduh, "How did you become a policeman, Mamduh?"

Darkly-handsome Mamduh felt sad and mad inside as he said, "My childhood was very unhappy since my parents favored my two brothers over me. Then, at eighteen years old in my last year of school, I was buying snacks at a convenience store when a masked robber attempted to steal money from the owner. He got away with money without anyone arresting him. At that point, I decided to get a degree in criminology and go to the police academy. Now, I'm trying to catch perps."

First Detective Srour recalled many unhappy events in his childhood and chimed in, "I too had a forgettable childhood, Mamduh. My father died when I was six; I barely remember him. To over-compensate for his absence, my mother used a barber's light-strap to beat us boys mercilessly, sometimes for no other reason than because she was angry at her life as a widow. I'm afraid I took out my anger on stray animals in the neighborhood and lit a few fires.... However, look at me today—a first detective fighting crime."

* * *

Then, Fahyim's mind returned to the time he entered his father's hospital room with his mother. He saw his eyes opening wide at the scene of his father lying flat on the hospital bed with several tubes and machines attached to him. Fahyim hid from his father behind his mother's robe. She said to him, "Don't be afraid, son. Be a man, since you are going to be the man of the house."

He looked wide-eyed at his mother, who pushed him forward to make an awkward, dishrag-like handshake with his father, who was in a near-coma.

* * *

"Fahyim, don't you dare hit your sister that way!" his mother yelled at him. She picked up the dreaded six-centimeter-wide barber's light-strap that she had bought at a garage sale. She swung it as hard as she could to crack Fahyim's backside ten times.

"Ow! That hurt!" he said, as he fought back his tears.

* * *

Fahyim also saw himself as a boy run after a stray dog a half-block from his house, catch it, slit its throat, and use a lighter to set it on fire. He laughed at the poor animal's fate.

* * *

Second Detective Huda decided to open up about his childhood, since others had done so. He said, "I too hated my parents because they were so changeable and never followed through on their threats to punish us. Did all of us have unhappy childhoods? More importantly, how were we able to turn our lives around?"

* * *

Huda's consciousness suddenly saw his mother shout, "You make that noise again, and you won't eat supper for a week." Because he made a shrieking sound, she yelled, "Okay, no TV for you tonight."

Abasi escaped to their house's front yard, where he found a cat looking for scraps. He caught it, wrung its neck, and buried it in the back yard. He then lit the neighbor's garage on fire and scampered home to enjoy the firetruck's arrival from behind the curtains of his house's side window.

* * *

Since Akilah also felt that she needed to share her experiences, she said, "I had a happy childhood, even though we moved here after experiencing a lot of fear in Turkey. Because of that situation, our family was very close."

Farhan also ventured with a handsome grin, "I also had unified and loving parents who let me decide what belief system to follow because they were nominal Muslims from Jordan."

* * *

During the fourth week of March, the task force showed up at the elaborate, five-bedroom, upscale mansion of their next host, First Detective Fahyim Srour, on New Tehran's south side. All of them put their sandals in the house-wide front porch's oak sandal-stand.

Fahyim led all of them on a tour of his place, while his wife, Fatima, prepared snacks and nonalcoholic drinks.

In Srour's large den, they saw a twentieth-century display on the far wall of antique British Bobby's police equipment and clothes. A manly mannequin wore a white shirt, a black tie, a reflective jacket, black pants, and body armor. Attached to its duty belt were a torch, arm restraints, speed-cuffs, a Taser, a telescoping Bobby policeman's baton, a personal radio, incapacitating spray, and a police notebook.

Fahyim felt a great amount of happiness as he explained, "I have a great interest in ancient British law enforcement and, as a result, have collected these antique items over the years."

Farhan—fast becoming the group's comedian—quipped, "With all those tools, it's a wonder he could stand up again when he fell over, like the medieval knights' problem with full armor. How could he run fast after a perp wearing all of that paraphernalia?"

Fahyim secretly envied Farhan's gentle humor but remarked with a smirk, "That's a good question, Farhan. Maybe they didn't have any 'runners' to chase."

They made their way back to the spacious living room, where Fahyim's wife served them coffee, tea, or water with tasty snacks and then disappeared into the family room.

Since First Policeman Ziya Touma secretly envied Fahyim, he said, "It's quite a place you have here, First Detective."

Srour's pride soared like a USA rocket to one of the six space stations. He told him, "Ziya, you can call me 'Fahyim' in my own home. Yes, Allah (praise to him) has blessed us."

Heavy-set Third Detective Basim Daher felt puzzled as he asked Fahyim, "How did you get interested in the British Bobby policeman's work that long ago?"

Since host Fahyim Srour thought he could reveal a little about his past while safe in his own home, he said, "When I was still in school, I read a lot about Jack the Ripper's unsolved serial killings and his letters to the police. That interest led me to learn about London law enforcement. The next step was my decision to become a New Tehran policeman attempting to catch perps."

In response to all of the members' personal revelations, Farhan's flight of fancy flew galaxy-high as he thought, *Interesting!*

Then, Fourth Detective Fayiz Maloof broached the sad subject of the seven-missing-women case. "We never met as a task force after we investigated the sixth and seventh women's disappearances. Did anyone come up with anything? Basim and I didn't find any clues."

All of them shook their heads with sober looks and remained silent for a while.

Finally, host Srour thought, *I need to divert our attention from those events a little while.* Therefore, he said, "The national camel-wrestling tournament is coming up. It takes place in New Tehran rather than up north this year. Which camel do you think is going to win?" The men then speculated about the eventual winner and discussed USA sports and world football, while Akilah visited with Fatima in the kitchen.

Second Detective Huda suddenly remembered his desire to host the task force at a special family celebration and said as they rose to leave, "You are all invited to rejoice in our son's circumcision three weeks from today at 7:00 P.M."

The guests then parted ways into cloudy, deep darkness.

* * *

As Farhan floated home in his old, fusion-powered hatchback on a laser lane, his mind germinated the seed of a possible solution to the missing-women case. After he entered his apartment building, he knocked on his next-door neighbor's door. When Muhammad opened it, he asked, "Muhammad, would you like to go out for an evening tea?"

Muhammad avoided eye-contact as he said, "Yes, why don't we walk to the cafe a block from here, where they have outdoor tables?"

"Agreed."

They walked to the restaurant on a warm, late-March night. On the way, they saw high in the air a pair of red-tailed hawks circling to find prey.

Farhan remarked, "Now, that's a rare sight in New Tehran." Muhammad nodded.

They sat at an outdoor table. One couple was engrossed in a conversation a few feet away on the wide sidewalk.

Farhan began their conversation with a grin, "I thought that we might get acquainted, since we live so close to each other, Muhammad. What do you do for a living?"

Muhammad fidgeted as he said, "I fly a camel cruiser from here to North GPN."

With Farhan's handsome grin, he asked, "The camels vacation up there?"

Muhammad showed a slight smile, "No, sometimes camel rentals are greater there than here, so I take them up north from the rental agencies around New Tehran."

"Interesting. So you take camels there and bring other things back?"

"No. The rental business is brisk enough to make one-way trips very profitable."

"I attended one of the camel-wrestling contests, and two of them almost trampled me. I felt that God helped me get out of the way just in time."

"May Allah be praised that you weren't hurt. That is one risk of watching one of those events."

"What kind of fuel does your camel cruiser use?"

Muhammad's voice matched his excitement, "A nitrogen and fusion mixture that makes it float fast to its destination."

"How long does it take to go from New Tehran here in the far-south to New Accra in the far-northern GPN?"

"One and a half minutes!"

"That's really fast! How can you and the camels keep from falling over?"

"We have special stabilizers to simulate gravity. No problem. I can take forty trips a day."

"Muhammad, that's amazing! What do you do to have other fun?"

"Of course, I watch world football at the local stadium and on television."

"I've seen some of that action. How do those players maintain their balance with jet packs on their backs?"

Muhammad's reserve eased off, as he said, "Aren't their abilities amazing?"

"Yeah, they are. I believe the God of the Bible created all of our bodies."

"I think Allah did too (may he be praised)."

"My understanding of the Bible makes me believe Jesus was involved in the creation of the human race also, Muhammad, as one Person of God."

"Jesus was certainly a great prophet, Farhan."

"What makes me especially interested in world football is the awesome laser-fields suspended two meters above the ground. Besides, the players' protective force-fields and jet packs would make it difficult too. I don't see how they can play on a field in the air."

A siren started up in the distance as Muhammad said, "I agree, Farhan."

"Have you always been in the camel-transport business?"

A police hover-sedan pulled up near the cafe.

Chapter Eleven

Experiencing legal injustice

"These wrist-restraints are too tight!" he said from the back seat of the Great Peninsula Nation police hover-sedan.

No response came from the two black spaces in the front seat.

"Why did you arrest me?" he asked with more intensity than usual.

"Proselytizing" came the one-word reply from the shadow in the front passenger seat.

"I wasn't proselytizing Muhammad Ibrahim. Because he's my next-door neighbor, we just shared our ideas with each other."

"You were overheard telling him about Jesus (peace to him) as the Creator."

Farhan thought, *Jesus told his disciples before he went back to heaven, "You will be my witnesses...."*

He, therefore, said aloud to the arresting officers, "I just told him that I believe Jesus as part of God was involved in the original creation of all things. I wasn't trying to change him from a Muslim to a Christian. I know that proselytizing is illegal. After all, I teach criminology at the Great Peninsula Nation University."

"Then, you should know better. Jesus (peace to him) is a prophet, he isn't Allah," the driving inquisitor said.

"Well, I believe that he is both fully God and fully human."

I guess one of my faults is being too bold sometimes. However, God wants us Christians to scatter his Word-

seeds. I hope he plants my words in these two officers' hearts and makes them grow.

* * *

The Shi'a-sharia judge, dressed in black turban and robe, marched from a side door of the second-floor courtroom to his place behind the broad, high desk. The prosecutor and defense lawyer—both dressed in black Muslim attire—took their seats at desks on either side of the central aisle. Farhan in his black business suit joined his defense attorney to the right-front of the judge.

The judge said, "Court is now in session. The first case this morning involves a proselytizing charge against the defendant, Farhan Issah, I believe. Mr. Prosecutor, why have you brought this case?"

The prosecutor jumped to his feet. He exercised his deep, penetrating voice, "Mr. Issah used the name of Jesus (peace to him) in an attempt to convert a man by the last name of Ibrahim from Islam to Christianity."

The somber judge turned to his right-front and asked for the defendant's plea. Farhan's emphatic voice echoed in the Star Chamber, "Not guilty!"

The judge ordered the prosecutor to produce his witnesses, both of whom said that they heard the defendant, known to be a Christian, invoke the name of Jesus in a conversation with the Muslim, who was also a spectator in the court gallery. Further witness testimony revealed that the two witnesses, a Shi'ite couple, sat at an outdoor, adjacent cafe table in New Tehran when the purported incident took place.

The judge then asked the defendant's lawyer to produce his witnesses. Farhan Issah's neighbor, Muhammad Ibrahim, said, "Farhan was merely telling me that he believed that Jesus (may he have peace) as part of God had made the universe. He never asked me to believe the same thing."

The defense lawyer called the defendant to the stand. He repeated Muhammad's testimony. The prosecutor, swishing in his black robe toward the defendant, asked, "Why did you talk about Jesus (peace be to him) with Mr. Ibrahim?"

With a calm smile, Farhan replied, "I shared with my next-door neighbor what I believe. I learned from other students at a United States of America university on the basis of the Bible that Jesus as part of God was the Maker of his world."

"Didn't you wish to influence him to become a Christian?"

"That was entirely up to him. I in no way tried to talk him into being a Christian. I never try to proselytize Muslims but do share what I believe as far as my faith is concerned. I always let them agree or disagree as they wish."

"You realize, of course, that the testimony of your views about Jesus (peace to him) as both God and man runs directly counter to Islam's belief that he was only a prophet, don't you?"

"Yes, I know that Muslims have that idea, but I was merely sharing my life and ideas with my neighbor."

"Do you really seriously believe that Jesus (peace to him) actually died on a cross and came back to life?"

"Yes, I do, because the Bible, which I believe is from God, says so."

"Since you are a professor of criminology at GPN University, I ask you, what is the Shi'a-sharia law's usual penalty for trying to change a Muslim to any other religion?"

"The most-severe, possible punishment is the death penalty."

"I have no other questions, your Honor."

After the defendant returned to his place, the judge asked him and his lawyer to rise as he pronounced his verdict, "I have no doubt that you were trying to influence a Muslim to turn away from his faith. As an expert in the law, the defendant should know better. Therefore, I declare that you are guilty of the proselytizing charge.

"However, the law gives me a range of punishments depending on the circumstances. Therefore, since this instance is your first offense of any kind, I choose to be merciful like Allah (praise be to him) and sentence you to five years in the prison for religious offenders, or you can choose two hundred hours of community service with five years of probation. In the latter case, your offense will not go on your record unless you break probation. How does the defendant respond?"

"Your Honor, I fail to see the reasons for your Honor's ruling....However, I accept probation and forgive you!" Farhan thought, *Thank you, Jesus, for giving me the willingness and courage to forgive the judge and to tell him so.*

A stunned silence continued for a few moments as everyone froze in place before the judge's gavel fell.

Chapter Twelve

Renewing a past connection

On a Monday morning in early April, Akilah's eyes almost popped out of her head as she shouted into her phone, "Is it really you, Shirley?!"

"Yes, it is," said grinning Shirley Jones, "and I'm in New Tehran now. I'd like to get together with you for lunch some day this week."

"Well, I teach today but am free tomorrow. Let's meet at noon in the cafe on Muhammad Street, where we hung out during our university years."

"Great! See you then."

* * *

Shirley Jones—a blonde-haired woman dressed in a blue, buttoned-up blouse and red slacks—entered the Ali Cafe. Akilah, who sat at a booth in the back, waved and smiled.

After they hugged and ordered sandwiches, eager Akilah said, "I have a thousand questions. We've kept in touch on Facebook since you graduated and moved back to the USA to teach school, but a face-to-face meeting is much better than social media. Why are you back here this spring?"

Grinning Shirley felt a settled peace as she explained, "It's spring break at our school, and I figured that I might return to enjoy spring among the palms....No, really, I've accepted a teaching job at a New Tehran elementary school for the upcoming school year and now have to look for an apartment."

Akilah gasped with a big smile, "That's the best news I've heard in a long time! How did it happen?"

Shirley lowered her eyes because of her painful memories, put her right hand to her cheek, and frowned. She thought, *I hate to hear reminders about that man's actions!*

Shirley shuddered and said, "Well, Akilah, I had a new principal this year who micro-managed all of the teaching with an extreme, child-centered approach. I couldn't teach fourth grade that way, because I believe that children need to memorize certain essential facts for life."

"I agree with you, Shirley."

Shirley remembered her extreme stress and frustration as she said, "I couldn't take any more of his constant visits to my classroom and his negative reports to the school board. In February, I saw on the World Web a job opening at New Tehran's Northwest Elementary School near the Everwaters. I applied and had a successful interview yesterday, during which the principal hired me on the spot, just before I called you. I guess God wants me to come back where he provided my GPNU education. However, what about you? How are you doing, Akilah?"

Akilah sat up straight with fond, friendly feelings, "I think that I shared with you the fact that I have a new partner consulting with the police in our attempts to catch criminals. His name is Farhan Issah, and—you won't believe it—he is a Christian like you!" Akilah and Shirley giggled like schoolchildren. Akilah continued, "He has a lot of interesting reasons for believing in the God of the Bible."

Since Shirley felt that she needed to discover Farhan and Akilah's exact relationship, she ventured, "Tell me the truth, Akilah. Are you two more than just friends?"

"No, we aren't. We're merely widowed GPNU criminology colleagues, who both enjoy solving puzzles like the seven-missing-women case."

"Oh, yeah. You said something about that case. Is it still a mystery?"

"Yes. The police, Farhan, and I are frustrated about the lack of leads in finding the women and our failure to discover the women's bodies, which we assume are in a hidden body dump. What's more, the perpetrator-predator seems to have gone on vacation from his perverse ways for several months. As a result, New Tehran is on edge waiting for a break in the case, while at the same time all of our possible clues have gone nowhere."

"Do you still play along with the GPN version of the USA's *Wheel of Fortune* and *Jeopardy*?"

"Of course, I do."

Shirley's thoughts returned to Akilah's partner, "Tell me a little more about this Farhan."

"He has a good analytical mind as a criminology professor and, therefore, is a good partner. On the other hand, he has a poor memory and isn't exactly a neat freak."

Akilah stopped as her jaw dropped, "A thought just occurred to me. You and I have enjoyed classical music since we were both students in the same GPNU music-appreciation class. I have a ticket for an all-Beethoven concert featuring his seventh symphony for this coming Saturday night. If I can get another seat with an extra ticket next to mine, would you be willing to go with me?"

"I don't have to fly back to the States until Sunday afternoon. That plan sounds heavenly!" Shirley gushed.

Akilah and Shirley spent another half-hour with small talk before parting with a heartfelt hug.

Chapter Thirteen

Camels clashing, spectators spectating

The LPTF gathered at Second Detective Abasi Huda's three-bedroom bungalow on New Tehran's southeast side near the Atlantic waterfront the following Friday night. A sandal stand was conspicuous by its absence.

During a brief tour, the group saw Abasi's United States baseball collection, including a baseball bat encased in a clear, plastic box with a backdoor for removal, in his study.

Lanky, bearded Abasi Huda felt elation in his whole body, lifted his head, and announced with a big grin, "During the third game of the 1932 World Series, the New York Yankees and Chicago Cubs were tied in the fifth inning with four runs each. Then, the great Babe Ruth pointed at the pitcher, the Cubs' dugout, or the Wrigley Field center-field bleachers, seemingly to predict his famous go-ahead home run. Then, the Sultan of Swat followed his brash gesture by using this bat to launch a gigantic smash to center field that traveled more than four hundred and forty feet. Lou Gehrig followed with another home run. The Yankees went on to win that game seven to five and the Series four games to none."

The task-force team then settled on the overstuffed blue furniture in Abasi's light-blue living room with coffee, tea, or water in their cups. Akilah asked, "Abasi, how did you get interested in USA baseball?"

The volume of Abasi's voice increased as he spoke, "I was surfing the channels one Saturday afternoon with nothing else to do as a teenager, when I came across an ancient replay of a baseball game that happened a century ago in 1984 between the St. Louis Cardinals and the Chicago Cubs.

"Willie McGee of the Cardinals hit a single, double, triple, and homer—a rare feat called the 'cycle' in baseball.

"Even more, the second baseman for the Cubs, Ryne Sandberg, who later became part of baseball's Hall of Fame, had three singles and then two home runs in the ninth and tenth innings. His homers tied the game both times off of one the best relief pitchers of all time, Bruce Sutter. That game, which the Cubs won by the huge score of eleven to ten, propelled Sandberg toward the Most Valuable Player award and the Cubs into the playoffs. That game hooked me on baseball."

Mamduh Ghanem snickered and piped up, "However, the Cubs haven't won the World Series since 2016 through 2019, a long time ago. Before those years, they hadn't won it since 1907 and 1908."

Abasi said with a slight grin, "You're right, Mamduh, but they're going to win the World Series this year."

Mamdah retorted with a frown, "That's what you Cub fans think every year, but my Yankees will win it instead."

Fahyim Srour felt that he had to be a peacemaker and interjected, "I'm sure that we can agree to disagree about sports, but the Colossal Camel Clash is coming up in two weeks, as I mentioned last time. Pulling a few strings, I've obtained eight tickets for all of us to go to that big tournament."

Farhan's harrowing camel experience flashed into his mind. He then said with pinched eyebrows, "I've been to one of the smaller camel competitions; and fast, fleeing camels almost trampled me. I don't want to have a camel-trampled death."

Fahyim replied with a smile, "The CCC, which showcases the most successful eight fusion-propelled camels during the season facing off against each other, takes place in a large stadium holding 40,000 fans. Concrete-brick walls protect spectators from any harm, Farhan."

Farhan responded with a slight grin, "Well, then, I'm game."

The other members nodded their heads.

Then, Huda projected for the team a three-dimensional, holographic recording of his son, dressed in a white robe with a gold design, wearing a matching golden hat with a feather, and riding a holographic horse around their neighborhood and up to their front porch. Then, the licensed circumciser led him into the front waiting room all decked out in kingly decor, and his "godfather" held him still in his arms. The hologram's next scene depicted the men and women dancing to a traditional Turkish song played on virtual musical instruments in celebration of the first stage of the young man's coming-of-age.

* * *

When the Thursday of the Colossal Camel Clash arrived in early May, at noon First Detective Srour picked up all of the task-force members in the police station parking lot with a large police fusion zip-van. When they arrived ten seconds later at Muslim Field across town, they used VIP parking at the stadium. They then joined many fans who were roasting camel meat and speculating on the outcome of the CCC in the parking lot before the game.

The task force sat halfway up the high stands in soft, theater-like seats that a dome of transparent aluminum protected during afternoon rains. The festivities began after a shrill soprano sang the GPN national anthem, "Praise be to Allah."

The first one of four matches in the preliminary round of the tournament pitted the camels named after twentieth century presidents Ronald Reagan and Mikhail Gorbachev. Farhan said to Fahyim on his right, "I heard at the other camel wrestling match why they name camels after prominent, political figures. Those names are two centuries old. It's because Turks name their camels after political figures in

Turkey for their camel contests. Apparently, we got that custom from them. Isn't that right, Fahyim?"

"That's right. Many of the names are from history a couple centuries ago."

As the sell-out crowd cheered for their favorites, two huge fusion-powered camels with fancy, multicolored saddles attached with a pair of slim zip-packs attacked each other at high speed to win a nearby female. At the same time, Farhan exclaimed above the din, "I want Ronald Reagan to win!"

Fahyim Srour thought that he would make the bout more interesting and replied, "Do you want to let some money back up your wish?"

"No, I'm not a betting man, and I thought that Muslims don't gamble."

Fahyim felt a little embarrassed and replied with a half-grin, "Well, that's usually the case."

Reagan attacked Gorbachev by slapping its neck against the latter's neck and kicking it. Gorbachev responded by biting Reagan's neck as it made a return neck-wave with its saliva flying. Reagan extended its left hoof to lock and pull Gorbachev's right leg, while Mikhail spit its toxic slime at Reagan's eyes.

Farhan yelled over the crowd's din, "When I saw the Smith and Levanshov camels fight, they didn't use their necks as weapons."

Next to him on his left, Second Policeman Mamduh said, "The best camels use that tactic too, though Levanshov did win enough during the camel-wrestling season to make the final eight. However, Smith finished well out of the running for the CCC."

Eventually, Reagan chased Gorbachev toward the concrete-brick wall closest to the task force. Gorbachev's violent collision with the wall knocked a couple of bricks out of it.

* * *

During the final match of the afternoon for the camel championship, Ronald Reagan, named after the States' famous President, faced off against Dick Nixon, named after an infamous U.S. President. Reagan charged Nixon at a gallop, knocked it down, and sat on it to the loud cheers of all of the spectators, especially Reagan rooters.

As the task force rose to leave the full stadium, Farhan said, "That was quite a spectacle. Thank you, Fahyim, for taking us to see it."

Fahyim Srour swelled with pride and said with a big smile, "You're very welcome!"

ChapterFourteen

A connection judged

Akilah and Shirley were having lunch at their favorite cafe on a Friday noon in mid-June, 2085, after Shirley's move to New Tehran. Farhan and two of his university friends entered. As they passed the two women's booth, Farhan's eyes lit up as he said, "Hi, Akilah!"

Akilah said, "Hello, Farhan. This is my friend Shirley Jones."

Farhan said with his big smile, "Nice to meet you, Shirley. Say, didn't I see you at our church this morning?" When Shirley nodded with her beautiful grin, Farhan continued as he pointed at his two friends, "These guys are two GPNU colleagues, Muheer and Malik. We've just come from church." The three men then found a booth farther back in the cafe.

Shirley felt a thrill run through her body and whispered to Akilah, "You didn't tell me Farhan was that handsome." They giggled like extinct African hyenas.

Muheer, Malik, and Farhan talked about camel and human sports as they enjoyed a hardy Friday lunch of beans and beefsteak.

* * *

Four days later on Tuesday, Farhan and Akilah were at the same restaurant at noon when she asked him, "How frustrated are you, Farhan, about the case?"

"I'm very frustrated. However, I believe that God has helped me germinate a theory about the murderer's identity."

"Tell me, Farhan."

Farhan looked around the restaurant like a spy, arose, edged around the table, leaned over her, and whispered in her right ear. Her eyes bugged out and her jaw dropped, "You can't be serious."

Farhan then shared with her the clues that made him suspicious. Akilah said, "Ah, I see why you are suspicious. However, we need proof, not just theories, Farhan."

Farhan grinned, "You're right. Say, Akilah, do you have Shirley Jones' cell phone number? I'd like to call her to make a date."

Akilah smirked as she checked her ultra-smart phone, "Sure, I hope you two have fun."

* * *

Farhan screwed up his courage as he said into his phone, "Hello, Shirley? This is Farhan Issah. Akilah gave me your number. Would you like to go on a date next week Wednesday evening to eat dinner?"

Shirley's heart skipped a beat, but she said, "Hello, Farhan. Yes, Akilah has told me a lot about you. I'm willing to go on a date with you."

"Akilah spilled the beans about me, and you're still willing?"

"Yes, Farhan."

"Is it okay if I pick you up at 7:00 P.M.?"

"That sounds like a good plan."

* * *

On Wednesday evening, June 25, 2085, Farhan, wearing a gray suit and a red tie, took Shirley, dressed in a glossy, red dress, to the fanciest restaurant in New Tehran. The maitre de ushered them to a table in a little, private cubicle. Farhan asked himself why he had asked this woman on a date, fumbled with Shirley's chair, and then sat down opposite her. They both ordered steak and settled in.

Shirley started the conversation, "Dating must be a little awkward for you, Farhan, after your wife died."

Farhan blushed several shades of red, "Yes, I do feel a little uncomfortable, but it's not often that I can find another Christian for real fellowship in a Muslim land. Besides, God has helped me grieve out my wife's death and find his peace. Tell me about how you became a Christian, Shirley."

Her soul experienced again the thrill of that first experience of new life. She gave Farhan her broad, beautiful grin with a nod, as her blonde hair bounced around her shoulders, "During middle school in Gatlinburg, Tennessee, where I grew up in the morning shadow of the Smoky Mountains, I was in church when our pastor's message was about Ephesians chapter two. He said, 'We are all born dead.'

"That statement aroused my curiosity. I waited to find out what he meant. He said, 'We are all spiritually-stillborn, that is, dead to God, not wanting to love and follow Jesus, but he makes us alive through Jesus by the Holy Spirit, when we begin believing in him.'

"When I skipped out of church that Sunday morning, my brother said, 'What's gotten into you, Shirl?'

"I said, 'The question is, who, not what, has gotten into me? Jesus came into my life during our pastor's message.' My brother's eyes bugged out as he turned away."

"As a result, I know that God made me really alive for the first time during that worship service. From that time on, I have been eager to worship God, listen to pastors' messages, read the Bible, serve in church, and follow Jesus. However, that path hasn't always been easy. What about you, Farhan?"

"I was a Muslim from the vast country of Jordan when my parents and I emigrated from our country to the USA. I began comparing the different religions in high school. However, when I attended Purdue University, not far from my hometown in Indiana, a friend invited me to a Bible study of a Christian campus group. God used that Bible study to make me search the Bible further to discover Christian beliefs. Then, I compared them with Muslim beliefs.

"During my personal and group Bible studies, God used the students' friendly acceptance, my growing conviction about the God of the Bible, and their enthusiasm for him to rescue me from my empty attempts to earn my way to Paradise.

"At one of their prayer meetings, I asked Jesus to remake my life from my performance-driven to God's-graceled. Then, Jesus entered my life and gave me real joy for the first time."

Shirley's muscles relaxed as she said, "That's great, Farhan! How has God used your time living in a Muslim country to help you?"

Farhan leaned toward her as he said, "That's a great question, Shirley. I guess he has strengthened my faith in him further by contrasting his truth in the Bible with various Muslim ideas. Since the two belief systems are so different, I've had to dig deeper into the Bible's truths to find what I really believed. What about you, Shirley? How has God strengthened your faith?"

"Well, in a similar way, I guess God used my time at GPNU in my discussions with Muslim friends like Akilah to make my faith in him stronger.

"By the way, Farhan, how is the murdered-women case coming along?"

Farhan felt a tiny glimmer of hope as he said, "Akilah and I have made a little progress on the case, but we have a long way to go. I believe that the murderer is getting overconfident about his success. However, he still does a very good job of covering his tracks."

* * *

As Farhan and Shirley approached her apartment house on the front sidewalk after their enjoyable three-hour dinner, she quivered with excitement and turned to face him. "I had a great time, Farhan."

He leaned forward as they embraced each other and kissed three times with each kiss longer than the previous one. Farhan noticed out of the corners of his eyes two apartment-house curtains flutter.

He felt so comfortable with her that he then asked, "Shirley, would you like to attend the symphony next week Saturday night with me?"

The full-moon light lit up her broad smile that reflected her heart's gushing waterfall of emotion, "I'd love to!"

* * *

Loud knocking on Shirley's second-floor apartment door accosted her Thursday morning, just after she had finished dressing for a day of teaching. When she opened the door, two New Tehran police officers Fadl Taslim and Dilawar Kaysan stood before her. The latter one said, "May we come in?"

When they had seated themselves on her couch, Policeman Kaysan came right to the point, "Ms. Jones, the C-POV alerted us that you and a man were hugging and kissing each other last night in front of the apartment house after ten o'clock."

Her sudden, perplexed foreboding said, "Yes,...Farhan Issah...and I ended our date...that way last night....What is the C-POV, and why do the police...care about our actions on a date?"

Policeman Taslim replied, "The C-POV is the Committee for the Prevention of Vice and the Promotion of Virtue. Don't you know that the law considers both kissing and hugging in public to be indecencies? Also, the New Tehran nightly curfew is 10:00 P.M."

Shirley's heart sank, as she said, "No, I didn't know that we violated the law. I also thought that the curfew was for under-aged people."

Policeman Kaysan said, "These misdemeanors are included in the Shi'a-sharia laws to protect the public's decency. I'll have to write you and this Farhan Issah a ticket. Both of you are to appear before the judge next Thursday at 11:00 A.M. for a trial."

"Why does that committee care that we kissed and hugged in public?"

Taslim preached, "The public-indecency laws and curfew are on the books to keep good order in our society."

Shirley scowled and said, "Those laws don't make any sense to me. If Farhan and I were having sex on the lawn, you'd have grounds to arrest us for public indecency and exposure, but giving a ticket for hugging and kissing seems extreme to me."

As Kaysan handed her the ticket, he said, "Nevertheless, you did violate the law. The judge will see you in a week."

* * *

When Farhan answered his cell phone on his lunch break, Shirley said with a quiver in her voice and her heart, "Hello, Farhan. You won't believe what happened this morning. Two New Tehran policemen issued us a ticket for two counts of public indecency and one of breaking the nighttime curfew."

Farhan's mind revisited his arrest and conviction about the trumped-up charge of trying to change his Muslim neighbor into a Christian. He said, "What?! You're right, Shirley. I can't believe it. I thought that I our nation had not held onto the sharia blue-laws of the past."

Shirley suddenly felt a weary contempt as she said, "Well, they said the government has these laws to 'protect the public decency.'"

Farhan's righteous indignation increased, "That makes no sense. We weren't a couple of young students out to make a lot of noise by disturbing the peace with a wild party."

Shirley sounded resigned to their conviction as she said, "Anyway, we are supposed to appear in court before a civil judge next week Thursday morning at 11:00 A.M. By the way, Farhan, I had a really good time last night."

"I did too, except for this ticket-business."

"Well, I guess we'll see each other again next Thursday morning. I hope you have a good week in spite of this irritation."

Farhan felt his sarcasm welling up inside him, "Yeah, the time before the civil judge will be a genuinely-joyful journey. Take care of yourself, Shirley. Goodbye."

* * *

Farhan and Shirley strode into the first-floor, civil courtroom at the appointed time. After the morning break, a clean-shaven prosecutor in a black robe and matching turban arrived at the same time. Then, the civil judge, dressed in his shiny, black robe with a matching turban, swished into the courtroom from a side door. He banged his gavel to bring the room to order.

He began with a slight smile, "Prosecutor, who do we have here, a couple of ne'er-do-wells?"

The stiff-standing, starchy lawyer tried to keep a straight face as he declared, "Multiple people reported seeing the defendants—Farhan Issah, a GPNU criminology professor, and Shirley Jones, a fourth-grade teacher—kissing and hugging in front of her apartment house after 10:00 P.M. last week Wednesday. Therefore, I charge them with three misdemeanors—two counts of public indecency and one violation of the curfew. I could charge them for each of their three kisses, but I won't."

The green-collared judge asked, "How do you plead, defendants?"

Farhan and Shirley looked at each other, nodded, and then said in unison, "We're guilty, your Honor."

The judge's bushy eyebrows lifted almost off his head, as he said, "That's the first 'guilty' plea that I have heard in a while. What do you say for yourselves?"

Shirley put on her earnest face and said, "We were unaware of your legal restrictions on public affection and your 10:00 P.M. curfew for adults. We are guilty of these misdemeanors."

Resisting the temptation to make a sarcastic remark, Farhan chimed in with his clean sense of humor, "However, we fail to see why the police and courts enforce these laws, since we were not creating a disturbance. Our kisses weren't that loud." Some people in the gallery snickered.

The judge glared at them and exclaimed, "Quiet in the court! Surely, you as a criminology professor were aware of these laws to protect the public good?!"

Farhan replied with a deeper-than-normal professor's voice, "I'm well-versed in criminal laws, not in these blue laws from a bygone era."

The judge shuffled a couple of papers and continued with his sonorous voice, "I see that you are both free of any other complaint, even traffic and parking tickets, except for one against you, Professor. I am ready to pronounce my verdict. Even though I can sentence you to a year in civil prison, I am inclined to be lenient. Therefore, I sentence you to one hundred hours of community service each. You are also on probation for a year. However, no more kissing or hugging in public, mind you.'"

Farhan said with a twinkle in his eye, "Thank you, your Honor. We don't see the need for those laws or the need for their enforcement, but we forgive you."

Everyone in the courtroom froze in space for a couple of seconds. Then, the gavel fell with a loud echo.

Chapter Fifteen

On probation

When Akilah and Farhan had their monthly lunch during the third week in June, she asked him, "What's this I hear about a ticket that the police gave you and Shirley for public indecency in addition to your previous 'crime'? Gossip is flowing around the 'small town' of the GPNU about you two."

Farhan's face got almost as red as a tomato as he said, "Yeah, after we hugged and kissed each other on the sidewalk in front of her apartment house a few minutes following curfew, the nosy neighbors reported us to the C-POV. However, God will judge them and the judge."

Akilah's natural indignation arose, "Those misdemeanors don't make any sense. So you had your day in court and are on another probation?"

"Yeah. Live and learn."

"How are you doing your mutual community service?"

"We're spending our Thursday afternoons at a local, second-hand thrift shop doing just about anything to help."

To calm Farhan's embarrassment, Akilah decided to return to the perplexing case of the missing murdered women, "Now, what are your thoughts about the presumed serial-killer case, Farhan?"

Farhan enjoyed returning to familiar legal territory, "I think that since all we have are circumstantial clues, we need to flush the murderer out of his sinful cesspool in some way."

"I agree. How do we 'flush him out'?"

"I'm not sure."

"Maybe we can get someone to be bait to catch that murderous shark."

"That's a good idea. We'll have to brainstorm further to figure out how we can hook him."

Then, Farhan changed the subject, "Akilah, I was wondering why Muslims believe that children are sinless and innocent until they reach the age of discernment. I've never had children, but I've observed young nieces and nephews back in Indiana. They seem far from innocent but very self-centered. I believe that we're all conceived and born tainted with selfish imperfection."

Akilah responded, "The Muslims that I know believe, as you say, that children are not born with self-centeredness but learn it from their environment."

"Akilah, I remember I visited my brother while I was home from college. When they put their baby in his crib at night, he would cry a little while and then wait a few seconds to see if my brother and his wife would let him get up. Then, he'd cry a little more and wait again trying to get his selfish way.

"I believe on the basis of the Bible that we're all born thinking that we're the center of the universe like my nephew and that parents have to teach their children that God is actually at the center of their world."

"Farhan, why do you believe that?"

"Well, Prophet David wrote in Psalm 51, after repenting of his adultery and murder, that he was conceived and born in sinfulness and that his sin made him guilty before God, the Judge. In the New Testament, Prophet Paul said that we are guilty all our lives unless Jesus' death takes that guilt away for us."**(Read the rest of the conversation on pages 234-236)**

Akilah felt anxious that his evidence was getting too strong for her. Therefore, she covered up her anxiety with her slight smile, "Well, we'd better get back to grading our final exams, or the administration's judges will come down hard on us."

* * *

"What is the price of this blue, lightweight, winter jacket? There's no price on it," said Shirley to the store manager in the used-clothes aisle, as she operated the ancient thrift-store cash register with raised, push-down keys.

He yelled back, "Two liras." Then, she rang up the sale for a disheveled, scarfed old woman. At the same time behind the store, Farhan—dressed in a short-sleeved shirt, jeans, and work gloves—unloaded a truckload of goods from an estate sale.

At afternoon tea time, Farhan asked Shirley how her afternoon was going. "Frustrating!" she exclaimed.

He said, "Yeah, a store in disarray like this one with no prices on half of the items is difficult. It's almost enough to make me neater at home and in my office."

"Almost?" Shirley asked with her beautiful grin.

"Well, I know where everything is there. It may look messy, but it has a certain orderly messiness."

She then looked deep into Farhan's eyes and said, "Your presence here with me makes even this store bearable, Farhan."

Farhan said with tight lips, "I wish that I could kiss you right now, but it would be ironic if we broke our probation with a public kiss while doing our community time. Those laws are unjust invasions of personal freedom."

Farhan combined seriousness and humor with his comment, "However, God wants us to obey the authorities over us, even when the laws are nonsense. Biblically, we can disobey them only when they clearly violate the Bible. Let's see. Doesn't the eleventh commandment say, 'You shall kiss and hug in public'?"

Chapter Sixteen

A new case and a big decision

In early July, a pregnant, thirty-year-old Sunni woman called a phone number that she saw in the *New Tehran Times*: "Hello, your ad said, 'medical procedure available.' I've been pregnant for seven months, and I don't want this inconvenient fetus. What kind of procedure do you offer?"

"We can take care of your problem."

"What are your hours, and where do I go?"

"You can come to our office any time from nine to five Saturday through Wednesday. Our office is at 39 West Ali Street."

"Okay. I'll be there."

Instead, she rode her zip-camel four blocks to the police station in five seconds. At the front desk, she told Second Policeman Ghanem, "I want to report a phone offer of an abortion."

Ghanem's adrenaline surged as he ushered her to his desk. He asked, "Tell me exactly what happened."

"I saw an ad in the *Times* that offered a medical procedure. Since I was curious about it, I called the number. I told the man on the other end that I was seven-months pregnant and didn't want my fetus.

"In reality, I'm happily married and want my baby, especially since we've been trying to have a baby for three years. I lied to him to see what he was up to. He said that they could take care of my problem. I wrote down their number and address for you."

Ghanem responded with a deeply-furrowed brow, "Thank you, ma'am, for this information. Of course, as you know, unlike many countries with Muslim majorities, abortion of babies is illegal in the GPN except when the mother is clearly in danger of dying. We will follow up on your information."

"Then, what do women who don't want their unborn babies do?"

"Adoption is the best option, since many couples who can't have babies are eager to love an adopted child. Adoptions fulfill a real need for unwanted children, but those couples often can't find a child to adopt. Another possible option is that the single woman can raise the child, and many of them do a good job. However, we believe that it's better for a child to have both a mother and a father."

"I know that the motherly instinct is very strong. How can women give their babies up?"

Ghanem replied, "Which displays more love to children—giving them up to a loving couple or selfishly keeping babies with the emotional and social problems that children have without a father?"

She asked, "What do you do about babies resulting from rape and incest?"

"Well, those babies also have a right to live and be adopted. It's not their fault they started the way they did."

"The USA allows unborn babies up to three months old to be aborted because they aren't viable outside the womb. Why not abort them, since they can't survive if they are born then?"

"They are still developing human beings, the vast majority of whom will become viable and be born. We don't believe that people should play Allah (may he be praised)."

Then, Ghanem rose and again thanked her for her information. She then waddled out of the station with a broad smile.

* * *

The following Tuesday afternoon, Akilah and Farhan arrived within a couple of minutes of each other at the police station for a task force meeting. First Detective Srour convened the LPTF, "Now, we have a new case of black-market abortionists soliciting women to commit baby-murders."

Akilah asked, "How can they justify killing developing human beings in the womb?"

Srour answered with a tight frown, "They fantasize that the baby is an object—a 'fetus'—not a human being growing in a woman's uterus. They think that the baby is a part of them, whereas he or she is only attached to them and has the right to live, just as everyone has that right. Because of our laws against killing unborn babies, adoptions by couples who are eager to have a baby are increasing. However, these black-market baby-killers violently prevent such eager parents-to-be from adopting their possible adopted children. They trash those lives instead."

Fourth Detective Maloof said with a big, frustrated frown, "We've tried to catch these baby-killers in the past, but every time we go to their killing place, they have disappeared."

Farhan chimed in, "Now, our task force has moved from attempting to catch a serial women-killer to protecting the life of a USA president to seeking justice for helpless, pre-born babies against baby-killers. In a way, all of our recent cases have dealt with illegal and attempted assaults on human life. We're living up to the name of our group."

Srour then asked, "Are we all agreed that we will pursue these murderers?" Everyone nodded.

Farhan said with profound sadness, "One of the real horrors in my home country is the modern holocaust that has killed many millions of helpless and hopeless babies, many more than the huge number of Jews that horrible Hitler killed. Both the Bible and the Qur'an describe a Creator-God who created each life from its beginning. Why do people devalue life so much?"

Everyone shook their heads with creased foreheads.

Perplexed Third Detective Daher said, "How are we going to find and arrest these baby murderers?"

Srour said, “Touma and Ghanem, follow up on the woman’s lead. Let’s all think about getting those abortionists and come back next Tuesday afternoon with strategies, okay? Anything else we need to discuss?”

After the meeting, First Policeman Touma made a quick phone call in a private conference room. Ghanem and he then ate a mid-afternoon lunch before departing for the purported crime scene.

* * *

When Touma and Ghanem walked into 39 West Ali Street, they observed an empty storefront. They called the two CSIs with little hope that they would find any evidence. The criminals knew how to cover up their illegal activities. The two policemen also went through the trash out back in the dumpster, one of the least-liked parts of their job. Then, they texted the other task force members to come and inspect the crime scene.

The rest of the life-protection task force and the two CSIs converged on 39 West Ali Street at the same time. Asima and Ameer dusted the place for fingerprints with little hope that their efforts would produce the criminals’ identities, since people could have left those prints there at any time in the past.

The team members perused the place. With a heavy, righteously-angry heart, Farhan said, “This front room must have been a waiting room, and the back room has to be where the doctor or medical person crushed the heads of the babies.”

Akilah grimaced and responded with irony, “You speak so delicately, Farhan. Asima and Ameer, can your laser light show up any blood stains?”

When the CSIs shone their light around the back room, several blood spatters appeared, radiating from the table at the center. With very little hope, Akilah asked, “Can you get any DNA samples?”

Asima replied, “If these perps made a quick getaway, they washed everything down very fast with bleach. We’ll try to get some DNA; but, again, our samples could be from people anytime in the past. I wouldn't hold my breath, if I were you. Perhaps, you're going to have to catch these criminals red-handed with their hands literally in the womb."

Akilah said as she felt a tiny glimmer of hope in spite of the dark killers' scene, "Not a bad idea, Asima."

* * *

Two days later, Farhan and Shirley in a mutual embrace sat on the carpet of their probationary rendezvous point behind the blue, lightweight, winter jackets. Farhan felt that it was the perfect time to break the delicious silence by proposing in a whisper, "Let's get married, Shirley. We are both committed to following and loving Jesus and each other. We have also avoided sexual intercourse before marriage because the Bible calls it sexual immorality. God certainly knows that we've been tempted to go beyond kissing and hugging, but he's kept us from going there by answering our prayers against temptation. What's to prevent us from getting married in September? How about Friday, September 5th?"

"Yes, let's get married then, Farhan! It will be early in our school year." Shirley grinned but then furrowed her brow, "That's only a little over two months from now. We have a million decisions to make."

Farhan smiled at his bride-to-be, "Well, we've decided the first one of those million; we only have 999,999 to go." They both laughed, muffling the sound with their hands. Farhan tentatively continued, "Can you let me tell Akilah about our decision?"

She thought that she'd have a little fun with him as she said with a little grin, "Why, Farhan, should I let you tell my best friend?"

"I have some pretty obvious reasons."

"Of course, I'll let you have your fun, but why don't you make sure the church and pastor are available for September 5th first? As you know, we have identical worship celebrations twice on Friday mornings, but usually the church is available Friday evening, since small groups usually meet in the members' homes then."

They then helped each other up with big grins and a final, long kiss; bent over so as not to be seen; and scurried to their appointed posts.

Chapter Seventeen

Pursuing and planning

Farhan smirked, "Akilah, may I have Shirley's hand in marriage on September 5th?"

Akilah was not surprised. She said, "Of course, Farhan. I'm overjoyed for you two! I'll be first in line at the church. I assume that's where the happy event is going to be."

Elated Farhan said, "Yes, it is. We decided last Thursday when we met at the far end of the thrift store for a little guilty time secretly transgressing our probation. However, now that I think about it, our time together there isn't really public—unless you count the jackets we hide behind as part of the public—since none of the public can see us behind those clothes."

Akilah teased him, "Maybe, I should report you two to the judge."

She then changed the subject, "By the way, Farhan, what do you think about our new case?"

"Well, Akilah, at least we know that a crime has definitely been committed this time. In the serial-rapist-killer case, we have only suspected that crimes were taking place since the seven bodies have not appeared.

"However, I wasn't surprised that we failed to find the outlaw abortionists at that address. They cleared out without a trace again."

"I wonder how they know that the police are coming. They must receive inside information, perhaps from someone within the department that they've paid off. Let's be alert for clues to identify him or her."

"Akilah, what strategy are we going to recommend to the task force to catch the criminals? Perhaps, we should keep our own strategy to ourselves, since the informant may be one of them."

She said, "Perhaps, we can have two strategies, one for them and another for us."

He scratched his head, raised his other fist to his cheek, and said, "Maybe, we could ask a pregnant woman to pose confidentially as a potential customer, give a false address to the rest of the team, and let us know the real place."

Akilah frowned with a glimmer in her eyes, "Farhan, you're a devious devil."

He responded with a slight grin, "I prefer not to be identified with that evil spirit....

"Say, Akilah, we talked about our differences over children's innocence or guilt. How can you believe that they are innocent when you teach criminology, in which we know that criminals are often formed beginning in childhood?"

"I know that parents often pervert children's lives with their self-centered abuse. However, my Muslim understanding is that kids start out innocent."

"As you know, that's where we differ, because I believe, according to the Bible, that all children are conceived and born infected with self-centeredness. Some grow up with their parents' loving limits, but they have to learn that God is the center of the universe rather than themselves. Others grow up to show their self-centeredness in outward rebellion like the criminals about whom we teach and whom we try to catch.

"I believe that for humanity's desperate need, the first Person of God sent the second divine Person to become Jesus in order to die in humanity's place, thus deflecting believers' guilty verdict away from them to him on the cruel, criminal's cross. Jesus certainly taught that children are our models but only as examples of dependence on parents, the way we are to trust in him and his Father."

"However, I still don't see how your God can be one and yet three, Farhan. He's not logical."

"You're right, Akilah, that he doesn't fit our limited, human reasoning; but God does conform to his own divine logic, which is far beyond what our minds can grasp."

"That theory is interesting, Farhan. In any case, we have to try to catch those baby-murderers."

"Akilah, I've been reading in Luke chapter one that the Virgin Mary, newly-pregnant with Jesus by the Holy Spirit, went to visit her cousin Elizabeth, who was six months pregnant with John the Baptist. When Mary entered Zechariah and Elizabeth's house, Elizabeth exclaimed that her baby leaped for joy in her womb because Jesus came near John.

"Perish the thought if abortion were available at that time to end Jesus' life because of the vicious gossip that must have taken place in the tiny town of Nazareth about Mary's pregnancy without being married! No wonder God sent angels to announce Jesus' birth to Mary and Joseph to convince them of his gift of the virgin birth."

* * *

Farhan and Shirley met for lunch the following Thursday at a restaurant near the thrift store to begin planning the special day. Shirley said, "Farhan, did you get the church for that Friday evening?"

"Yeah, it's available and I reserved it. Our pastor is also planning on September 5 at 7:00 P.M. Where are we going to live?"

"Good question. Should we buy a house?"

Farhan suddenly felt overwhelmed by the big decisions that they needed to make. He asked her, "Should it be a little or larger one? How many children are we going to have?"

Shirley felt that a whirlwind had caught them up. She asked him, "Um, how many do you want? We're already in our thirties. The ticking biological clock limits the number."

"You mean we can't have thirteen?"

"No, silly, we can't, unless you give birth to the last ten or so."

"Then, it's settled. With God's blessing, we'll have three children."

Farhan's impishness could not stay put as he said, "However, remember Abraham and Sarah, who gave birth to Isaac when Abraham was one hundred and she was ninety years old." Then, his serious side reasserted itself, "Of course, we could always move from a small to a medium-sized house when our family grows. I don't think we want a fancy house."

Shirley nodded with a thankful heart that they were both flexible, "That size family sounds reasonable. We'll have to go house-hunting. Maybe, we can get tips from watching that cable network that majors in that topic."

They looked at each other and burst out laughing. Shirley continued, "Now, our wedding doesn't have to be fancy or big. Let's invite your university buddies and my teacher friends. Who else? Oh, yes, we could invite the police and our church members."

"Who should the best man and maid or matron of honor be?"

"Of course, I'll invite Akilah to be my matron of honor and my third-grade teacher friend as my bridesmaid. Who do you want to be your best man and groomsman, Farhan?"

"I don't know."

"You could invite your Muslim university friends that you introduced to Shirley and me."

"That's a good idea. By the way, my school board gave me the following week off for our honeymoon. Can you get that week off at the university?"

"I'll get it off if I have to get a substitute professor myself. Where should we go? Maybe, we can go to Iceland and observe the volcanoes and ice."

They looked at each other with the joy of a couple deeply in love.

Chapter Eighteen

Catching body-invaders?

On the following Tuesday, July 15—a sultry, oppressive day—the task force met to discuss how they might catch the baby-killers. Farhan announced to the group that he and Shirley were going to get married. The group smiled and nodded their heads.

First Policeman Touma asked, "How are your plans going?"

Farhan grinned with his impishness showing through, "Well, we have the wedding party, the church, and the minister. What else could we possibly need?"

Akilah said with a tiny grin, "You men! Of course, you need a theme, wedding clothes, flowers, invitations, and many other things, including a place to celebrate afterwards."

Farhan continued his humor, "Oh, I suppose. We should get married wearing zip-snowshoes, as if we were up north." They erupted in belly laughs.

First Detective Srour moved them to the subject at hand, "Now, what strategy can we devise to bring the abortionists to justice for their illegal baby-murdering?"

Akilah volunteered, "Farhan and I think that we need to find a pregnant woman who will be willing to lead us to the crooked, illegal abortionists."

Fourth Detective Maloof said, "If we're going to pull that feat off, how do we find such a person brave enough to lead us to them?" Silence ensued.

He continued, "Also, I want to report about our trip to an empty storefront minus abortionists. As we all observed, they left quickly and left no clues behind for us to catch them except some laser-revealed blood spatters."

All of the members shook their heads.

Huda said, "Does anyone know a pregnant woman who fits our need?"

All members again shook their frowning heads.

* * *

For Shirley and Farhan, August blew by with the tornado of details needed for the big event. On one Friday-morning church date in mid-August, when they left the auditorium after worship, they greeted a young couple named Mel and Janice Whiting. With a big smile, Farhan said, "Tell us about yourselves. What do you do for a living?"

Warming to Farhan and Shirley's natural friendliness, Mel said, "We just moved here after I got a job as an engineer at Ali Manufacturing on—you guessed it—Ali Street; Janice is expecting in October, as you might have suspected."

In spite of Janice's strong backache, she said, "I found a job teaching pre-school on the west side. We're really looking forward to having our first child."

Seeing a possible opportunity, Farhan looked at Shirley with a wink and said, "You're invited to come now to my apartment for coffee or whatever you want to drink, except any kind of hard stuff."

Mel said, "Sure, we'll follow you there."

* * *

When they had settled with coffee in Farhan's small living room after Farhan had picked up his criminology books scattered there, tall, blonde-haired Mel asked, "What do you two do for a living?"

Shirley's friendliness opened like flower from a stem as she said, "I'm a fourth-grade teacher at a school on the

New Tehran outskirts, and Farhan is an assistant criminology professor at GPNU and an assistant criminology consultant for the police department."

Not realizing where the conversation was going, Janice said, "Really! What cases have you worked on with the police?"

Farhan thought of the Latin clause *Carpe diem* or "seize the day" and answered, "I've only worked here a year, but we have a big one about a serial kidnapper-murderer that continues to stump us without any solid evidence.

"However, now, while the serial killer eludes us, we protected USA President Smith's life during his state visit but now have black-market abortionists giving us the slip. The way I understand it, our strict abortion laws were a huge reaction against the United States' loosening of abortion restrictions back in the 1970s. The reason was that virtually everyone here believes in an all-powerful Creator who made human life begin at conception.

"Right now, since GPN laws against abortion are very strict compared to the United States and to just about every other country, we're now trying to catch these baby-killers. The problem is that every time we get a lead and move in on them, they have already cleaned up after themselves and vanished into thick air."

Mel thought, *I think I know where this conversation is leading. We'll have to be open to God's leading.* He said with a wrinkled brow, "You're right about the air here. However, we're pro-life too and wouldn't think of aborting our dear baby. What are the laws here?"

Farhan returned Mel's seriousness, "Abortion is an illegal felony because it's considered first-degree murder except when the birth clearly threatens the mother's life."

* * *

Janice's thoughts drifted to her past. In her imagination, she saw Mel and herself sitting in their USA living room. Mel said in his frustration, "We've tried so hard for a whole year to have a baby to love but haven't been able to. What are we doing wrong, dear?"

She said, "I don't think we're doing anything wrong. It's just not God's time yet."

"Why would he prevent us from having a baby when he put that desire in our hearts?"

"Maybe, he's trying to teach us patience, Mel."

"I guess many Bible people also had to wait. Abraham and Sarah had to wait twenty-five years. I hope that God doesn't wait that long to give us a little one."

"I hope so too."

"Of course, before we wait that long, we could adopt an unwanted baby."

"We could."

* * *

With her mind back in the present, red-haired Janice remarked with clenched fists, "Why would anyone want to kill a helpless child, a developing human life? Why don't women give the child up for adoption to fulfill a barren couple's desires instead of killing their children?"

Shirley said, "We're going to get married September 5th, have been looking for a house, and then also hope to start a family."

Sensing that the time had arrived to suggest Janice's involvement, Farhan sent a prayer heavenward, cleared his throat, and spoke just above a whisper, while looking at her with a little grin, "Actually,...our task force has been looking for a pregnant woman who will pose as one of the abortionists' possible clients."

Janice was afraid that Farhan was going to make some suggestion that might involve her and replied, "If you're suggesting that I might be that woman, I'd have to pray a lot about being involved."

Farhan said, "Of course, don't feel any pressure. It just seems to me that maybe God has provided you at this time with the need to catch them, but maybe not. Feel free to decline my suggestion with no hard feelings at all."

Janice dropped the level of her voice as well as her shiny, red hair on her shoulders, "Well, what would be involved?"

"The pregnant woman would answer the baby-killers' newspaper ad by phone; find out the address; tell it to my partner, Akilah, and me; go to the abortionists' office; pretend to be a client; and wear a wire so that we can hear the abortionist's plans. We will follow her at a safe distance. Then, we and a couple of trusted detectives will take over from there. In addition, she might have to testify at a trial."

Fearful that too many strangers might be involved, Mel interjected, "Who's Akilah?"

"She's a GPNU criminology and Islamic-studies professor, my consultant-partner, and our good friend."

Janice said, "We'll pray about your suggestion and proceed on the basis of what we decide God wants us to do."

"Fair enough. I hate to dump this decision on you so soon after we've met, but we need someone to help us. Here's my card in case you decide to assist us."

Chapter Nineteen

Agreements and disagreements

Janice gathered her wits and faced down her fears until she called Farhan and heard his calm, comforting voice, "Hello."

"Hello, Farhan. This is Janice Whiting. We've prayed a lot about your suggestion and have decided that God wants me to be part of your scheme to catch the baby-killers."

Farhan nearly fell out of his recliner with joy as he said, "Thank you, Janice. Thanks a lot! We'll try to put it into action a week from Sunday, August 28. Please don't tell anyone about our plans, which have to remain secret for obvious reasons."

"I understand. When do I get the microphone?"

"We'll get together on Saturday evening, the 27th, at my apartment to make final plans and let you put on the wire. Are you available that night?"

"Yes, we'll be there, God willing."

* * *

The following Tuesday noon, Akilah and Farhan met for lunch. Farhan began their conversation, "Akilah, I've wondered since we first met why you ride a fusion-cycle instead of driving a hover-car."

Akilah laughed, "Why didn't you ask me about it earlier?"

"Well, I didn't know how you would react."

"I ride a cycle because of our warm climate and the wonderful panorama that a car decreases. Besides, it enables me to get around faster than a zip-camel would."

"I see. I've also seen in our conversations that your Muslim beliefs and my Christian ones have a number of ideas in common, though we differ on others."

Akilah narrowed her eyebrows, "Yes, we both believe in one God, though Christians believe that he's also three Persons."

Farhan responded, "I find commendable Muhammad's attempts to overcome the many false gods of the Arabian tribes and to replace them with one God."

"We share belief in evil spirits. We call them jinn, while you call them demons. However, jinn can be different shades of good and evil, whereas your evil beings are all bad."

"Also, we both believe that Satan leads the rebellious spirits against God."

"We Muslims honor the prophets Adam, Noah, Job, Abraham, Jacob, Joseph, Moses, David, and Jesus, as you Christians do. However, we also honor Ishmael as a prophet and Muhammad as the final prophet in contrast to you Christians, who honor the others, especially Jesus as the divine Prophet." **(Read the other comparisons and contrasts on pages 236-238)**

"Those comparisons and contrasts are true....

"Farhan, I've begun reading the Bible one chapter a day. Since you have read the whole Qur'an in an English translation, I have tackled the latest of many NIV translations of the Bible."

"That's great, Akilah! As I understand it, the NIV is a very good translation of the original Bible's Greek and Hebrew. If you have any questions about your reading, I'll be happy to discuss them with you. By the way, I invite you to come to my apartment to be involved in our attempt to catch the baby-murderers Thursday morning. Are you available?"

Looking at her holo-smart phone, Akilah said, "Yes, I'll be there both times."

Chapter Twenty

A just ruse

On Saturday evening, Farhan, Akilah, and Third and Fourth Detectives Daher and Maloof met with Mel and Jan Whiting. Farhan began, "Jan, we really appreciate your willingness to help us catch the slippery abortionists."

Since righteous anger had displaced fear in Jan, she responded with a tight frown, "I'm happy to help you, but those people better not harm my baby! You can't imagine a pregnant woman's wrath until someone threatens her baby. Mother bears and I have that reaction in common."

When Akilah took from the coffee table an ultra-fi wire, she said, "Here's the wire."

Jan got up with Mel's help, "I'll use your bathroom. Could you help me, Akilah? I'm sure you know where it will be safe and out of sight."

When they returned, Farhan asked, "How are we to proceed?"

With confidence born of experience, Third Detective Daher leaned his ample frame forward, "Well, we need to know what each of us is going to do. How does this plan sound to you? First thing tomorrow morning, you will answer the newspaper ad about a medical procedure, find out the address, phone Akilah's police station telephone number with that information, and proceed to the abortionists' city block.

"Second, Farhan and Akilah will tell the rest of the task force that it is a different address on the other side of town, preferably a vacant lot.

"Third, after they have left the station, Maloof and I and our criminologist consultants will float to the real address in separate, unmarked fusion-cars.

"Fourth, you will drive to the baby-killers' storefront address.

"Fifth, we will wait at a safe, unwatched distance until they offer to do the 'procedure.' (You will want to get them to be specific about it.)

"Sixth, we will rush the establishment—two of us at the front and the other two at the back—to cut off both avenues of escape.

"Seventh, we'll arrest them and haul their baby-destroying hides off to jail cells."

The crew members were silent for a few moments. Then, Farhan said with a big smile, "Basim, that plan is brilliant. It's extremely important that we tell no one, especially other members of our task force, about our ruse. Our wrinkle in the plan does not go beyond these walls. Does anyone have any questions? My only question is, how can we involve zip-camels?"

Everyone snickered with nervous smiles.

* * *

The next day, Sunday, at 9:00 A.M. sharp, Jan called the newspaper ad's phone number. The voice on the other end said, "Hello."

With an arrow-prayer sent to heaven, Jan said with a calm voice, "Is this where I can get a 'medical procedure' that takes care of my pregnancy problem?"

"We can correct your situation for you."

"What is your address?"

"We're at 407 Palm Tree Avenue."

"I'll be coming today."

After hanging up, Jan called Akilah's police-station phone number and put her message on voice mail.

A few minutes later, Akilah checked her voice mail and told the rest of the task force her bogus address. After preparing to leave, Huda, Touma, and Ghanem went on the futile wild-camel chase, while Srour did paperwork at the station.

Then, the four justice-pursuers arrived at the real address. After they saw Jan enter the abortionists' office, they heard her say, "No one's here!" When Farhan, filled with frustration, came into the office, he gasped, "How did they get wind of our plan?!"

* * *

The inner crew gathered the following Monday evening at Farhan's apartment with bewilderment in their hearts. Basim began, "It's really frustrating. Why did our plan fail? What went wrong?"

All shook their heads, but Farhan said, "A USA saying applies here, 'don't cry over spilled camel milk.' I added one of the words. In other words, let's think about any holes in our previous plan and then correct them instead of dwelling on our failure. Does anyone have any idea how we can improve the plan to catch those crooks?"

Fayiz Maloof suddenly had an insight and said, "I thought that Basim's previous plan was fool-proof, but I think that maybe someone is intercepting Akilah's voice mails or our communications. I can't see any other way."

Akilah brightened and responded, "You might have something there, Fayiz."

Farhan smiled, "We have a little matter of a gathering on Friday followed by a honeymoon. Let's meet again in three weeks and come up with a better plan to apprehend those death-for-a-fee people. Let's pray and brainstorm for a fully-fool-proof plan between now and then."

Chapter Twenty-One

A joyful celebration

The greatly-anticipated, sunny day arrived with comfortably-warm temperatures and the usual afternoon rain shower.

Farhan and Shirley's families and friends filled the center of the church's large sanctuary. Shirley, Akilah, and Shirley's third-grade-teacher-friend, Aarifa Abraham, put on their dresses in a nearby Sunday school classroom. Shirley's whole being was swirling with joy, anxiety, and anticipation.

In another classroom, Farhan, full of eagerness, said to his friends, "Are you guys ready for the main event?"

Best man Muher replied, "Are you, Farhan? That's a more important question. As for me, I have the rings, apparently important items in the wedding."

Farhan shot back with his biggest grin and joy in his heart, "I'm more than ready! Hey, Shirley and I should have ridden a hydrogen-powered zip-camel through the center aisle at the end of the ceremony. Why didn't I have that idea earlier?" They all shared broad smiles.

The men walked around to the side entrance to join up with Pastor Bob Bramble, a graying, middle-aged man whom they followed into the auditorium, which Shirley had decorated with two bouquets, one at either side of the front stage. At the front of the steps, they turned to look at the back and waited for the music to change to "Pachelbel's Canon," played on the organ. Then, after Akilah and Aarifa walked down the center aisle, the crowd rose with Pastor Bob's encouragement and turned to look at the beautiful, beaming, blonde bride, dressed in a frilly, white wedding dress.

Grinning Farhan moved forward to interlace Shirley's right arm with his left arm. They both faced the pastor, who explained, "Dear loved ones, we are gathered here to join Farhan Issah and Shirley Jones in holy marriage.

"Before we proceed, Akilah and Farhan have asked me to say a few words about the Bible's love passage, 1 Corinthians 13:4-7. God inspired Prophet Paul to write, 'Love is patient, and love is kind. It does not envy, and it does not boast. It is not proud, and it is not rude. It is not self-seeking, it is not easily angered, and it keeps no record of wrongs. Love does not delight in evil but rejoices with the truth. It always protects, always trusts, always hopes, and always perseveres.'

"These goals along with the many other commands in the Bible are God's objectives for your marriage, Farhan and Shirley, and for everyone's life. Gaining patience and kindness; giving up envy, boasting, pride, rudeness, selfishness, anger, and grudges; replacing evil with truth; and protecting, trusting, hoping, and persevering are all very hard goals for our lives, especially our marriages. How can we make progress?

"Well, as Christians, our divine Ruler Jesus the Messiah resisted all of the self-centered temptations to give up his mission. Instead, he showed his love for us by going to definite death by Roman torture and rising from that same death on the third day. He has gone ahead of us to Paradise in God's presence and earned believers' places there.

"Now, we who trust only in him as our divine Deliverer—who set us free from God's just verdict of 'guilty' by his death, has given us new life by coming back to life, and has earned our way to God—can have the power of his resurrection to make progress toward our love-goals."

Pastor Bramble smiled at both of them, "I know by meeting with you that you, Farhan and Shirley, have committed your lives to follow Jesus and to live together as husband and wife. The key to experiencing Jesus' love in our married lives is to ask for the divine power of Jesus' victory daily through prayer.

"His results become the three Cs of marriage: communication, commitment, and comedy (involving a sense of humor)—all with the only true God of the Bible at the center of our lifelong relationship.

"Therefore, I ask you, Farhan, do you promise to love, honor, and protect Shirley, as Jesus does for his church, in all the ups and downs of life, as long as both of you will live?"

Thankful that he had grieved out Trish's death, Farhan looked at his beautiful, beaming bride and said with a loud church-echo, "I certainly do!" A few chuckles arose from the crowd.

"Shirley, do you promise to love, honor, and submit to Farhan, as the church does to Jesus, in all of the ups and downs of life, as long as you both live?"

Full of joy that Shirley had found the love of her life, she said with joyful tears creeping down her face, "I do."

"May I have the rings please?"

* * *

After the ceremony, Farhan and Shirley Issah celebrated their new marriage with their guests in the church's fellowship hall by eating a simple chicken meal and wedding cake. The gathered celebrants sent them off to their week-long honeymoon at an air-floating resort on the Great Peninsula's Gulf of Mexico side.

* * *

Farhan in a yellow swimsuit lounged on an outdoor, reclining chair floating two meters above the sand on a Gulf beach, as sleek Shirley sunned herself on a magic-blanket like ancient Aladdin's rug next to him, wearing a one-piece, dark-blue swimsuit. Farhan said, "Both of our killers' cases bug me, dear. More specifically, why do the baby-murderers get away so easily?"

Shirley with puzzled thoughts faced him and pursed her lips into a grin, "You can't just relax on a Gulf beach with your new wife without thinking about your consulting work, can you, honey?"

"No, I guess I can't."

She gave him her cute half-grin, "Well, tell me what you're thinking about the abortionists' case."

God, thank you for giving me such an understanding, beautiful bride! He got down, lay next to her on his stomach on another magic-blanket with his arm around her mid-back and said, "I'm thinking that they must have an inside policeman monitoring our conversations and movements. Maybe, they've put bugs and SGPS tracking devices in our vehicles."

"Ooh, I hate bugs! By the way, a super-sized one is buzzing around you."

He swatted it away and then kissed his bride on her mouth and neck. He looked around with a grin, "Are we breaking the law here, sweetheart?" They both gave out big belly laughs.

* * *

Two weeks later, a squat, fat, bare-headed woman—distressed at the Muslim Mall's high prices and dressed in a white, full-length robe—window-shopped on the mall-long conveyor belt. A man dressed in black turban and robe approached her from the opposite direction, pointed at her protruding stomach, and said, "We can correct your problem."

Enveloped with sudden anger at his aggressiveness, she yelled with a big frown, "I'm not pregnant, you dummy!" She then slapped his jaw with a force that knocked him flat on his back on the spongy surface. His body bounced on the conveyor belt and then back onto his feet. She then stalked off.

After he sat for a while on a bench to recover next to the belt, the same man approached a woman with a large belly under a yellow, buttoned-up, head-to-foot dress with a full, brown burqa on her head. He said as he pointed down, "We can overcome your unwanted problem."

She lowered her eyes and said with a squeak, "How can you get rid of it?"

"We have very safe ways."

"Well, then, where is your office, and how can I get in touch with you?"

"Here is our business card; call us for an appointment during business hours."

Chapter Twenty-Two

Perps pursued

As the LPTF met at mid-afternoon on Tuesday, September 23, 2085, the pregnant woman from the mall—full of fury with flashing, black eyes—entered the police station and asked for a police officer. Second Policeman Ghanem rose and asked her, "How may I help you, ma'am?"

She said, "As I window-shopped in the mall today, a man in black clothes approached me and offered to get me a safe abortion. I knew that it was illegal but played along with him. Here's his card."

Ghanem with a surge of eagerness took the card and said, "Thank you. We may be in touch with you. What are your phone number, World-Web-mail, and physical addresses?" She wrote that information on the back of the card and stomped out.

He scurried to the group and shared her information with them. First Detective Srour piped up, "Maybe now we can catch them. Let's think during the next week about a good, successful plan."

* * *

That afternoon at 5:30 P.M., Farhan entered his new home, a modest, two-bedroom row house just outside of downtown New Tehran, and called, "Hi, honey. I'm home."

Shirley dropped everything and ran to his embrace and full-face kisses. He said, "I think our task force got a break today from a pregnant woman who gave us information about an abortion operation. A man in black approached her in the mall and offered to get rid of her 'problem.'"

"That woman's info sounds like the opportunity you've been waiting for."

"Yeah, I hope so." He motioned toward the front door. Then, they exited the house and sat on the front-porch, two-person zip-swing. Farhan whispered, "After our dinner, I'm going to search our two cars and our house for SGPS devices and wireless bugs someone might have planted. The other people in our inner circle are going to do the same."

Shirley deadpanned, "Don't let those bugs bite you."

With renewed hope that maybe now they can catch the perps, he returned her deadpan look, "I'll try not to."

* * *

Farhan stooped and slouched while searching his rusty fusion-hatchback and her new, green hydrogen-sedan in their carport. Under the back seats in both cars, he discovered a tiny, wireless transmitter-filament, which he crushed with his size-twelve right shoe and cut it into many pieces. He said, "Ah, ha! I found your ultrasonic eaves-dropping devices!" He also found and destroyed two SGPS tracking devices in the cars' back-left wheel-wells. He then locked his cars.

* * *

The task force inner-circle met the following Saturday evening at Farhan and Shirley's house to compare notes. Farhan and Shirley gave them a "grand tour" of their bungalow. Then, as they settled in the living room with coffee or tea and dessert, Farhan asked, "What electronic devices did you find in your vehicles?"

Daher said with a hint of triumphant joy, "I found both SGPS and listening devices in my vehicles. Did you find any in your house, Farhan?"

"Nope, I guess the assistant perps haven't caught up with our new residence. Did the rest of you find electronic eaves-dropping and SGPS devices in your vehicles?" They all nodded.

Maloof suggested, "Why don't all of us raid the baby-killers' office Tuesday morning at 9:00 A.M. before our task force meets, the way we did last time—only this time without listening devices to warn them in advance?"

Farhan said, "Great idea, Fayiz!" As he raised his right index finger to his lips, "Mum's the word until then." Everyone nodded.

* * *

On Tuesday morning, October 6, at 8:30 A.M., the inner circle met at Farhan and Shirley's house. They then air-floated to the killers' business address and parked down the block. At exactly 9:00 A.M., Daher and Maloof circled to the back of the building, while Farhan and Akilah burst into the abortionist's front door. The gray-scarfed and robed assistant fled into the back room, as the detectives entered the back door and caught the abortionist, dressed in blue turban and operating garb, and his assistant heading out the back.

Daher with great indignation yelled at them, "Kneel on the floor with your hands behind your heads!" They obeyed without hesitation.

Farhan and Akilah gasped at the backroom scene. Before them was a large, pregnant woman in a hospital gown sprawled on a surgical table with her legs spread high on two stirrups. Farhan said to her, "We will help you down. Just get dressed, give us your contact information, and go home. I advise you to use the adoption option instead. You won't be charged with a crime if you will testify against the criminals."

* * *

Later that morning, a parade of the slouching, scowling abortionist and his assistant secured with virtual handcuffs followed by smiling, upright Farhan, Akilah, Basim, and Fayiz shuffled and marched into the New Tehran police station. Everyone stared at the procession. They then stood and burst into applause and cheers.

Then, the two detectives and the alleged killers with understandably-contrasting moods sat in the interrogation room. Third Detective Basim Daher began with a victorious half-grin, "We caught you red-handed offering and attempting to abort an innocent child. What do you have to say for yourselves?"

The disgusted doctor grimaced, folded his arms, and said, "Nothing."

Fourth Detective Fayiz Maloof relied on his interviewing experience by saying, "We know that you have had help in the police force. If you will give up your accomplices, we'll tell the judges that you cooperated with us. You might get off with a lighter sentence. Who is your police helper, or are there two?"

The scared-stiff receptionist said, "I'll tell you, but I must have a written offer of a reduced sentence from the prosecutor first."

The baby-killer glared scalpels at her.

Basim thought, *we've got them now*, and said with a hint of a smile, "So you're admitting that you aided and abetted this man in killing helpless, unborn children?"

She thought that she would do time anyway, decided to get the best deal that she could, and said with a deep frown, "I'll tell you everything if you will get the prosecutor to reduce his probable charge against me in writing."

The death-doctor's murderous anger welled up inside of him as he turned to her and raised his virtual-handcuffed hands as if to strangle her. The detectives rose to protect her. Then, before they could reach her, the doctor with resignation and an anguished frown slumped forward and said barely above a whisper, "I guess I'll do the same as she's doing."

The detectives with smiles on their faces exited the room, called the prosecutor, and hurried back with a charge of attempted manslaughter in the first degree instead of attempted first-degree murder in exchange for their full confession and information on their accomplices.

The doctor slumped and said, "We have decided to sign a confession and this plea agreement. The officer who helped us was...." Then, two shots rang out from the ceiling air vent to kill the baby-killers. Both of them slumped on the table, bleeding from their heads.

Maloof—scared that their successful plan had suddenly crumbled to dust and ashes—rushed to check their pulses and shook his head with a deeply-furrowed brow. Daher, filled with deep foreboding, called for a zip-bus and the medical examiner.

They then exited the interrogation room to inform the other police, who had all gathered at the interrogation room door when they heard the shots, of this tragic turn of events.

In the basement boiler room, Daher also discovered an open air vent but saw no one.

Since CSI Asima was smaller by far than CSI Ameer, she had the unenviable task of dusting the whole length of the air vent for fingerprints. She emerged in the boiler room proclaiming, "It's a good thing that I'm not claustrophobic!" Ameer examined the air vent in the interrogation room for gunshot residue and gun shells and dusted the boiler-room air vent for fingerprints, only finding a partial print.

The medical examiner pronounced the suspects dead and remarked with great disgust, "Why do people devalue life so much? We've tried to protect women, a president, and now babies and baby-killers. Who's next?"

Basim sat down at First Policeman Touma's squad-room desk and asked him, "Touma, where were you when the shots rang out?"

Touma sat up straight in his office chair, folded his arms, and said, "I was in the men's restroom using our powerful, new fusion-toilet."

Basim asked, "Did anyone see you?"

Touma said with a tight face, "No, I like privacy for that activity. By the way, it works well!"

Basim approached Second Detective Huda next and asked, "Where were you when the suspects died?"

Huda, feeling a little indignant at the question but realizing that Basim was just doing his job, said, "I was right here sitting at my desk writing reports. You can ask anyone."

"Since your desk is at the end of the room, you have a view of everyone. Who was missing?"

"As far as I can remember, Touma was the only one absent....Come to think of it, I remember that when we first got the other woman's lead to the abortionists, Touma went into that interrogation room to make a private call before eating his lunch and then accompanying the rest of us to the empty baby-killers' office. I thought at the time that his action was unusual."

Chapter Twenty-Three

Suspects confronted

Late that same Tuesday, smiling First Policeman Ziya Touma sat in the unfamiliar chair of a suspect in the interrogation room across the table from Third and Fourth Detectives Daher and Maloof. Basim Daher stood and said, "These are the facts, Touma. You disappeared to make a phone call after the task force previously discovered the abortionists' address when we received a woman's tip. That errand was fruitless.

"Several of us found listening filaments and SGPS devices in our vehicles that someone planted there. You were the only policeman absent from your desk when the abortionist and his receptionist died with bullets that ballistics will match with your gun.

"Not only that, but the CSIs will check the partial fingerprint found on the boiler room air vent to see if it is a match to your thumbprint.

"Also, your bank statements show substantial deposits incompatible with your salary.

"We have you dead-to-rights. What do you say to these clues that point at you as the baby-killers' accomplice and murderer?"

Feeling as if he had to protect himself at all costs against the detectives' accusations, Touma slouched, folded his arms, and said with a scowl, "I don't know what to say. I am not guilty."

Bearded Fourth Detective Maloof waded in, while tapping the table between them, "We suspect that you have another abortionist accomplice on the force and that you two shared your surveillance of us. If you will confess and tell us who that person is, the prosecutor can reduce the charges. Come on, Touma. We've been on the force together for several years. Tell us what we want to know, and the law will go easier on you."

As Touma's defensiveness increased like a Caribbean hurricane, he leaned forward and frowned, "I want a lawyer."

* * *

A week later, three black-robed judges filed into the first-floor courtroom from a side door. The middle judge said, "What is going on in New Tehran, prosecutor? Do we have a suspect accused of being a corrupt, criminal cop?"

The prosecutor in his silky, neatly-pressed, black robe and turban replied with contempt in his heavy heart, "Yes, I'm afraid so, your Honors. We charge First Policeman Ziya Touma with aiding and abetting abortionists and then murdering them in the police station in broad daylight."

"How do you plead?"

"Not guilty."

The judges glanced at each other and nodded. Their spokesman said, "You are arraigned and held without bond, because of the charges' severity, for a preliminary hearing two weeks from today to determine whether or not you will stand trial. Court is adjourned." The three gavels fell with loud thuds.

* * *

On Thursday, October 16, a stocky, solemn man, wearing gray robe and turban, knocked on the door of Farhan's GPNU office. Farhan said, "Come in." He then cleared a stack of student papers from a chair and two piles of books from his desk. The man entered, extended his hand for a firm handshake, and sat on the wooden chair opposite Farhan's desk. "I'm Nawfa Amjad, one of the Sunni spiritual leaders in New Tehran."

Farhan's feelings were a mixture of apprehension and foreboding. He said, "Nice to meet you. Why did you come to visit me?"

Amjad thought as he glanced around, *this man is a messy, forgetful professor.* However, he said, "I have come to express my concern about your conversations with Akilah Jamal concerning Christian and Muslim beliefs. We have laws against proselytizing in the GPN. I am worried that you are trying to change her from a Muslim to a Christian."

Farhan paused briefly as he prayed that he would be able to control his defensiveness and explain his conversations with calmness. He then proceeded, "I've only shared with her as a friend my beliefs and reasons for my faith, just as I have with many Muslim friends. How she reacts is entirely up to her. Why? What did she tell you?"

"Well, she shared with me some of your reasons for believing that Jesus is God as well as man. I fear that your ideas are confusing her about her commitment to Allah (thanks be to him) and the Prophet Muhammad (peace to him)."

"She can believe what she wants to. I'm not trying to make her into a follower of Jesus. Such a decision would be entirely up to her. I've told her that I am in no way trying to talk her into anything, and I meant that statement. We're just sharing ideas as good friends do."

"I could have turned you in to the C-POV, but I wanted to get your side of the story first. Like Akilah, I also used to be an Alevi Muslim.

"Dr. Issah, my fear is that you're trying to seduce her religiously."

"I understand your concern and in no way wish to make her do what she doesn't want to do."

"Well, you confirm Akilah's words to me. Thank you for your time."

* * *

Akilah and Farhan had their usual lunch the following Tuesday noon. Farhan began, "Did you hear, Akilah, that the judges held Touma over for trial in December?" Akilah nodded. "Also, your Sunni spiritual leader visited me last Thursday. He expressed his concern that I was trying to change you from a Muslim to a Christian."

Akilah felt a surge of anger at her Sunni leader, frowned, and said, "He came to see you, Farhan? I didn't mean for him to talk to you. I just shared with him some of your reasons for believing in Jesus as God and man. I didn't want him to confront you about them."

"Well, I assured him that I was just sharing my ideas with you. I in no way want to convert you against your will, Akilah, as I've told you already."

She felt relief that they had this conversation and said, "Yes, I know, Farhan....

"By the way, now we have a police criminal in custody. I wonder how often that circumstance has happened."

"It's quite rare, especially here in the GPN."

Her curiosity increased as she leaned forward and made full eye contact with him. She said, "Farhan, I've been reading Mark's book. One event caught my eye. It said that four people brought a fully-paralyzed man with great effort through the crowd to Jesus, who said a very peculiar thing to him, 'Your sins are forgiven.' He sensed that the religious teachers who were present mentally condemned him for saying it because only God can forgive our failings. Then, he claimed that he, 'the Son of man,' had the authority to forgive sins and proved it by healing him on the spot. My question is, how could he have forgiven the man's sins as God when he called himself 'the Son of man,' a title that implies to me that he was a mere man?"

Farhan thought *I learned that information in a Bible study with Purdue students. What was it again? Oh, yes.* He put his hands to his face and replied, "I learned to let the Bible interpret itself, Akilah, because I believe it's all God's Book. Jesus took that title from the Old Testament. In Daniel 7, God gave Prophet Daniel a vision. I know that all Muslims put a great emphasis on Muhammad's visions that you believe came from Allah. Also, I know you believe that Daniel was one of the prophets."

At Akilah's nod, Farhan said with relief that God helped him recall the answer from the Bible, "Well, Jesus referred to that passage in Daniel every time he took the title 'Son of man,' which, by the way, was his favorite title for himself. There, the Ancient of Days, a title for God, sat on his throne to judge. Another person 'like a Son of man' came to occupy his throne with him. Daniel said that in his vision the nations worshiped that Son of man. Therefore, I believe that those verses in Daniel 7 show that when Jesus re-entered heaven after he rose from death, he resumed his high position of ruling the universe with his Father.

"Also, in Matthew 16:13, Jesus asked his followers, 'Who do men say the Son of Man is?' His disciples immediately knew to whom he referred, himself, and named a few possibilities. Then he asked them, 'But what about you?...Who do you say I am?' Then, Peter declared, 'You are the Christ, the Son of the living God.'

"When he gave himself the title 'Son of man,' he claimed to be the same divine person as the second of the three Persons of God, two of whom he pictured for Daniel in that vision."

Akilah frowned and asked, "If he was the second of the three, wasn't he inferior to the Father?"

"No, the three Persons of God are equal in status but different in their roles. The Father is the Source; Jesus, his Agent; and the Spirit, the personal 'Atmosphere' in whom he works for his creatures and church."

"You are full of answers to my questions, Farhan. However, I'm not persuaded that Jesus ever was God."

"You don't have to accept my reasoning if you don't want to, Akilah, but the Bible teaches that truth."

Chapter Twenty-Four

Thankfulness

On USA's Thanksgiving Day, November 27, 2085, Farhan and Shirley looked at their friends around their air-floating, legless kitchen table extended by a similar card table, as he said, "Let's pray. Dear God, we praise you for your goodness in providing this feast, and we thank you for all of your free blessings in taking care of all of our needs and so much more. Bless this Thanksgiving food so that we can give our lives more and more fully to you. Through Jesus alone, amen."

He continued with a big smile, "We miss the United States Thanksgiving. As a result, we decided to invite all of you to celebrate it with us. Dig in and enjoy!" They passed turkey, sweet potatoes, cranberries, stuffing, and vegetables around the extended kitchen table.

Clockwise from Farhan at one end were Akilah, Muher, Malik, Daher, Maloof, and Shirley on his right. The other men wore informal shirts, sweaters, and pants instead of the robes and turbans of their daily professional lives.

Shirley piped up between bites, "Farhan cooked this whole feast. I didn't know that you could cook, honey."

Farhan said with a grin, "The Worldwide Web is a wonderful source of information, dear, and everything was readily available at the only American market in town. One of my many weaknesses is poor memory, though; I'm one of those absent-minded professors. I also tend to be a little messy."

Shirley piped up with affection for him and a big grin, "A little?!"

Farhan felt great joy as he said, "I'm just thankful for my neat homemaker to keep me on the straight and narrow," and leaned over to hug her. "Oops. Are you the 'public'?" They all laughed.

He felt somehow that he needed to explain his cooking prowess, "Anyway, I used to help my mother cook, especially on Thanksgiving. In fact, one of my childhood desires was to be a chef. However, I can't remember recipes for very long. Forgetting the recipe and losing my place in the middle of it from the beginning of the recipe to the end doesn't provide good food."

Akilah chimed in with a friendly gleam in her eye, "Ah, our criminologist hero has faults?!"

Farhan admitted as he glanced at Akilah with a smirk, "Oh, yes, many of them. One of them is impatience. I wish that we had solved the missing-women case a long time ago."

He then said to all of them, "Say, I notice that the GPNU Fighting Camels' zip-soccer—er, fast-football—team plays this afternoon at four. Another USA tradition is football."

Muher interjected with a tongue-in-cheek smile, "Is that USA sport the one in which men throw, kick, and catch a funny-shaped ball; zip around a floating field; and knock each other down?"

Farhan deadpanned, "Yep. That's the one; it's a war game. Why don't we go watch the Fighting Camels play?" The men nodded.

Akilah and Shirley looked at each other as the latter one said, "You boys can go watch them, while Akilah and I clean up and chat."

At the end of the Thanksgiving meal, Farhan read a fitting psalm from the Bible. Then, he said, "One of our Indiana-family Thanksgiving traditions is to go around the table and describe blessings for which we are thankful to God. "

Akilah thought for a moment and said, "I'm thankful to Allah (may he be praised) for my friends."

Fully-bearded, muscular Muher Jan, a GPNU economics professor, said, "I'm thankful for health, family, and friends."

Short, clean-shaven Medical Examiner Dr. Malik Nejem said, "I'm thankful for a job that I love."

Heavy-set Third Detective Basim Daher said, "I'm thankful that we caught the baby-killers, though I'm sad that one of our own was involved in their murders."

Bearded Fourth Detective Fayiz Maloof said, as he glanced at Farhan and Akilah, "I'm thankful that we have two professor-consultants."

Shirley said with adoring glances at her friend and husband, "I'm very thankful that God sent Akilah and Farhan into my life."

Farhan finished up, "I'm very thankful for you, Shirley, as well as for all of you and all my friends and family back in Indiana. Shirley, you and I can be in touch with them by Ultra-Skype this evening." She nodded. Then, he prayed a prayer of thanks to God through Jesus the Messiah.

* * *

Sitting in the GPNU football stands on floating seats under a bubble-dome, the men rooted for zip-pack-equipped students as they kicked a round ball around a rectangular, floating field, playing keep-away much of the time. After ninety minutes with only three shots on goal for each team, the game ended in a nil-nil tie, for which each team got one point in the university standings. Farhan asked Basim next to him, "Why does a team get a point for getting no goals?"

"Maybe it's because they keep the other team from scoring."

"I guess you might be right, because they do spend a lot of time keeping the ball away from the other team. It seems like a lot of zip for nothing. I praise God for giving such tumble-talents to people, but I personally prefer USA fusion-football, which almost-always has more scoring than this sport. Maybe, my preference is also because I didn't grow up playing or watching world fast-football."

* * *

That same evening after a light meal of Turkey sandwiches and the departure of Farhan and Shirley's friends, they called their USA families on Ultra-Skype. Farhan said to his parents, "Dad and Mom, how are you?"

His dad said, "We're doing well, son, though the aches and pains of being sixty-plus are catching up with us. We have a lot to be thankful for on this Thanksgiving Day, especially since we have a new daughter-in-law!"

"I see that my alma mater, Purdue, is having another one of those years in fast-football."

"Yeah, wait until next year in football. However, I do still have some hope for Purdue's basketball team, but it may be that we also have to wait for next year in that sport too."

"We have a perplexing serial-women-murderer case that I hope doesn't wait until next year to be solved."

Chapter Twenty-Five

A prosecuted predator

On Tuesday, December 2, the three black-robed, criminal-court judges banged their gavels. Their senior spokesman said, "The courtroom will now be in order. The trial of New Tehran's First Policeman Ziya Touma will now proceed. Prosecutor, make your opening statement."

The dark-green robed and turbaned prosecutor swaggered near the judges, made full eye-contact, and said, "This case is an open-and-shut case concerning Mr. Touma's greed and perfidy in assisting black-market profiteers who kill babies for a living and whom he killed to keep them quiet about his involvement. The prosecution will call witnesses to prove the defendant's involvement in multiple murders of unborn babies and two abortionists."

The black-robed and turbaned defense attorney said, "All clues that the prosecution has in this case are circumstantial. They have no real physical evidence except a questionable, partial fingerprint that he could have left in the boiler room at any time in the past. The defense will give your Honors many considerations beyond the shadow of a doubt to acquit the defendant."

The prosecutor called his first witness, CSI Ameer Muhammad, "What evidence did you find at the police-station crime scene?"

"We found a partial thumbprint on the open-air vent in the basement boiler room that was a five-point match to the defendant's left thumb. Also, when we tested his hands for gunshot residue, the tests were positive."

"What other evidence pointed at the defendant as the abortionists' accomplice?"

"He had four large bank deposits in the past year that were inconsistent with his income."

"No more questions, your Honors."

The defense lawyer asked, "What evidence did you find that the abortionists gave the defendant those large sums of money?"

"Uh,...we really didn't, but...."

"How can you be sure that Mr. Touma left the thumbprint at the time of the murders?"

"Uh,...we really can't, but...."

"Couldn't the gunshot residue have gotten on his hands at any time in the past, during his practice shooting on the range?"

"I suppose, but...."

"Thank you. No more questions."

The prosecutor said, "Re-direct, your Honors?" At their nods, he proceeded, "What were you going to say when the defense so rudely interrupted you, CSI Muhammad?"

"Objection, your Honors! The prosecution is criticizing our cross examination."

The judges nodded ever so slightly. Their spokesman said, "Okay, okay, gentlemen. Let's proceed during this trial with respect for each other in the pursuit of justice. Please continue."

The prosecutor repeated his question. Ameer glared at the defense attorney as he answered, "The first time he interrupted me I was going to say that, nonetheless, Mr. Touma's income did not justify such large deposits. The second time, my reply was going to be that I found the thumbprint on the frame of the open, boiler-room air vent through which the murderer entered to crawl to the interrogation room air vent from which he shot the abortionists in cold blood. The third time, I was going to observe that gunshot residue washes off, so that it had to be recent."

The defense attorney shouted, "Objection, your Honors! Such a characterization of the shooting 'in cold blood' is prejudicial against my client!"

"Sustained" was the middle judge's one-word reply.

The prosecutor felt that his witness had made the point about the evidence sufficiently enough. Thus, he said, "No more questions of this witness. I call Third Detective Fayiz Maloof to the stand." Then, when Maloof was settled, the prosecutor asked, "What did you observe when you questioned the death-doctor and his receptionist in the police-station interrogation room?"

"Well, the abortionists had decided to plead guilty to first-degree manslaughter in the unborn infants' deaths. We had asked them to give up their police accomplice in return for the lesser charge. The doctor was about to reveal the two people's names when shots rang out from the room's large air vent to kill both of the baby-killers. My partner, Basim Daher, checked their pulses to no avail."

The prosecutor proceeded, "What other evidence did you discover at the crime scene?"

"We discovered two bullets that ballistics matched to the defendant's gun."

The defense attorney faced Maloof and asked, "The defendant claims that someone took his gun, which he found missing when he returned to his desk. It then re-appeared the next day. How do you respond to his claim?"

Maloof answered, "I don't know how to respond except to give you the facts that point to him as the abortionists' accomplice and murderer."

"Then, how do you know that the four deposits in the defendant's account were from the abortionists?"

Maloof felt a little defensive and said, "Well, where else would they come from, then?"

The defense attorney felt that he had made his point and continued, "Did you see the assailant who shot the deceased?"

"No. The air vent blocked my view."

Satisfied that he had decreased this witness' impact on the judges, he said, "I have no other questions."

The prosecutor felt a little panic but said, "I now call Third Detective Basim Daher to the stand. What did your further investigation of the double-murder reveal?"

"I questioned First Detective Huda, who confirmed that the defendant was the only police officer or detective absent from the squad room when the shots rang out in the interrogation room. He also recalled that the last time we got a lead on the abortionists, Touma had left the task force to make a call and then eat lunch before pursuing the baby-killing perps, who cleared out before we could arrest them."

The stiff and starchy defense attorney said, "Your Honors, I move to strike the witness' last two observations as irrelevant."

The judges shook their heads to each other. Then, the spokesman said, "Denied."

The defense attorney frowned and asked Daher, "Do you have any evidence, other than a questionable fingerprint and a ballistics report, to place the defendant in the boiler room, the air vent, and the interrogation room at the time of the shooting?"

"No, not direct evidence."

"What did the defendant say about his actions when you questioned him?"

"He said that he was busy with bodily functions in the rest room." A faint titter came from the gallery at this revelation.

"Could he produce any witnesses to confirm his alibi?"

"No, he couldn't. He said that he preferred privacy for that activity." Again, a soft chuckle filled the courtroom.

The prosecutor proceeded, "I call criminology professor and police consultant Dr. Farhan Issah to the stand." Then, he addressed Farhan, "What evidence did you find to implicate the defendant?"

Farhan replied, "I found listening devices and SGPS units in our cars. The reason I suspect the defendant is because he could have easily put them there in the police parking lot on my many visits to the police station as a member of the special life-protection task force."

The defense attorney marched to the front, "Isn't your conclusion about your suspicions mere speculation? Isn't it true that anyone could have bugged your vehicles?"

"I guess so. However, the defendant made a phone call after our meeting dealing with a woman's lead to the abortionists. In addition, all of the police and consultants' cars had hidden devices except for the defendant's car."

"Going back to his phone call, do you know the person to whom he called? Did you hear his conversation?"

"'No' to both questions, but I can add two and two to get four, if you get my drift."

When Farhan—satisfied that he had done his best and thanking God—returned to the gallery, the prosecutor said, "Your Honors, we have no more witnesses."

The middle judge said to the defense attorney, "You may call your witnesses."

Then, with a cocky assurance that his case was going well, the lawyer paraded three character witnesses before the judges. They extolled Touma's virtues as a husband, father, family man with a wife and three children, and an all-around good-guy.

With the judges' permission, the prosecuting attorney began his closing argument, "Your Honors, we have here a detective whose greed and guilt are obvious. The listening devices and GPS units in the other police cars without any being in his car point to his involvement in an inside job to prevent the apprehension of the baby-killers.

"The defendant's four large deposits in his bank account demonstrate payoffs to enable him to protect the criminals.

"You must consider that he was the only policeman absent from the police squad room during the murders, that he had no confirmed alibi, that electronic devices appeared in all of the task force cars except for his, and that the CSIs found his fingerprint on the edge of the boiler-room air vent.

"Also, no matter how much the defendant claims that his gun vanished into thin air and mysteriously re-appeared, the ballistics report points to his gun as the murder weapon. Also, tests showed that gunpowder residue was on his hands. How else would his gun be used, residue get on his hands, and his fingerprint get on the air vent if he were not the murderer?

"Your Honors, the evidence must inevitably bring about a guilty verdict."

The public defender strutted to the front, made eye-contact with the three judges, and said, "My client is not guilty. The so-called 'evidence' is merely speculative and indirect. The fingerprint is only a five-point match to the defendant. If it does belong to him, he could have left it there at any time when he was talking with the janitor in a friendly conversation, as he often did.

"No direct proof has shown that the missing gun and the gunshot residue point to him. He contends that his gun went missing and that he shot his gun the previous day at the shooting range.

"He was absent from the police squad room during the murders, as was his gun from his desk, but he had an urgent matter that couldn't wait, a need to which we can all relate," he said with a grin. The gallery again emitted muffled laughter.

"Your Honors, the prosecution (or the 'persecution') has presented a flimsy, circumstantial case, about which your Honors should have considerable doubts. Please declare him 'not guilty.' Thank you."

The prosecutor jumped to his feet and shouted, "Objection to the defense attorney's disrespectful characterization of our case and of us as persecutors!"

The judges all shouted, "Sustained!"

Then, the judges' spokesman said, "We will take this case under advisement." They banged their gavels and exited to their right into the conference room.

When Farhan and Akilah conferred in the hallway, he asked her, "What verdict do you think the judges will bring back?"

She said, "I think that the fingerprint and the ballistics will convince them to declare him 'guilty.'"

He said, "You might be right, but the defense attorney was right to say that the case is mostly circumstantial."

Ninety minutes later, the judges marched into the courtroom. Their spokesman asked the defendant and his lawyer to rise and then said, "Ziya Touma, we understand your lawyer's defense that the case has been largely circumstantial, but we can't get past the discovery of your thumbprint on the boiler-room air vent and the facts that the bullets came from your gun and that you had gunpowder on your hands. Therefore, we are unanimous in declaring you guilty of aiding, abetting, and murdering two criminal serial-baby-killers. We sentence you to life in prison without parole."

A huge gasp filled the courtroom, as the prosecution team and task force shook each other's hands with huge grins. Touma slumped into his chair, where the court bailiff revived him with super-smelling-salts.

Chapter Twenty-Six

A hopeful break in the case

On Tuesday, December 16, Akilah again visited Harley David and Sons' Camel and Cycle Sales and Service to have her vehicle serviced. This time the attendant was ready with an answer for her question about the building's three square lookout towers. When she sat down to pay her bill, he said, "I remembered to ask your question. The towers mean that we are always looking out for you. The owner also thought that three was a good number."

"I see. Interesting," said Aliyah. Afterward, she walked out on the performance platform to enjoy the view of the palm grove to the west and the suspended six-lane highway to the north.

* * *

Thursday and Friday were New Tehran children's days off from school, and they attended school from September through the end of June. On a Thursday in mid-December with a slight chill in the air, Sunni Muslim brothers, twelve-year-old Daleel and ten-year-old Umair Sahm, decided to play in the palm grove west of the camel and cycle establishment, one block north of their treehouse. They had built a small treehouse in the only oak tree among the palms, to which they brought lunch and lemonade. They zoomed on their hover-boards up to their house. However, they fought pitched battles all afternoon with some hungry and thirsty bees.

On their way back to their home late that afternoon on their laser hover-boards, a short-cut took them past the west side of the performance platform at ground level. Daleel glanced under the stage and exclaimed, "Umair, do you see what I see?!"

Ten-year-old Umair's curiosity heightened as he asked Daleel, "Is that a plastic bag sticking out of the ground?"

"It sure looks like it. Why would a plastic bag be under here?"

"I don't know. Let's yank on it to see what it is."

They jumped off of their boards, grabbed the object, and pulled hard. A zipper appeared. They unzipped part of it, revealing a human hand. Sheer panic seized them as they shrieked, dropped the bag, and zipped home at the record speed of one second.

* * *

Srour and Huda were first on the scene at Harley's Place that Thursday evening, followed closely by the rest of the task force. The police dug under the performance platform until they uncovered seven body bags and laid them on the stage.

The medical examiner, Dr. Kaysan Nejem, examined the carved-up bodies. When he finished, First Detective Fahyim Srour asked him, "What happened to these women, doc?"

Kaysan said to the task force, who gathered inside the new, bright red, crime-scene tape around the platform, "The seven women are the missing ones that you have been seeking. The perp repeatedly abused the victims physically and sexually. Then, he stabbed them and cut them up with a large, sharp knife. I'll know more after I examine them at the morgue and get DNA results."

Then, the team huddled as Srour said, "This is probably the break we've been waiting for! We now have to wait a little longer for the doc's continued examination of the bodies and DNA findings." They then examined the whole area around Harley's Place for clues with their laser-lights but came up with nothing except a number of footprints from a dozen people below the platform.

Farhan felt great sadness as he exclaimed to the rest of the crew when they had finished investigating the area, "What a sad place the serial-killer's performance platform is! It's almost too much to take in to think that bands played their music above the buried women's savaged and abused bodies!"

* * *

The LPTF gathered with Medical Examiner Dr. Nejem on the next Tuesday afternoon in the police squad room to discuss the crime-scene evidence. Nejem, dressed in a blue doctor's robe with a matching turban, began, "No other DNA was in or on the body bags besides that of the seven women and the boys. The killer must have used sterile latex gloves the way we do.

"However, the only discovery I made apart from the expected body wounds was a series of unexpected perforations or holes on the tops and insides of all of the women's uteruses made by a pointed object. Someone brutally beat and abused them over a period of time, maybe a month. DNA tests showed conclusively that they were all of the missing women that we have been looking for."

First Detective Srour frowned, "It's disappointing that we have no conclusive evidence from the body dump to point to the perpetrator."

Fourth Detective Fayiz Maloof chimed in with determined desperation, "What about the footprints? Also, we need to interview the boys and canvas the area, including the motel past the palm grove to the west and the suburban subdivision to the south. Perhaps, some all-night motel employee saw the murderer. However, this perp knew what he was doing. That little ridge hides the performance platform from traffic on the highway all the time."

"Good thinking, Maloof." Srour answered with orders, "Jamal and Issah, interview everyone at Harley's Place to find out if they saw anyone suspicious. Ghanem and Huda, see if the boys ever saw anyone lurking around the dealership or their neighborhood. Daher and Maloof, interview everyone that you can find in the vicinity of the body dump, including the boys' neighborhood and the nearby businesses. I will try to piece together the information that you discover. Holo-phone or tele-text me any new clues here at the police station. Let's get this murderer. Any questions?"

* * *

Farhan and Shirley attended the New Tehran Symphony Orchestra's concert featuring Dvorak and Brahms that Saturday evening. As they stood and waited to get out of the auditorium after the concert, Farhan said, "Shirley, the murdered-women case is maddening. I've been thinking about it during the whole concert. It almost seems as if the killer knows how police collect evidence in order to cover his tracks."

"Yes, he's a slick one. Maybe, Akilah and you can track him down. I hope so. All of the women I know are scared that he might go on another killing spree. As you know, I'm certainly taking precautions to protect myself—laser light, for example."

"I'm glad that you have taken that step, Dear. It's frustrating that we didn't make much progress even after we discovered the bodies. Maybe Akilah and I can discover some clues tomorrow afternoon at Harley's Place."

* * *

Mid-afternoon on Sunday, Farhan picked Akilah up in his old, tan fusion-hatchback. At the dealership, they interviewed all of the employees. No one had seen any suspicious characters there. Harvey's Place closed at six o'clock Saturday through Wednesday and at nine o'clock on Thursdays. Everyone deserted it the rest of the time with no one protecting the building.

They stopped for dinner at their favorite bistro on their way home. Farhan's frustrated frown looked like that of a lion that went a month without a kill. He observed, "This case is just as mystifying as it was before those boys found the body dump. What are we missing?"

"We're missing key evidence like the perp's hidden performance place, where he beats, abuses, and kills his victims. At least, we found his evil performance platform."

"To change the subject, Akilah, I've been wondering about something since I moved to this Muslim country. Why do some Muslims hate Christians and their western European and American nations? For example, the Islamic State controlling the whole Middle East has been threatening to raise their black flag over the White House and the Vatican for more than a century. Where does their rage in beheading people who refuse to convert to Islam come from?"

Akilah thought, *the wrong of the extremist, terrorist Muslims' rage is a subject on which we can both agree.* Then, she said, "Well, five major Muslim teachers in the time following Prophet Muhammad (peace to him) expounded on the Qur'an as well as the Hadith tradition following the Qur'an's completion and the death of Muhammad (may he have peace). Only one of them interpreted the Qur'an to advocate violence in spreading the Muslim faith. The other four all urged Muslims to spread our beliefs through peaceful means.

"In fact, 'jihad,' which the terrorist Muslims wrongly interpret to mean 'holy war,' literally means 'struggle' to obey Allah's will (praise to him). When our good actions outweigh our bad ones, he will be merciful to us."

"You mean that the terrorists are only about 20% of all Muslims? If that's accurate, they have gotten a lot more attention than they deserve."

"Yes, that's true. However, to answer your question, many of those extremist Islamic terrorists hold long-term grudges toward Christian nations' actions against Muslims in the Middle Ages—for example, the Crusades that attempted to conquer Muslim-held Jerusalem and Islamic nations. Later, the Inquisition persecuted non-Christians, including Muslims, in Christian nations, considering them to be traitors."

Farhan felt a little depressed as his eyes and mouth opened wide, "I believe that the worst mistake the Christian churches ever made was to allow themselves to be the established religion first in the Roman Empire and then in England, France, Germany, Italy, Holland, Scandinavia, and other European areas.

"On behalf of the Christian church, I apologize to all Muslims that those Christian countries used armies to try to force their religion on Islam and other people in the Crusades and the Inquisition. The Christian churches should never have become their countries' established religions. Christians are far from perfect too, you know. Sadly, because theirs was the official religion, anyone who differed from them was considered a traitor, the way extreme, terrorist Muslims do today."

Akilah felt gratified that Farhan apologized on behalf of those established Christian churches and their abusive nations. Therefore, she said, "Farhan, I also feel ashamed that some Muslim nations have persecuted and killed Christians in the name of Allah (thanks be to him). After all, the Qur'an honors 'the people of the Book,' a clear reference to Jews and Christians."

Farhan responded to her apology, "As a result, it seems to me that those facts about Christian abuse of their power are only ways to understand some Muslims' hatred. However, they don't excuse that great anger, which also shows up in their persecuting Christians in Muslim nations and their attacks on the West. Doesn't the Qur'an teach that a future Day of Judgment is coming when God will judge everyone?"

Akilah answered with an emphatic nod.

"Then, why don't those minority, terrorist Muslims wait until that last time to let God judge Christians?...Akilah, all of those formerly-Christian countries as well as the United States now have secular governments like the one in Turkey. Even in England, King Ralph VI has no real political power as the so-called head of the church and the nation. His royal role is still only pomp and pageantry.

"Don't terrorist Muslims understand that the Christian churches throughout Europe and the USA aren't one with their nations' governments in any meaningful way, the way they were hand-in-glove with them during the Crusades and the Inquisition?"

"Apparently not, Farhan. They describe their jihad as a crusade against the Christian West, even though the West is no longer Christian, at least politically. I agree that Muslims should wait until the Final Judgment for Allah's justice to be done."

Chapter Twenty-Seven

Any witnesses?

Huda and Ghanem walked up the sidewalk to the Muslim children's small two-bedroom house in the middle-class neighborhood a block south of Harley's Place. When they knocked on the door, a middle-aged woman, Aarifa Sahm, wearing a brown scarf and robe, came to the door. The two detectives placed their sandals on the provided stand inside the front door.

When they had settled in the living room, she called the two boys to come from their bedroom.

After they all sat together on the floor with their robes covering their feet, Huda asked them, "Daleel and Umair, how are you doing?"

Twelve-year-old Umair spoke up, "I'm having nightmares about those bodies coming alive and chasing me."

* * *

The boy's imagination went to his recurring nocturnal struggles. *He suddenly saw the seven dead women floating out of their body bags at Harley's Place. He scurried as fast as he could toward the motel to the west to escape them. No matter how hard he ran, the women—risen from the dead and wearing glowing, glistening gowns—caught up with him and passed him. They turned around. He stopped. Their jaws dropped to their knees, and they shrieked at him.*

He turned around and zipped past Harley's Place and south toward his home, which had burned to ashes before he arrived. Then, he saw himself in bed shouting in grief as he woke up, shaking with fear.

His mind returned to the present with sweat on his brow.

Ghanem leaned forward and replied, "Nightmares can be really scary, Umair."

Ten-year-old Daleel with his heart beating wildly in his throat because of his fear asked, "Why did someone kill those women?"

Daleel, we're trying to find out why the murderer killed those victims in order to catch him. Did you see any person that you didn't recognize in your neighborhood or around Harvey's Place last year?"

The boys shook their heads. However, then Umair's eyes opened wide, "I remember now that one night when I couldn't sleep, I looked out the front window and saw an old, rusty fusion-car parked at the north end of our block facing north toward Harley's Place, which is a block away. I also saw a shadowy figure walking north with a flashlight. The night is very dark at that end of our street."

Huda felt that they were now getting somewhere. He sat up straight, smiled, and asked, "What did that man look like?"

"He looked like a tall, dark ghost; but I didn't think anything about it, because he wasn't coming toward our house. Then I went to bed."

Ghanem asked, "Can you tell us anything about his fusion-car?"

The boy's memory tried to recall every detail of that scene. However, he scratched and shook his head, "No, it looked old and I think it was gray."

Huda said, "Thank you, boys. You've been a big help. I hope your nightmares go away. I'm sure they seem real, but they aren't. We certainly hope to catch this criminal soon so that the real-life nightmare ends for women."

Handing his holo-card to their mother, Touma said to the boys, "If you remember anything else, please call us."

* * *

Daheer and Maloof walked into the Travelodge motel west of Harley's Place. The person on duty, a young, bare-headed woman, greeted them. Maloof asked her, "Do you ever work during the middle of the night here?"

She said with a hint of a smile, "Yes, we all take two nights a week to sleep—I mean, work—here and to get breakfast ready."

Maloof cracked with a grin, "We could arrest you for sleeping on the job..., but we won't. During your nights on duty last year, did you see any activity, flashlights, or people east of here at Harley's Place?"

The woman shuddered because the body dump was so close to her place of work. She said, "I heard the whole ruckus about those poor women's bodies the boys found there. I'm taking self-defense classes, as all of my women-friends are, to get ready for any attempts to kidnap me. As you know, this front desk faces southeast. No, I don't remember anything out of the ordinary over there....

"Wait a minute! One night I did see a light bobbing around to the east out of the corner of my eye. I thought it was peculiar. I went out that office door and saw a long shadow gliding through the darkness at Harley's."

Daheer and Maloof's detective-antennae activated. Therefore, they stopped slouching and leaned forward, as Maloof said, "What can you tell us about that person?"

"I could only see him faintly through the trees. The flashlight was shining toward Harley's parking lot. The man, dressed in black, was digging with a shovel under the platform."

Daheer chimed in, "What else can you say about him?"

"I just looked for a couple seconds. I don't know anything more."

Maloof said, "Well, if you remember anything else at all, here's my holo-card."

* * *

A petite, bareheaded woman in her 50s, wearing blue jeans and a buttoned-up yellow blouse, rode her hydrogen-powered zip-camel just above a dusty path out into the Everwaters. A tiny sliver of a new moon and a hint of after-glow in the sky on a warm Monday evening in late December barely lit the well-trodden walkway.

A long, human phantom on a medium-sized boulder along the left side of the trail jumped onto the camel's back behind her and wrestled with her, as she squirted his eyes with laser-light. At the same time, a six-foot alligator wriggled out of the water to attack the camel, which bucked the woman and the apparition off of its back.

First, to protect the camel's owner, it kicked and spat at the human intruder, who then limped back up the trail.

Second, again defending its female owner, the snorting camel with foaming mouth and nostrils turned on the other reptilian enemy to dispatch it with several kicks, spits, and bites. Then, the young, defeated alligator retreated into the nearby quagmire.

The Alevi woman rocked back and forth, as she flew her valiant life-protector back to fully-dry land. The attacked woman thought with chagrin, *So much for an uneventful, leisurely, evening ride out into the Everwaters.*

* * *

On Tuesday morning at 10:00 A.M., solemn Ghanem sat behind the squad-room front-desk when the accosted Alevi woman entered the New Tehran police station. She said, "I want to report an attempted assault and kidnapping."

Ghanem directed her to a hover-chair next to his own floating desk. He frowned, "How did this alleged attack happen?"

She then related the heroic camel's role in attacking the two reptilian attackers. Ghanem then tele-texted the other members of the task force except for First Detective Srour, who was taking a personal day, "COME TO QUESTION ATTACKED WOMAN."

When they had all floated in, Fourth Detective Maloof asked the woman, "What did your attacker look like?"

She knew what he meant but thought that she should break the thick tension of her ordeal with humor. Therefore, she responded, "It was about six feet long, brown, and scaly."

Maloof showed his appreciation of her pluck as he chuckled and said, "No, I mean your *human* attacker."

She grinned, "Oh, he jumped on my camel behind me. I really didn't get much of a look at him until we both fell off of my bucking camel, leaving both of us sprawled on the camel path. Even then, his face was a blur in the dim light. He was a tall, clean-shaven man with short hair. He limped as he retreated up the trail."

"Could you tell a sketch artist what you saw?"

"As I say, I didn't get a good look at his face. The new-moon light wasn't strong enough. I don't see how my description would help."

Hopeful Third Detective Daher asked, "Are these the clothes you were wearing last night during your adventure?"

The woman tightened her facial muscles, "No, as soon as I got home, I threw my clothes in the washer because I didn't want to have anything from that man on me or in my apartment." A tiny groan came from the task-force members.

Third Detective Daher waddled to his desk, retrieved a picture album, climbed back into his floating office chair, and placed it in front of the woman. "See if you can recognize any of these people."

The woman pointed at one of the pictures and said, "This man may have been the one."

Second Detective Huda asked, "Can you think of anything else about your assailant that you haven't told us?" When the woman shook her head, he said, "Well, thank you for coming in."

After she left, the task force gathered to discuss the latest development. Akilah was puzzled at Srour's absence and therefore asked, "Why didn't Srour come in today?"

Huda said, "He called in to say that he has a personal emergency."

Farhan made a mental note of the whole morning's events but said aloud, "If only we had that woman's clothes for the perp's DNA."

Huda, who was always careful about details, replied, "Of course, we don't know if this perp is the same one who killed those seven women. He may or may not be starting another spree. He may also be a copycat killer or a different man beginning his kidnapping and murdering ways."

Akilah said, "If I were a betting woman—but I'm not—I would place a wager that he's the same 'reptile.'" Everyone nodded with drawn smiles.

Huda then phoned for a hover-van and a driver to pick them up and go to the listed address of the ex-con tentatively fingered by the Alevi woman.

He concluded the meeting by looking around the circle, "We're going to catch this perp. We may have just gotten our big break. Maybe he's getting a little overconfident and sloppy. Everyone, keep the faith. "

Chapter Twenty-Eight

Togetherness

The task force rode in the police hover-fusion-van in silence on the edges of their seats, while the SWAT team's black hydrogen-van with large, white letters spelling "SWAT" on both sides traveled behind them to the last known address of the fingered man.

At the small house on the west side of New Tehran, Huda banged on the front door and yelled, "New Tehran police! Open up!" As the door edged open, a burly, clean-shaven Shi'ite Muslim in red turban and robe thought, *here we go again;* centimetered out; and raised his arms.

Huda said, "You need to come down to the police station for a few questions, Mujahib Harb!" They then handcuffed him and loaded him into a police hydrogen zip-car.

* * *

At the station, Second Detective Huda and Third Detective Daher entered the interrogation room where the suspect was waiting, while the rest of the team waited in the next room separated by one-way glass. Huda began, "Where were you last night just after sunset?"

"I was at my girlfriend's house, where you found me. In fact, we were watching a USA holo-movie. She and her female housemate can verify that I was there. What's this about anyway?"

Daher said, "We'll be asking the questions, Harb. Let's see you walk around this room."

Swarthy, muscular Mujahib marched up and down behind the table without hesitation. While he walked, he thought, *here we go again. Wait a minute! This must be about those missing women.* He then returned to his seat and asked, "Is this about those murdered women?"

Huda replied, "What if it is?"

"Well, as you probably know, I just got out of prison on parole earlier this past summer. As a result, I couldn't have killed those women in 2084. I've paid my debt to the GPN, and I'm now trying to find a job. Do you have one for me?"

Daher retorted, "Don't try to get us off the subject, Harb! To cover your tracks, you could've had someone else murder them and then tried to resume your murderous ways in attacking a woman last night out by the Everwaters."

Frustrated at police officers' occasional "tunnel vision," Harb's calm voice covered up his inner anger, "However, anyone in the neighborhood will tell you that I was at my girlfriend's house all evening."

"We will find out if you're lying."

* * *

On Thursday, the team canvassed the girlfriend's neighborhood and executed a search warrant on her house. On Sunday afternoon, they reconvened at the station to pool their information.

First Detective Srour walked with a hitch as he assembled them in the conference room. First, he asked the policemen to report on their interviews. Ghanem said, "Both next-door neighbors confirm the suspect's alibi. They agree that he arrived at his girlfriend's house at about 5:30 P.M. and left at 11:30 P.M. His human-propelled camel was in the driveway the whole time."

Srour thought, *we have to pin this case on him. It's gone on way too long.* He asked, "Could he have slipped out of the back door to take a vehicle on the next street?"

Third Detective Daher said, “The neighbor directly behind the house saw no one in the alley or alongside his house during the evening.”

Fourth Detective Maloof reported, “Our search of the house revealed nothing incriminating.”

Akilah said, “Our investigation along with our interview of the girlfriend and her housemate showed us that the man did nothing wrong.”

Srour opined, “Come on, folks. You mean that we struck out again?”

Farhan answered him, “I’m afraid that’s the case. By the way, what happened to your foot or leg, First Detective?”

Srour looked down and frowned, “It was dumb and embarrassing. I was carrying a box down our steps into the basement. The box blocked my view, when I thought that I was on the last step. Instead, I stepped off of the second step, lunged forward, and twisted my ankle while attempting to catch myself.”

Everyone winced in sympathetic pain.

Chapter Twenty-Nine

Planning a ruse

Farhan and Shirley had just settled into their theater-style seats in the third row of the Muslim Concert Hall Auditorium when the orchestra's first violinist came on stage to the crowd's applause. Then, the conductor entered from the spectators' left side to a louder ovation, bowed to the audience, mounted the small platform, and raised his baton. From Farhan and Shirley's perspective, they saw the right side of his profile dressed in a purple turban and matching robe, but they could see no pages of music. The New Tehran Symphony Orchestra lifted their instruments.

The expert players cruised through Mozart's thirty-ninth symphony and Tchaikovsky's fourth symphony. As Farhan thought about the still-mysterious case and, at the same time, stared at the concert master's energetic and passionate direction of the harmonious and powerful classical music, a light came into his previously-perplexed brain. He grinned like a boy getting his first puppy as he whispered to Shirley, "I believe I just solved the murdered-women case!"

* * *

The following Thursday morning on the USA Christmas Day, Farhan and Shirley attended the New Tehran Christian Church's Christmas service. They then welcomed their friends to their home for Christmas dinner with a choice of ham or chicken, depending on the people's religious persuasion.

After they all sat at the kitchen table, Farhan prayed, "God of miracles, we praise you for that astounding miracle that you performed more than 2,000 years ago, the birth of Jesus, the Messiah by way of Mary and the Holy Spirit. Thank you for your gift, the God-baby. Bless our food and fellowship this noon and afternoon. Use the health you give us through this food so that you may receive all of our praise in our daily lives. In Jesus' grace and love, amen!"

As they began eating, he asked their friends, "What does Christmas mean to you?"

Between bites of chicken and vegetables, Fourth Detective Fayiz Maloof spoke up, "It means more to me since I heard your minister's words at your wedding and since our Thanksgiving dinner together."

After he chewed a bite of mashed potatoes, Third Detective Basim Daher said, "My opinion about Jesus has grown lately. Therefore, Christmas means more to me now."

Akilah said as she glanced at Farhan and Shirley, "Because of my Christian friends, my ideas about Jesus have stretched to examine the Christian faith more closely."

Shirley joined in, "Of course, Christmas has always been special to me. However, when I was a little girl, my parents pretended that Santa Claus brought all of the gifts that came at midnight on Christmas Eve. When I grew older, I discovered that Santa was a myth. As a result, when we have children, we're going to tell our children the truth, 'Santa is pretend, and Jesus is real.'"

Farhan said, "I forgot what I wanted to say....Oh, yeah! What I appreciate about the GPN is that we don't have the USA's secular materialism with all of the commercial Christmas hype and the drive to buy presents for everyone and receive them too. What I don't enjoy is the complete lack of Christmas here. I guess every place a person lives has both good and bad." Everyone nodded.

After the rest of the crew left at mid-afternoon, Farhan said to the two women in his life, "Why don't we go to the local camel-racing track for an evening of spectacle?"

At the track, unlike horse-racing tracks in the USA, no betting took place. Spectators merely picked out their favorites for each of the eight races and rooted them on, as the zip-camels floated two meters above the ground 200 kilometers an hour three times around a suspended oval track.

After they sat down, the loud-speaker system blared, "Welcome, patrons, to today's first race, featuring six worthy fusion-propelled camels with ancient political names. Nearest the inner fence is a veteran camel, FDR [polite clapping]. Next to it is New Tehran's own LBJ [a thunderous ovation]. Third is Abe Lincoln [moderate applause]. Fourth is this year's CCC winner, Ronald Reagan [ear-splitting din]. Fifth is Adolph Hitler [complete silence]. Sixth and not the least is Hillary Clinton, our only female racer [muffled clapping]. On the mark, get set, go!"

* * *

The first race took Farhan's mind back to his narrow escape from the fleeing camels on a Sunday afternoon. However, this time his imagination made the camels trample him and other spectators.

Then, his mind went fast-forward to a hospital scene in a long room with a dozen beds. Interestingly, though Farhan didn't know Shirley then, she came to visit him. His bandaged feet were elevated in slings. Bandages covered much of his body.

Shirley put her hands to her head and shed a few tears at seeing Farhan. She whispered to him, "How do you feel, honey?"

He croaked, "I'm thankful I'm alive, dear."

Farhan's "day-mare" made him shiver. He then whispered his thankfulness to God for his narrow escape.

* * *

The fusion-camels—with small, multicolored jockeys riding on top of colorful fusion-saddles—jetted at about 200 kilometers an hour three times around the track to loud cheers, "Go, go, go, Reagan!" and "Go get 'em, LBJ!" Finally, Abe Lincoln came from fourth to first place in the last fifty meters to win by one tiny millimeter over second-place Reagan. Adolph and Hillary came in tied for fifth.

After the first race, Farhan confided to the women with a voice just above a whisper, "Shirley and Akilah, I invited you both here to explain my theory about the identity of the perpetrator." He then explained to them the clues that he put together, especially the one that dawned on him at the symphony concert.

He continued, "However, theories aren't enough. The case is all circumstantial without any hard evidence or solid, credible witnesses. We're going to have to catch the perp in the act."

Akilah whispered, "How can we trap him? It would have to involve a woman who would be willing to be a decoy. It's risky."

Shirley said to herself, *it's now time for me to do my part in catching this slimy monster.* She straightened up and volunteered, "I'm willing to be the guinea pig to help catch him."

Akilah and Farhan nodded with wide grins. Farhan's desire for justice overcame his mixed feelings about letting his wife be even a temporary victim, as he said to reassure himself and her, "We'll make sure you're safe, Shirley!"

* * *

The following Tuesday, Farhan texted some of the life-protection task force members to meet him for supper on Wednesday at an out-of-the-way restaurant on dry land out in the Everwaters. Together, they planned their strategy to flush out a sewer-rat who had killed seven women and assaulted another one.

* * *

Shirley Issah taught fourth grade at the grade school that bordered the eighteen-acre palm grove where the perpetrator abducted the seventh woman. Her evening habit on

Saturday, Monday, and Wednesday was to stay late correcting assignments and tests.

After sunset on a cool Tuesday, January 6, 2086, she put on her zip-running shoes in the female teachers' restroom. She then exited the building to run through the deserted parking lot, down the dusty path, through the palm trees, and toward the opposite subdivision on the outskirts of New Tehran.

A hundred meters into the grove, a lanky, black-clad figure emerged from behind a tall palm to say to her, "My old fusion-car in that subdivision won't start. Could you please help me?"

At that very moment, he grabbed her with an iron grip. After a struggle, she went limp in his arms. He picked her up and began lugging her through the palms.

Simultaneously, two people emerged from the sides of the school; two others, from the other end of the woods; and a jet-powered camel with a rider, from the palm-tree depths. The dim silhouette of a female camel also appeared just off the trail.

As the perpetrator ran with his limp load toward the subdivision, the camel—urged on by its rider-policeman—ran at him toward the school. As they collided, the camel hissed its vomit at the murderer's eyes, bit his head, kicked his lower body, and—when Shirley dropped to the dust with a thud—sat on the fallen perp. The four task-force members scampered to aid Shirley, who awoke in a few minutes. Frantic Farhan thought, *I regret letting her get involved in this case!* He cradled her in his arms.

Akilah with great relief in her heart then used a flashlight to illumine the dark figure. The task force focused on him as she removed the bandana on his dazed face. She proclaimed, "As we suspected, we have caught you red-handed as you tried to abduct another victim, First Detective Fahyim Srour!"

* * *

Deeply-depressed and angry Srour sat in the police-station interrogation room in the unfamiliar seat of a suspect/perpetrator. When Third Detective Daher and Fourth Detective Maloof entered the room, they sat on chairs opposite Srour at the table. Huda, the other policemen, Akilah, and Farhan observed through one-way glass in the next room.

With mixed feelings of relief that they had solved the case, profound anger at Srour for his tangible evil against women, and sadness that their leader had led such a double life, heavy-set Daher began, "First Detective, you had us all fooled by your complete hypocrisy. How could you have pretended to seek the perp so eagerly when you were the guilty one all along?"

Srour remained silent, as he relied on his expertise at evading detection to get him out of this deep, justice hole into which he had fallen.

Deeply-saddened, bearded Maloof said, "We have executed a search warrant on your house and your grandparents' farm that you inherited. We found your farmhouse basement dungeon rooms. The CSIs will do a thorough job gathering evidence that will put you out of commission permanently. We'll also run DNA tests on what we find. Why don't you come clean and save us a lot of time and effort?"

Suspended Srour folded his arms and replied with a tight, solemn face, "My defense will be that my fellow police officers entrapped me out of jealousy for my position. Furthermore, I am confident that you will find no evidence linking me to the women's murders. I want to speak to my lawyer."

Enraged Farhan barged into the interrogation room, "Srour, we all saw you attack and try to abduct my wife, Shirley Issah, and we will testify to that fact! You made the fatal mistake of returning to the scene of one of your horrible crimes!" Maloof and Daher struggled to keep Farhan from pummeling the suspected serial killer, who sat still with his arms tightly folded.

* * *

The task force minus Srour met in the police squad room after he again invoked an attorney and returned to his cell.

Tall and lean Second Detective Huda declared, "Well, I didn't see that arrest coming! Srour pulled the camel's hair over my eyes. We have to make sure that we get as much evidence as possible from his home and dungeon to nail him to the concrete-block wall, so to speak."

Mystified Second Policeman Ghanem asked Farhan, "What clues led you to suspect our leader Srour? I missed them completely."

Farhan felt a surge of confidence that Srour was a good collar and recounted most of his observations, "First, I observed one of them when the killer showed us through his home and workshop. That one will come out at the trial.

"Second, you'll remember that Srour described the absence of his father, his mother's abuse of him, and his abuse of animals—all when he was a boy.

"Third, he admitted that he lit fires in his neighborhood and read all about Jack the Ripper in high school.

"Fourth, his fancy house just didn't seem to fit a detective's salary. As a result, I suspected that he might be a crooked cop.

"Fifth, at the Colossal Camel Clash, he said that he sometimes bets money. As you know, gambling is against Muslim principles. His mistake showed me that Srour didn't always follow the rules.

"Sixth, the personal day that he took after he attacked the eighth woman along with his limp the next day made me suspect him more.

"Seventh, the final clue came as I watched the New Tehran Symphony Orchestra and thought about the case. That last clue will also come out at Srour's trial.

"I believe that God helped me put those details together to seek justice for those victims."

All of the other members' eyes bugged out with wide-open mouths that gave out huge sighs expressing relief that their long, frustrating investigation now seemed to be wrapping up.

Chapter Thirty

Examining evidence

The following Thursday morning, the CSI team of Ameer and Asima and the task force minus Srour and Touma arrived at Srour's house in two police fusion-hover-vans with search warrants in hand. Srour's wife wept many tears at her family's situation when they arrived.

Farhan thought, *we have to be cagier than Srour to get the goods to bring him to justice.* Thus, he told lanky, intent Ameer and raven-haired, alert Asima, "Take the pieces of the perpetrator's display in his den as well as every tool in his basement workshop. Then, examine each one carefully for any evidence." Then, they bagged each item with great care for lab analysis.

In addition, they dusted Srour's whole house for fingerprints, took DNA samples, and bagged every large knife they found there.

When they finished examining the Srour house, they traveled out to the apparent dungeon. On the way, Akilah shuddered with horror at what they might find on his farm and said, "I can sense that Srour's grandparents must be turning over in their graves because of the alleged tortures at their farm."

Farhan said with clenched fists, "Yeah, serial murderers are genuine monsters. Yet, Srour seems so normal. He's apparently like the character in the book *Dr. Jekyll and Mr. Hyde* about a dedicated scientist during the day and a near-monster at night."

At the farmhouse north of the New Tehran city limits, they investigated the basement-dungeon. They went through all of the forensic techniques until they discovered with super-red light the remnants of a great amount of blood. The spatter patterns radiated from a table with stirrups at the center.

* * *

Ameer visualized Srour as he danced around a woman, brutalized her with his weapon, hacked her to pieces, put the body-pieces in a body bag, transported her to the body dump at Harley's Place, and buried her. His imagined scenario sent shivers up and down his spine.

* * *

The CSIs' investigation showed, however, that the perp had washed the whole room, the adjoining bedroom, and all of the furniture with bleach, thus making blood DNA hard to find. Ameer and Asima took DNA samples and dusted for fingerprints anyway.

Frustrated yet still hopeful, Farhan declared, "The worst kind of elusive criminal is a policeman gone bad. That kind of criminal can hide his brutality and abuse from our techniques."

Akilah responded, "I think that we will have enough evidence to send him away wherever he's going. Personally, I have an idea what his ultimate destination is going to be."

* * *

Back at the police lab, the forensic pair took a lot of time to examine all of the items that they took from Srour's house and farmhouse. Ameer shouted to Asima, when he examined one of the pieces, "Eureka! I think I've found the 'smoking gun' that should do the trick, but we'll have to keep it under wraps until the trial. Be sure to keep it from all of the camels!" he said with a wide grin.

"No one else besides us, even the camels, has to find out except Farhan." Asima nodded.

* * *

Farhan and Shirley attended the next classical concert. On the way home in Farhan's old car afterwards, he said, "How are you feeling, Shirley?"

Shirley smiled her sweet smile and said, "I'm thankful that I've fully recovered from Srour's attack."

Still feeling a little guilty for his suggestion that led to her involvement, Farhan said, as one tear fell as a drop from his tear-ocean, "Shirley, I'm sorry that my suggestion led you to that ordeal."

With a determined voice, she said, "I volunteered to do it, Farhan. He had to be stopped."

* * *

When Farhan and Akilah had their usual Tuesday lunch, she asked him, "How satisfied are you that the case against Srour is solid?"

He replied, "I'm pretty satisfied that the evidence will convince the three judges chosen to decide his fate, but you never know for sure how they will decide....

"Akilah, I have a question about Muslim beliefs that stems from your comment in the dungeon about Srour's probable, final destination. I've been wondering, how will your Allah decide who will go to Paradise and who will end up in hell?"

"Well, the Qur'an is very clear that he will weigh our good actions against our bad ones, as a person would weigh two objects on old-time scales. If the good ones outweigh the bad ones, he will send us to Paradise. Sadly, if the bad ones are weightier, our destination is hell."

"How do you know what are really bad actions? I assume that you know what the good ones are."

"Yes, we can get guidance about the good ones from the Qur'an, and the bad ones are the opposite, I guess."

"I prefer the Christian, biblical teaching about God's love."

"What is that love, Farhan? I've often wondered about that Christian concept, which is lacking in Muslim thought. To me, it sounds so soft, slippery, and unjust."

"Well, John 3:16 in the Bible says, 'For God so loved the world that he gave his one and only Son that whoever believes in him should not perish but have eternal life.' The words following that verse say that people who refuse to believe in Jesus as our Substitute and the Way to heaven will, sadly, experience eternal separation from God, in other words, 'perish.'"

"However, is love a feeling, or what?"

"No, I discovered that love in the Bible at its most basic involves decisions of the will and actions, but feelings often go along with it. God the Father sent Jesus into this world, not because he had warm, fuzzy feelings toward his human race that was running fast away from him. Instead, he decided to rescue many humans through Jesus, even though not one of them deserves it. He decided to send Jesus from the holy heights of heaven to the dark depths of death on two wooden cross-pieces about 2,050 years ago. The only motive for making such sacrifice was his love or decision to act for his fallen human creatures."

"Such a love is mind-boggling and out of this world. I prefer to think that it's up to us whether we make it into Paradise." **(Read the rest of the conversation on pages 241-244)**

Chapter Thirty-One

Probation broken and justice pursued

While Farhan and Shirley were working in the thrift store the following Thursday afternoon, a scarcity of customers and a temporary absence of other workers prompted them to scurry on opposite sides of the store to the back aisle like two hunchbacks. They met behind the notorious stack of blue, lightweight, winter jackets. That pile was still just as tall as it was before they began meeting there.

They kissed each other, and Farhan hugged her tight. Wide-eyed Shirley felt a warm glow all over her body and whispered with a tiny grin, "It feels so good to break probation with you, Farhan."

"Yeah, I love you too, Shirley."

"Farhan, I have a favor to ask of you. Would you be willing to come to my fourth-grade class on our career day next Tuesday to speak and answer questions about your criminology teaching and police-consulting work? I think the children will be fascinated."

Farhan grinned, "Of course, sweetheart. I'd be honored."

They kissed several seconds and then, separately imitating bent-over people with arthritis in their spines, returned to their probationary activities.

* * *

In front of Shirley's twenty cherubs, Farhan said, "I teach university students how to catch people who break the law. How many of you have done something that your parents didn't think was right?" Twenty hands shot up. "Well, I would be like a spiritual leader or your grandparents who taught your parents right from wrong so that they can guide you to do right things and avoid naughty actions. I also help the police catch bad people. What questions do you have?"

One little eager guy raised his hand, "Did you help the police catch the man who killed those women?"

Farhan grinned, "Yes, we all worked together to get him. However, we're now trying to get the evidence to prove that he is the killer. Then, the lawyers will present that evidence to the judges, who will then decide whether he is the bad guy and how to punish him."

A perplexed little girl asked, "What's 'evidence'?"

Farhan thought, *these kids are really perceptive; Shirley has taught them well.* He glanced with a grin at his wife and then said to all of the students, "Well, pieces of evidence are things at the place where the murderer hurt people and wherever he has been that prove he is the killer."

A grinning boy shot his hand in the air. When Farhan pointed at him, he said, "I heard that you caught the guy right here in the palm grove. Is that true?"

"Yes, Mrs. Issah was here late, and the man grabbed her when she tried to run for exercise on the path among the palms. The police, a jet-powered camel, my partner, and I rescued her. Your teacher is a hero."

Forty wide-open eyes, twenty gaping mouths, and forty raised eyebrows stared at Mrs. Issah, who was leaning against the front of her desk, and then at the windows that looked out on the palm stand.

Another student asked, "What did the camel do?"

"It bit, kicked, spat at, neck-wrestled, and sat on the man at the urging of its policeman rider to protect its nearby female." The whole class chuckled.

Another little eager beaver asked, "What will happen to the man if they prove that he did it?"

"That's up to the judges, but he may have to die because he took other people's lives."

One little girl asked with a smirk, "Do you and Mrs. Issah love each other and kiss a lot?"

Farhan blushed several red shades. However, he managed to spit out, "Yes, we do." The class giggled.

Shirley knew that it was time to resume regular classwork for more than one reason. As she turned red, she leaped to her feet and said, "Thank you, Mr. Issah. Let's give him a hand."

The class burst out in applause and cheers. Farhan bowed and, after a grin at Shirley, exited the classroom with a huge sigh.

* * *

The middle man of the three judges banged his gavel and said, "The courtroom will come to order." The chatter stopped in mid-sentence. "Mr. Prosecutor, what is happening in New Tehran that we have a second police corruption and murder case before us? At any rate, our next matter of business is a preliminary hearing to determine whether we should bind Mr. Fahyim Srour over for trial on charges of multiple kidnappings, rapes, and murders. The prosecutor will now proceed."

The prosecutor, resplendent in silky, purple turban and robe, said, "Your Honors, we intend to present evidence to demonstrate that that man, Fahyim Srour, must be tried for the kidnappings, rapes, and murders of seven women and the assaults and attempted kidnappings of two more. I call as my first witness GPNU assistant criminology professor Dr. Farhan Issah."

Farhan, who was sitting in the second row of the gallery, sent an urgent arrow-prayer heavenward and found his seat in the witness box to the three judges' left. After the prosecutor marched to his side, he asked, "What did you witness on the night of January 6th on the edge of New Tehran?"

"I stood at the side of the elementary school, as the fourth-grade teacher, Mrs. Shirley Issah, left the school to jog on a dusty path through the palm grove near the school.

As she entered the path among the palms, a tall, dark, shadowy figure approached her. Suddenly, he grabbed her and put his hand to her face; she swooned. He picked her up to carry her farther away from the school, when another police consultant, Dr. Akilah Jamal, and I ran to assist Mrs. Issah. Before we could reach her, a jet-propelled police camel with a rider raced from the other direction toward the assailant and Mrs. Issah. The camel, at its rider's urging and with the incentive of a nearby female camel, made short work of the man. My partner ran to shine her flashlight in the darkness and to unveil the attempted kidnapper."

"Please point to him if he is in the courtroom."

"He is that man, Fahyim Srour!" The gallery gasped. Srour folded his arms and leaned back in his chair.

"What crime took place on that same path last year?"

"It was the kidnapping of the sixth victim as well."

"What clues did you previously observe about Mr. Srour that made you suspect him?"

After Farhan repeated some of the clues that he shared with the task force, the prosecutor said, "No more questions, your Honors."

The fully-bearded defense attorney strutted to the front and asked, "Dr. Issah, what is your relationship with said teacher?"

"We're married."

"Ah ha! So you and she have a conflict of interest. Couldn't your love for her have concocted this tale to accuse fine, upstanding First Detective Srour?"

"No, it happened just the way I said."

"No more questions, your Honors."

The erect, proper prosecutor thought, *now I'll finish the job of getting Srour bound over for trial as the next step to seeking justice for those victims.* He then called his next witness, "I call Crime Scene Investigator Ameer Muhammad to the stand." When he settled there, the prosecuting attorney said, "When you investigated and took samples at the suspect's home and his inherited farm, what did you find?"

"At his house, we took several samples from his den and his basement workroom. At his inherited farm, we found basement rooms in the farmhouse that had a single bed in one and a table with attached stirrups in the main room. With laser light, we also found abundant blood spatters that radiated out from the table."

"What is your conclusion from your observation of the evidence?"

"Well, he spent a lot of time at both scenes. The farmhouse basement was completely washed with bleach, but the blood pattern suggested a lot of carnage on the table."

The defense attorney jumped up and shouted, "Objection, your Honors! The CSI's description assumes evidence not yet introduced."

The middle judge said, "Denied. His conclusion is logical given the evidence."

The defense lawyer realized that he had a high hill to climb in proving that his client should not stand trial. He slouched toward the witness and said with an almost-inaudible voice, "So you didn't really find any evidence at the suspect's home and farm directly tying him to the abductions and murders?"

"No, not direct evidence."

"Your Honors, because of this case's completely circumstantial clues, I move that the charges be dropped and that this upstanding police detective receive a 'not guilty' verdict."

With glances to the judges on either side, the spokesman answered with a steady voice, "Denied."

The defense attorney then called to the stand a string of witnesses, who all testified to the fine, moral character of the defendant.

The judges' spokesman called on the lawyers to make their final arguments. The prosecutor enumerated the evidence from eyewitnesses' accounts about the attempted abduction and the evidence at the defendant's farm and then said, "Your Honors, the defendant was caught red-handed kidnapping the ninth victim. Therefore, I respectfully request that you keep the defendant in jail because of the nature of the crimes and that he be remanded for trial because of the horrendous crimes."

The defense lawyer felt backed into a corner but rose to exclaim, "Your Honors, this preliminary hearing is the result of a witch hunt! The investigators have not demonstrated a shred of physical evidence that directly ties the defendant to the murders.

"Furthermore, the teacher's experience among the palms was clear entrapment. The police tried to pin the defendant with the kidnappings and murders because of their frustration with the lack of progress in the case and because of their professional envy of their leader, Mr. Srour. Your Honors, I again move for the dismissal of all charges."

The three judges glanced at each other and shook their heads a couple of millimeters. Their spokesman again said, "Denied. We will take this matter under advisement." The three judges then left the room to confer in an adjacent room to the gallery's left.

Conversations had hardly started before the judges returned. The middle, senior judge, who asked the defendant and his attorney to rise, said, "We believe that the prosecution has presented enough evidence about two of the crime scenes to bind the defendant over for trial and to keep him in jail because of the nature of the crimes. However, we make no assumptions about the eventual outcome of that trial, which will begin on Tuesday, April 14, 2086." Three gavels resounded in unison.

Chapter Thirty-Two

Protecting more people's lives

On a cool February 8, 2086, a dark, shadowy outline of a person drifted into the room of two Ali-Nursing-Facility residents, closed the curtain between the two, moved to the first patient's intravenous machine, stooped over that person for a moment, and then slid out like a slow, slimy snail.

* * *

On Tuesday morning, February 10, the LPTF members all read a text that said, "LPTF, COME TO THE STATION THIS AFT AT THREE."

At the appointed hour, all of the remaining team arrived. Acting First Detective Huda looked at his dwindling crew with great sadness because of the two missing members. Nevertheless, he convened the meeting, "Second Policeman Ghanem will report on suspicious deaths in New Tehran."

Ghanem with eagerness cleared his throat and said, "I have received three separate, anonymous calls from people who said they were patients in three different nursing facilities. They described a large number of senior citizens' deaths for no apparent reason."

Fourth Detective Maloof asked with a tiny smile, "Could it be that they died from old age?" Everyone grinned.

Ghanem felt that the group wasn't taking him and the patients seriously and responded with emphasis, "Well, these elderly people's bodies were apparently in comparatively-good health, but their minds were not. People's minds usually can't kill their own bodies."

Maloof still couldn't wrap his mind around any real reason that they should be involved. Therefore, he rejoined, "Many of those people have very poor quality-of-life. Wouldn't it be okay to help them die?"

Farhan felt frustration just as he did when people made light of any death and said with a furrowed brow, "Then, where do we stop? Their lives are still worth protecting. I've seen my grandparents lose their abilities to remember and to live productive lives. Yet, their weakness gave other people the opportunity to show them love, even though they couldn't return the favor.

"We need to protect human life, no matter how disabled people become."

Maloof pursued the subject by asking Farhan, "How is euthanizing animals different from letting humans die when they get old?"

Farhan felt fervent as he answered, "Well, I know that the Bible, which I know Muslims respect, says that God made humanity to be like him in some ways but didn't do the same for animals. That difference between humans and animals means a lot to me."

Since Huda felt that he had to defend the laws against assisted suicide and against those who kill incapacitated older people, he said, "Besides those good reasons, it is illegal to kill any humans, no matter what their stage in life is, from their conceptions to natural deaths.

"Then, how do we proceed? The ranks of our LPTF have decreased by one-fourth. Therefore, our ability to investigate crime has dwindled. The rest of you aren't planning to commit any crimes, are you?" All of them grinned and shook their heads.

Akilah sensed that they still could investigate those nursing homes and said, "We are now six life-protection task force members. We could investigate the three nursing homes in pairs."

Because Huda felt more optimistic because of Akilah's suggestion, he said with a tiny grin, "Good thought, Jamal.

Why don't Daher and I go to the Eternal Rest Nursing Home? Maloof and Ghanem, why don't you ask questions at Muhammad Manor? Jamal and Issah, you can investigate the Ali Nursing Facility on the street by the same name. Let's all think about good questions to ask that will confirm that this case involves serial murders.

"Also, I'll ask the medical examiner for his reports and also find the death certificates. We may even have to dig bodies up and give them more-extensive autopsies, if we find anything suspicious at the nursing facilities. At our meeting next Tuesday, I'll ask the M.E. to meet with us. Let's keep in touch, gentlemen and lady."

As they rose to leave, Farhan said, "Well, here's another possible life-protection case. I hope we can get to the bottom of it to protect our older people's lives, if murders did take place."

* * *

Late Tuesday afternoon, Akilah and Farhan walked into the Ali Nursing Facility and asked the woman at the office for the administrator. As they sat in the waiting room, they read Muslim magazines until the receptionist ushered them into the chief administrator's office lined with bookcases filled with books about old age and geriatric medical matters. The administrator, Mustafa Kamal, was a thin, medium-height, middle-aged man wearing matching orange turban and robe.

He asked with his high-pitched voice, "Why do we merit a visit from two illustrious criminology consultants to the police?"

Farhan was suddenly somehow uncomfortable but shrugged the feeling off. He looked around at the neatly-kept, well-stocked bookshelves and said, "Well, it's more of a 'de-merit.' A person from here called the police with an accusation that senior citizens who were living here had died suspiciously."

Mr. Kamal's eyebrows almost jumped off of his forehead. He cleared his throat, looked down at his desk, and said with a scratchy voice, "It's the first time I have heard of such an accusation. We run an efficient facility here. If people are killing our residents, we need to find and prosecute them for murder!"

Akilah felt the same undefined discomfort but asked, "Could you give us a list of the people who have died in the last six months and the nursing staff whom you share with the Muhammad and Eternal Rest nursing homes?"

Mr. Kamal thought that he could protect his turf but decided to cooperate with these famous investigators to protect his good reputation. He sputtered, "Of course, I'll be happy to share with you any relevant information. You can also interview any of our staff. We have nothing to hide here at Ali." He then raised his voice, "Ghaliya, would you please come in here?"

When the administrator's secretary entered his office, he said, "Please give these two police consultants any information they want," as he ushered them out.

As Farhan and Akilah sat at Ghaliya's desk, Akilah said to her, "We need a list of the people who have died here in the last six months, another one of the nursing staff that you share with the Muhammad and Eternal Rest nursing homes, and a list of all your staff."

"Of course, I'll have to look at all of the staff's records in our database and call the other nursing facilities. I can get your information by tomorrow."

Farhan voiced a sudden thought, "We also need their room numbers and the names of the staff who took care of them those same nights. Now, we'll walk around your building and ask your patients about the people who recently died. Thank you, Ghaliya."

* * *

As they walked, Akilah's lips quivered as she admitted to Farhan with pursed lips, "These places make me uneasy."

"Why, Akilah? Dying is a part of living."

"However, I don't want it to be part of my life, as it was in my husband's life. Living in this kind of place would be a symbol to me of the last step before I die."

"We Christians have a great, tangible hope for the next life because of Jesus' real resurrection from death. Therefore, I'm not scared of that future event in my life. God used my wife's death to help me face death and to find his gifts of peace and hope for my own death. On the other hand, the only matter that I'm uncertain about is the whole process of my future death."

"Farhan, you never cease to amaze me."

The nursing home was a large, square building with the main entry in the northwest corner, connecting hallways, and a central flower garden with the ever-present palm trees. When they entered the first room in the north hallway, they found an unresponsive, older woman in the first bed and a barely-conscious, older woman in the bed near the window.

In the second room near the window, a middle-aged, graying quadriplegic man sitting in his wheelchair greeted them, "Hi, there."

Since Akilah was pleasantly surprised to find a younger man with whom they could converse, she began, "Hello. I'm Akilah and this is Farhan. We work for the police. The sign on the doorpost says that your name is Fadl Taslim."

The paralyzed man straightened himself as much as he could and said with a straight face, "I confess. I took two packets of sugar from the dining room. I admit that I'm a sugarholic. I'm sorry that I can't raise my arms and put them behind my back for you to arrest me."

Farhan and Akilah grinned. Farhan said, "Fadl, we're not here for your sugarholism, though I suppose we could search the laws for an anti-sugar one. Instead, we want to know if you were friends with any of the people who died here recently."

"Yeah, I knew three of them. Their bodies were all in comparatively-good health, even though they were in their nineties. On the other hand, their minds weren't at all good anymore. I was the person who called the police station."

Akilah asked, "What made you suspect foul play in their deaths?"

Fadl felt that he needed to defend his friends as he said, "Well, one day they were doing well and were contented because they didn't know any better, but the next day they were gone. I sometimes think it's better to be in a place like this and not have your right mind than to be like me."

Farhan said, "Was one of them your roommate?"

"Yeah. Kazim was my friend. He didn't talk much but was a good listener."

Akilah thought that they needed to find out whether Fadl might be an eyewitness to murder and asked, "On the night he passed away, did you see or hear anything suspicious in your room?"

Fadl managed a tiny grin, "No, I'm afraid not. I sleep like a dead alligator and camel all rolled into one. However, I did have a strange dream in the middle of that night. I was in my own bed when a brief shaft of light came from the hallway. A dark silhouette with a slight build glided into the room, leaned over Kazim, and then edged out."

Akilah's investigative instinct kicked into high geared as she asked, "Why did you consider the dream strange?"

Fadl thought about all of the dreams that he could remember and answered with a grin, "Well, it seemed too ordinary to be a dream."

Farhan said, "Have you ever considered the possibility that you didn't dream it but that it really happened?"

"Hey, you might have something there."

Farhan felt fervor build within him as he pressed his point, "What do you remember about that night, Fadl? Any memory might be helpful to us, in case it wasn't a dream."

"Hmm. Let me think. I do remember that the shadow was thin, but I couldn't make out a face in the dark."

Akilah asked with the eagerness of an LPTF member, "What was the date your roommate Kazim died?"

"I remember that it was the night of Sunday, February 8th, because the next day, the 9th, was my birthday."

Since Akilah felt completely at ease with this interesting gentleman, she said with the biggest grin that Farhan had seen her make, "Well, Fadl, happy birthday! Sorry we're a little late for it. I guess my wish is for your next birthday."

Fadl beamed, "Thank you!"

Farhan said, "Is there anything unusual you can remember about the events surrounding Kazim's death?"

Fadl closed his eyes, frowned, and said, "No. I can't."

Farhan felt reluctance as he said, "Who discovered his body in the morning, Fadl?"

Fadl's thoughts returned to that sad scene, shivered, and said, "I'm sorry to say that I did. He was paralyzed and unresponsive. Then, he died."

Akilah's own fears of death came back to haunt her. However, partly to divert them from the subject of death, she managed to ask, "Who were the staff members taking care of you two that day, the night he died, and the next day, Fadl?"

Fadl shrugged mentally and said, "I don't remember. It's a whirlwind of people here."

Farhan's curiosity increased as he leaned forward and said, "Fadl, may I ask what happened to paralyze you?"

Fadl grunted as he recalled that fateful event. He replied, "Sure. I was a twelve-year-old boy riding in the front passenger seat of our old fusion-car, while my mother was driving here in New Tehran. Another driver ran a red flag and crashed into my side of the car. I'm thankful that Allah (praise him) kept me alive, but I needed a lot more help than my parents could give me. So, I ended up here as a long-term resident. I sometimes wonder why I'm still alive."

An idea brightened Farhan's mixed emotions as he said, "Perhaps, it's to be a friend to people like Kazim."

Fadl's eyes widened as he said, "Maybe so."

Akilah hated to tear them away from this engaging man but said, "It's been a pleasure talking with you, Fadl. Thank you for your help. Here's my holo-card on your nightstand. Please be on alert for other unusual activities. If you remember anything else about your friend's death or witness any other suspicious events, please call me."

Fadl said with a gleam in his eyes, "Happy to be of any service to the police. I certainly will!"

After a few fruitless attempts at conversations with other patients, Akilah and Farhan returned to the secretary's office. Then, they discovered that it would be the next day before she would be able to give them their needed information.

They arranged to come back on Thursday for the secretary's information, since they would be teaching on Wednesday.

Chapter Thirty-Three

Another serial killer pursued

Akilah and Farhan spent much of Thursday in his cluttered GPNU office analyzing the nursing-home secretary's gathered information. Akilah threw those papers into a pile on his desk separate from Farhan's other paper piles and said, "This case is just as murky as the 'dream' that Fadl had. What about you, Farhan?"

"I don't see any pattern to the deaths, if they were murders. Not one of the nursing home staff members works in more than one of the facilities. We have to put our heads together as an LPTF to find some way to catch this murderer, if he actually exists. Maybe, the M.E.'s more-extensive autopsies will help us make this case a real one. What do you think, Akilah?"

"We need to interview the Ali staff members who were on duty on February 8th and 9th to find out if they saw anything out of the ordinary on either day or during the night."

"Good thinking, Akilah. Let's head out there."

* * *

Late Thursday night, Akilah and Farhan sat at a coffee table in the Ali staff lounge with Nurse Aisha Abrahim. Farhan said, "We have information that you worked on the night shift the night of February 8th-9th. Is that correct?"

Aisha, a small woman, dressed in a multicolored headscarf and a matching robe, thought, *I don't see how I can help the police*, lowered her eyes, and said, "Yes, I checked my schedule and did work all that night."

Akilah asked, "What suspicious activities or unusual visitors did you see then?"

"I don't remember any. I really didn't see much. As I remember, though, the residents were particularly restless that night."

Farhan's investigative juices increased as he asked, "What do you mean?"

"The other resident, Fadl, in the room of the deceased patient, Kazim, kept turning on his call light for help, but he didn't seem to need any assistance. He only seemed to be experiencing nightmares."

"Why did Fadl want your help? What did he see that disturbed him?"

Aisha thought for a moment with a creased brow, avoided eye contact, and then said just above a whisper, "He said that he had seen another person in his room near his roommate's bed. I just thought he was dreaming."

Akilah asked, "Did you see anyone in the hall or that room that night?"

Her voice increased in volume as she said, "Wait! Now that I think about it, I did see a man going down the north corridor toward the northeast entry door! He was leaving the building."

Farhan thought that they might have gotten their first break in this suddenly-hot case and said, "What did he look like?"

The multicolor-dressed nurse replied, "I only caught a split-second glimpse of him. He was thin, had average height, and was dressed in a black robe and turban. He was walking away from the nurses' station in the northwest corner of Ali where I was filling prescriptions. As a result, I didn't get a look at his face. I thought it was very unusual to see a visitor that time of night."

Akilah said, "About what time was it?"

"About three o'clock. I remember because I was about to make my three o'clock rounds to check on the residents."

Akilah asked, "Did you notice anything unusual in Fadl and Kazim's room?"

"Now that you mention it, I did see that someone had moved the intravenous machine and that the curtain between the two beds was closed, when it had been open earlier."

Farhan with a satisfied feeling said, "Thank you, Aisha. You're very observant. You've been helpful. Here's my holo-card. Call us if you remember anything else."

* * *

On the following Tuesday, February 17, 2015, the task force gathered at 3:00 P.M. Huda felt like a bloodhound ready to follow a scent-trail and said, "Daher, why don't you report on our visit to Eternal Rest?"

Since Farhan's sense of humor suddenly sharpened, he cracked, "I want to hear this. What was eternal rest like, Basim?"

Everyone chuckled.

Daher enjoyed Farhan's question, looked at his notepad, and deadpanned his answer to him, "Quiet." To the whole group, he said, "We interviewed the administrator, who, of course, knew nothing and defended his turf. On the other hand, the deceased man's roommate said he glimpsed a shadowy man near the dead man's bed on the night he died. That person definitely wasn't a nurse."

Huda said, "Maloof and Ghanem, what did you find out?"

Mamduh Ghanem frowned with his wrinkled forehead and said, "No one that we talked to knew anything at the Muhammad Manor. They didn't see anyone who wasn't normally there during that night. The patient in the room of the deceased observed nothing because he slept the whole night."

"What did you discover, Issah and Jamal?"

Akilah felt a sense of accomplishment as she observed, "Well, the case got really warm at the Ali Nursing Facility. The administrator said he was open to our investigation and had his secretary collect information for us. We met and interviewed the deceased man's roommate, Fadl, a quadriplegic. I thanked Allah (praise him) that Fadl had his right mind and that he remembered having a 'dream' of a black-dressed man who came to his friend's bed in his room. He admitted that he could have been awake instead of dreaming because his dreams were usually much more unusual. This one seemed too ordinary to him.

"Later, we interviewed a nurse who was on duty the night of Kazim's death. She saw a thin, dark-dressed man with medium height leaving the building from that same hallway where the man died. She also said that someone had changed the positions of the curtain and IV machine in the room."

Huda smiled an investigator's grin as he said, "This case suddenly became a genuine one because of what you and Dr. Nejem found out. Go ahead, doctor."

Dr. Nejem looked at his notes and said, "The unearthed bodies of the three deceased people had traces of the drug succinylcholine V, an extremely-strong muscle relaxant that can paralyze and kill older people who have little resistance.

Farhan said with a tight smile, "Sucky what?! This perp really sucks! Are you sure the murderer isn't Srour?" Everyone smiled.

Nejem continued, "Of course, we missed the drug in our previous exams because we assumed that the patients all died of old age with no other apparent symptoms, since they were all in their nineties."

With genuine satisfaction at their progress, Huda said, "Now, we seem to have a case of a serial murderer, an 'angel of death.' How should we proceed?"

An investigative bulb lit up in Akilah's mind as she said, "Perhaps, we need to send an undercover person to work or become a resident at a nursing home to catch the murderer in the act. Don't consider me, since I already have a day job."

Huda asked, "That's a good idea. Who could be an undercover agent to pose as a resident in a bed or in an adjacent one when our perp tries to do his thing? It has to be someone outside of this circle, since we've already interviewed patients and staff. Let's think about that possibility. What else can we do?"

Ghanem brightened and said, "Have we investigated all of the deaths? Maybe, we can get more clues by pursuing information about more nursing-home residents' deaths."

Huda appreciated his group's creativity as he responded, "Good, Ghanem. We have at least three definite murders; let's widen our search to other deaths in the last year. Continue to dig for information in your respective nursing homes. Maybe we can catch a break."

* * *

Huda and Daher entered the room that another deceased Eternal Rest resident had occupied. The dead man's roommate, Matin Farooq, greeted them with a smile, "Hi, gentlemen! I'm always glad to have visitors. This place can be very lonely." The detectives retrieved two padded folding chairs that hung behind doors.

Then, Huda said, "I'm Abasi Huda and this is Basim Daher. We're police detectives investigating suspicious deaths in this facility. Our information is that your roommate died during a recent night."

Matin felt suddenly sad at the thought of his roommate's death. He paused but then said, "Yeah, it was a little while ago, but I lose track of time in this place."

Daher said, "I can understand that. What do you remember about that night?"

Matin puffed up with pride that the police depended on him as a witness and answered, "Well, my short-term memory is usually bad. However, a skinny, black-clad apparition woke me up in the middle of that night with a bright light shining on me from the hall and then with deep darkness. I could barely make out his movements with very dim light from the central courtyard, as he glided to the bed of my friend, Ghufran Kafeel; did something with the IV, an action he shielded from my sight with his body; and then floated out of the room with a scraping sound like an evil jinn. Of course, I pretended to be asleep with slitted eyes the whole time."

Huda was thankful that they had found a man with a good memory but was curious that he remembered so much. Therefore, he said, "Your memory is remarkably good."

"Yeah, my memory gets good when someone wakes me up in the middle of my beauty rest. After all, we're in Eternal Rest. People shouldn't disturb mine."

Daher said, "Is there anything else you remember about that intruder, Matin?"

"No. Nothing out of the ordinary. I certainly couldn't remember his face, which was away from my sight all of the time....Wait! I do remember that he shuffled his feet as he walked. He was, indeed, a very evil jinn."

Huda remarked, "Well, thank you. You've been very helpful. Here's my holo-card, if you remember anything else."

They rose with Daher's continued curiosity as he said, "It must be hard for you with your good mind to live here with so many people whose minds are really shot."

Matin felt that his situation, like all situations, had good and bad aspects. He said, "I've gotten used to it. Three or four of us men can discuss and watch sports together, especially camel sports and world football. At least, we can easily forget the losses in our favorite sports because of our poor memories, which sometimes come in handy. My roommate's mind, however, was gone. Alzheimer's is a bad disease."

Chapter Thirty-Four

Further investigation

Fayiz Maloof and Mamduh Ghanem entered a room in the south and short side of the L-shaped Muhammad Manor to investigate the deaths that occurred six months to a year ago. A bareheaded woman in her 80s greeted them from her wheelchair at the foot of her bed by the window, “Hi there. What can I do for you gentlemen?” They both sat on her bed as she turned to face them.

Mamduh said, “I’m Mamduh Ghanem and this is Fayiz Maloof. We are GPN policemen and would like to ask you a few questions.”

“Okay, sonny. Fire away. I assume that you’re here to investigate my roommate’s death. That was a shocker because she was 103 years young but still in good physical health, though her mind had gone the way of many here. (I’m a spring chicken at 89.) News about the suspicious deaths has traveled like a camel manure pile on fire here. This place is like a small town.”

Enjoying her directness, Fayiz asked, “Did you grow up in a small GPN town, ma’am?”

A twinkle appeared in Bibi’s eyes as she said, “Enough of this ‘ma’am’ business. You can call me Bibi, my first name. I never had any desire to be formal. With a name like my first one, how could I?...To answer your question, I grew up in a town with a population of forty, including cats and dogs, exactly in the middle of Great Peninsula and the Everwaters. That location was our claim to fame as an important, huge city.”

Mamduh chuckled and said, "Did your roommate die suddenly?"

Bibi's cheerfulness turned somber as she said, "You don't beat around the camel's fodder, do you, young man?...Yes, my roommate died suddenly about seven months ago."

Fayiz's curiosity clicked in as he asked, "What do you remember about that night?"

Bibi answered, "Well, it was my birthday. I had Swiss steak for dinner and Rocky Road ice cream, my favorite, for dessert...."

Mamduh grinned in spite of himself as he interjected, "I mean, what happened while your roommate and you were in bed that night?"

"Oh, I see, I hafta get right to the point. I was fast asleep when a dark ghost woke me up by suddenly swooping into the room; pausing near my roommate, Anisa; and escaping through the door."

Mamduh said, "Was there anything different about the 'ghost'?"

Bibi paused with lowered eyes, pointed with her right index finger at Mamduh, and said, "He said something that I couldn't quite make out except for the word 'IV.' He seemed to be frustrated that his attempt to use the intravenous machine was not going well. However, he managed to accomplish his task because he then exhaled a big sigh."

Fayiz asked, "What did his voice sound like—high-pitched, medium, or base?"

"I'd say it was high-pitched like chalk on a white-board, or is it a holo-board? That's why I thought it was a ghost. They were white-boards in my day. I can't keep up with the latest newfangled inventions, you know."

Fayiz persisted in following his investigative instincts, "Could you recognize his voice if you heard it again?" She nodded. "Was there anything else that you noticed about the man?"

"Well, when he walked, he made a scraping sound. Oh, yes, he had glowing eyes just like a ghost. I don't remember anything else. It's a wonder I remember that much that long ago. I guess that experience stuck with me."

Mamduh wanted to report on their interview back at the station. Therefore, he said, "Well, thank you, Bibi. We'll be going along now. If you remember anything else, here's my holo-card. Give me a call...."

Feeling a little disappointed, Bibi said, "You mean you're not staying for afternoon teatime? We love to have visitors stay for that fun time."

Mamduh said, "I'm afraid not...."

Fayiz jumped up with a grin and a wink at his partner, "Mamduh, maybe we can stay for a little while to meet some of the other residents. Where does teatime take place?"

"I'll show you if you're willing to float me there."

* * *

Bibi proudly announced, "Hi, everyone. These two gentlemen have been visiting with me. They're from the police and are looking into the nursing-home residents' deaths."

The circle of six jet-wheelchairs parted to accept Bibi's wheelchair and two floating, folding chairs. Fayiz said, "How are all of you today?" In response to their nods, he continued, "We've been talking with Bibi about the strange happenings the night her roommate, Anisa, died. How many of you have been roommates with someone who died suddenly or have seen strange happenings in your rooms?" Two hands went up.

Fayiz turned to the resident on his right and asked, "What's your name, ma'am?"

The bare-headed woman made eye contact with him and said, "I'm Hikmat. I awoke one night when a dark figure entered our room around 3:00 A.M. I know the time because I looked at my alarm clock.

"After the door closed, I could barely see someone I assumed was a staff member going near my roommate's bed by the window. Suddenly, she woke up and shouted at the top of her lungs, which didn't have a lot of air, 'Someone's trying to kill me!' Then, she pushed her button to summon the staff, but the dark figure vanished into the hall."

Mamduh joined in, "You must have gotten a look at that person, since your bed was closer to the door. What did the dark figure look like?"

"Yes. He was a thin man of average height dressed all in black."

"Did you see his face?"

"I'll never forget him."

Fayiz said, "If I bring pictures, do you think that you could point out that man to me, if he is among them?"

Hikmat grinned with the importance of a witness who can help the police as she said, "I believe so. It was dark that night in our room. However, as he went out the door, I caught a good glimpse of him. Sure, I'd be willing to look at your pictures. This is the most fun we've had around here in a long time. Not that our roommates' deaths are fun, mind you. But I want to do anything I can to help catch criminals who kill old people."

Mamduh thought with increased enthusiasm, *maybe we can solve this case.* He then looked at the other woman who raised her hand and asked her, "What is your name, ma'am?"

She lowered her scarfed head and replied just above a whisper without making eye contact, "Ayda. Hikmat and I had similar experiences. However, the dark figure moved right next to my roommate, but then she woke up and shouted. After the figure disappeared into the hallway, we eventually settled down. However, my roommate was severely paralyzed in the morning and died in the hover-ambulance on the way to the hospital."

Fayiz said, "Would you be able to spot the man in a picture, Ayda?"

"I think so. It all happened so quickly, though."

Mamduh asked, looking at both Hikmat and Ayda, "How would you describe your roommates?"

Hikmat spoke up, "My roommate's mind disappeared because of Alzheimer's disease. You can count on your fingers the people in this place who don't have some stage of dementia or Alzheimer's. In fact, those people are pretty much all of us in this circle, I guess, plus a couple of men."

Ayda softly echoed Hikmat without looking up, "Yes, most of us have poor memories, but that disease is much more severe. Loved ones and friends gradually lose those poor people—mentally."

Satisfied that they had made real progress solving the murders, Fayiz said, "What else did you notice about the man that you saw?"

Hikmat said, "I did notice that his walking made a scraping sound."

Ayda said, "I didn't notice anything else."

At that moment, kitchen staff brought tea and goodies. Fayiz exclaimed, "I'm glad that we stayed, Maloof! Look at those cookies and that cake!"

* * *

On the way out of Muhammad Manor at the facility's southwest corner, Fayiz and Mamduh stopped at the secretary's office to ask her for holo-pictures of all the nursing-home staff. She agreed to supply them. Fayiz said to her, "We'll pick them up in a couple days when we come back. Thanks."

* * *

When Fayiz and Mamduh returned to Muhammad Manor, they picked up the pictures from the secretary and headed to Hikmat's room first. There, they couldn't find her, and her sheets and covers had disappeared. As they approached the nearest nurses' station, Mamduh asked the nurse on duty about Hikmat, "We couldn't find Hikmat in her room. Do you know where we can find her?"

The short nurse, dressed in blue burqa and robe, said, "She died. We found her severely paralyzed this morning.

She died before the ambulance arrived. Another patient, Ayda, also died in a similar way last night."

Mamduh's heart sank as he said, "That's terribly tragic. Did anyone report anything unusual happening during the night?"

"No, not that I know about."

They stopped by to see Bibi, who was not in her room either. In fact, the staff had also stripped her bed. A nurse told them about her tragic death the night after they had talked to her.

Fayiz and Mamduh were disgusted and looked at each other with deeply-furrowed brows. The latter said, "That's the straw that broke the camel's neck, Fayiz. It's very sad. I guess we'd better go back to the station."

Chapter Thirty-Five

Re-grouping

On Tuesday, February 17, the task force met again at the usual time. Huda had hope in his heart as he said, "Let's hear what you have discovered. I'll write them on the holo-board. What have you learned about the victims?"

"They were all in their nineties except for one over a hundred, and all of them had lost the use of their minds."

"They were all in relatively-good health, except for the use of intravenous machines to hydrate and medicate them."

"They had the usual old-age problems of leg paralysis and arthritis."

"Nevertheless, their deaths were all a big shock to people who knew them."

Huda felt disgusted as he focused on the killer, "Now, what do we know about the murderer? I'll start. He is a thin man with a medium build, who dresses in black and shuffles his feet with a scraping sound. Right?"

Farhan felt an investigator filament-bulb go on in his brain and said, "Hey, that description of his body fits all of the nursing-facility administrators and half of the male employees. We certainly have our work cut out for us."

With the crew's nods, he asked the M.E., "Doctor, tell us again about his weapon."

The good doctor said, "He uses a powerful muscle relaxant to paralyze and kill his victims."

Then, the group resumed their brainstorming, "He uses his drug-weapon around 3:00 A.M."

"He certainly has medical knowledge and the ability to use an intravenous machine."

"His voice is high-pitched like laser light piercing the old whiteboards." Everyone shuddered because of childhood experiences.

"One resident reported that he has glowing eyes."

"More than likely, he killed three Muhammad Manor residents who said they might be able to identify him."

Dr. Nejem said, "You're right, because I found traces of succinylcholine in their blood streams too. Apparently, he's not aware of our drug-discovery, or he would have changed it."

Akilah said, "He must also use a different form of the drug, since those more-recent patients weren't on intravenous machines. Or were they?"

Ghanem said, "No, they weren't."

Huda then asked, "Doctor, I assume the drug comes in pill form too. Right?"

"No. However, the killer could knock his victims out with a handkerchief full of chloroform held to their noses and then inject them with a solution of a powdery form of the drug."

Huda said, "Ah, that possibility does make a lot of sense. Ghanem and Maloof, it also appears to me that the geriatric serial-murderer knew about your conversations with the possible witnesses of his killings. How can he possibly know what they said?"

Farhan spoke up, "The way I see it, he must have access to the surveillance cameras and have hidden microphones in the nursing homes. But how can he cover all three? Only God is everywhere. If the perp can, he is certainly playing God in more ways than one."

Ghanem said, "Perhaps, we have a conspiracy of people in all three of the homes."

Huda said, "Hey, maybe you're on to something, Ghanem. Let's go back to the residences with these new insights, investigate their camera systems, look for mikes, and find out who has access to the electronics. Find out any other information that you can."

Chapter Thirty-Six

Three disagreements

The following Wednesday, Farhan passed part of the Everwaters as he floated his fusion-hatchback from his house to teach at GPNU. As he passed a business parking lot, he saw two camels confronting a stray, twelve-foot alligator. The male camel, protecting his nearby female, used his usual weapons. However, the adult alligator leaped high, grabbed the camel's left leg, and shook it in spite of the camel's attempts to get away as it blasted its two jet packs. The camel's attempts to bite, kick, and spit at the reptile, as it tried to retreat, did not deter its advances.

Farhan thought, *Oh, no! Someone, help the poor camel!* He felt very helpless. The alligator continued to shake the camel and then grabbed the camel's other front leg with its powerful jaws. The camel fell to the pavement and swooned as the alligator shook and gobbled its legs. The end for the camel came quickly.

Because Farhan had called 2-1-1, a brown animal-control truck showed up. Then, three gunshots administered the reptile's prompt death penalty and provided future retailers with a few alligator-skin purses. Sad Farhan thought, *it's a sin to kill a camel.*

* * *

Akilah and Farhan met for lunch on Thursday, February 19, 2086, before they planned to return to the Ali Nursing Facility on the following Sunday. Akilah said, "How should we proceed, Farhan?"

"I think that our LPTF meeting was on the right track."

"But what do we do if the administrator refuses to let us look at the electronics?"

"We say in the States that we'll cross that bridge when we come to it."

Akilah wanted enlightenment on another subject as she said, "Farhan, on a different subject, I read in the book of Mark that Jesus calmed a ferocious storm on Galilee lake. However, his followers were terrified and asked who he was. They didn't believe in him. You've said that believers in Jesus as the Messiah become God's children, but why does Mark say that they didn't have faith in him?"

Farhan scratched his head, sent up an arrow-prayer, and replied, "It's my understanding from my studies of that book that Mark emphasized their unbelief to comfort his Roman readers, who were struggling with severe persecution that tested their faith in Jesus.

"Moreover, Jesus' close followers and the other Jews hoped that the Messiah would be an earthly ruler ruining the Roman rulers and restoring their rights. They followed Jesus with that hope, not because they believed in him as God and man. Yet, his command that calmed the severe storm should have been one of many clues for them to Jesus' deity." **(Read the rest of the conversation on pages 244-245)**

Farhan's curiosity then changed the subject, "Akilah, what do you think about the big trial that's supposed to happen in April? I think that we have a better case against Srour than we had against Touma, but you never know about judges. I wish we had a jury system, instead, like the States with a judge and twelve citizens. In fact, the USA's jury system was a reaction to the judges-only British system. Leaving criminal cases in the hands of only three judges like the justice systems of Turkey and some European countries seems to me to be inadequate. At least when the Shi'ites gained power here, they kept three judges instead of one, the way it is in Iran."

Because Akilah felt the need to defend GPN justice, she said, "There are pluses and minuses to any justice system, Farhan. Juries can sometimes make mistakes too. I think your observation is right, however, about some high-profile, serious cases here in the GPN. I admit that politics can enter into our way of pursuing justice at times. I'm grateful it hasn't yet entered into our police cases. When the police break the law, they need to be punished too."

* * *

That same Thursday evening, Farhan felt frustrated as he sat at his desk in the spare bedroom. Many bills littered the desk's surface. He had piled several stacks of books and student papers on the floor in front of the full bookcases that lined all four walls. He called to Shirley, who was preparing supper, "Hey, Shirley, could you come here please, sweetheart?"

After he had cleared away a stack of papers on the spare chair, she sat next to him. He asked, "Honey, how could you have spent eight hundred lira on our credit card?"

Since she felt a jolt of fear and the need to defend her spending, she said, "I needed a new coat and saw some other things at the department store that we could use."

He frowned at her and said, "But we don't have that kind of money available in our bank account."

"I saw on TV that we could spend lira on a holo-credit-card and pay for those purchases with easy payments."

Filled with the desire to inform his bride gently, Farhan lowered his voice, "Honey, you realize that our holo-credit-card has an outrageous rate of twenty-three percent yearly interest, especially considering our present low interest rates in our stagnant economy. For example, our mortgage is only three percent. We need to spend money on the holo-credit-card only when we have the money in the bank to cover it in order to avoid the high interest rate of payments to the holo-credit-card company. I guess that we should've discussed this subject earlier."

"I admit that I'm pretty impulsive in my buying habits. I'll try to do better to stay within our means, honey." Shirley took her holo-credit-card out of her purse, fumbled as she grabbed a scissors from a desk drawer, and administered the card's death penalty. "There, I can't use it anymore. Dear, I'll only write holo-checks when we have the money."

Farhan's eyes opened wide. As he looked at Shirley, he kissed her with a full-face, tongue-tying, wet kiss. He then exclaimed with wide eyes, "Hey, we just had our first argument!

"Dear, you might also, through persistent prayer, turn your impulsiveness over to God and ask him to replace that quality with the Holy Spirit's gift of self-control through Jesus' victory.

"Shirl, I have to do the same with my impatience and frustration, asking God to replace them with peaceful submission to God's will."

She grinned, nodded, and rested her pretty head on Farhan's shoulder as he hugged her. Then, they decided to postpone supper for an enjoyable bedroom session in two parts as they moved from one bedroom to the other.

Afterwards, at the supper table, Farhan said with a wink, "Did we break the law? Were we each other's 'public'?!"

Chapter Thirty-Seven

Pursuing the perp

On Sunday afternoon, February 22, Farhan and Akilah walked into the Ali Nursing Facility and asked the secretary to see Administrator Mustafa Kamal. She said, "He's in a meeting but will be available shortly."

When she ushered them into his office, Mr. Kamal, dressed in a bright-yellow turban and matching robe, wondered to himself what these nosy investigators wanted to know now. However, he rose to give them hardy handshakes and say in his high-pitched voice, "Well, have you found the culprit who is apparently killing elderly people?"

Akilah said, "No, not yet. However, we have a question about your surveillance cameras. Who monitors them, and what do you do with the recordings?"

He said, "Well, our cameras are in place to protect our residents, of course. Our IT man is also our security coordinator. He and two assistants watch the monitors round the clock to observe and protect our residents from hurting each other or disappearing into the night."

Farhan asked, "May we look at your central security center where he watches all of the monitors?"

"Of course, you may. I'm curious. Why do you ask about that part of our operation?"

Akilah wondered why he asked the question but said, "Oh, we're just covering all of the bases in our investigation. Do you have recordings of the nights when the suspicious deaths occurred? If so, have you checked them for images of a mysterious man dressed in black? If not, may we have those recordings to examine?"

Mr. Kamal was tempted to make some defensive comment but, instead, answered with a smooth smile, "We hadn't thought to check those recordings. Of course, you may examine any of them that you want to. We want you to get to the bottom of the case because our reputation is on the line."

Rising, he ushered them to the third room between the rehab rooms on the north side of the north hall with a sign saying, "Authorized Personnel Only." He left as they entered a room full of small monitors showing all of the hallways, the dining room, the activity room, and the patients' rooms.

An overweight, short man in chartreuse robe and turban rose to greet them, "Hi, I'm Abid Arshad. What can I do for you today?"

Akilah took the lead by saying, "We're Farhan and Akilah. We work for the police and are investigating recent suspicious deaths here and at two other nursing homes in New Tehran. Could you please describe how your surveillance system works to protect your residents?"

"Of course. The new, 5-D cameras all feed the signals into these monitors, which we watch for any suspicious activity and for any residents who wander out the door."

Farhan asked, "Who is on duty overnight? Can we get the recordings of the residents' rooms in the middle of the nights when the deaths occurred? It seems that the intruder came around three in the night."

"My second assistant is on over-night duty. These cameras even show everyone's emotions and thoughts in colors. Yeah, give me those dates and the room numbers, and I'll retrieve those for you."

Akilah produced a paper from her robe pocket and said, "Here is a list of the dates. All of the six residents died suspicious deaths around 3:00 A.M. How can we get those videos?"

"I can send them to your computer if you give me your IP address, or I can send them as attachments to your W-W-mail addresses."

Farhan said, "W-W-mails would be great. Our addresses are also on that sheet. Who has access to this room?"

"Everyone on the staff can use it."

Farhan and Akilah winced. They then thanked Abid for his time and visited the patients' rooms and the activity room to look for microphones. They came up empty and left the building by way of the north corridor through the northeast entrance.

* * *

At noon on Monday, Farhan and Akilah both checked their W-W-mails. The subject line of one said, "From Ali Nursing Facility." When they both clicked on the subject line, Abid Arshad's message read, "All of the recordings have eighteen-minute erasures of the time around 3:00 AM. Sorry. It's a mystery to me how those gaps happened. The cameras and recording equipment were working properly. If I can be of service to you in any other way, let me know, Abid."

Both consultants forwarded Abid's message to each other and asked, "What do we do now?" Both answered, "I don't know."

* * *

At Farhan and Akilah's usual Tuesday noon lunch, he began with a perplexed heart, "What can we propose to the LPTF as our next steps, Akilah? I'm at a loss."

"Obviously, a staff member erased those recordings. I think that we can have one person pose as a patient or staff member of one of the nursing homes to try to catch the perps in the act. That action is the only way we're going to flush this angel of death out of his deep darkness. He's a clever one like Srour."

"I think you're right, Akilah."

"On another topic, Farhan, I've read several more chapters in Mark's book, but I found chapter seven especially fascinating."

"Refresh my poor memory about that chapter."

"Well, the Jews had a number of ceremonial washings, just as the vast majority of Muslims do today. Similarly, they also avoid pork and other kinds of meat as unclean. However, Jesus' disciples didn't do those washings before eating to become clean in their God's eyes."

"Yes, I remember now." Then, he grinned, "By the way, I was reading through Prophet Moses' book Deuteronomy and discovered this time reading through the Bible that camel meat, especially from jet-propelled camels, was unclean for Israel....

"What did you find fascinating about Mark chapter seven, Akilah?"

"There, Jesus said that only what comes out of the heart is unclean, not what goes into the body from the outside. Alevi Muslims heritage would agree that their kind of Islam also mainly deals with their inner life, not outward rituals, which I adopted when I turned Sunni. Thus, Alevi worship expresses their inner joy in Allah (praise him) as their Creator."

Getting out his pocket New Testament, Farhan said, "Akilah, Jesus brought a new order or covenant with his people that comes out of God's covenant with Abraham. Christians and Jews believe, on the basis of the Bible, that the covenant continued with Abraham's son Isaac to the Jews and eventually to the Christians."

"We believe the Qur'an's description that the covenant continued with Ishmael, instead." **(Read the rest of the discussion on pages 247-248)**

* * *

When the LPTF convened in the police squad room at exactly 3:00 P.M., Huda announced, "All of our attempts to get video and microphone evidence have been futile. One or more persons erased the incriminating recordings and probably removed any microphones before we had a chance to find them. At least, we know that the killer or killers have to be on the nursing homes' staffs. What do we do now?"

Akilah spoke up, "Farhan and I think we need undercover people to pose as members of the staff or patients to try to catch the perp or perps."

Maloof felt a mixture of hope and doubt as he said, "That's a good idea, but how can we carry it out? People have seen all of us at the nursing homes. Also, we will need people who can be workers or pose as residents all night long to try to nab the perp or perps."

Huda said, "Could any members of the police force or retired police be undercover agents? I'm just thinking aloud."

Daher said to Huda, "Could you ask the other police staff or retired police confidentially to volunteer?"

"Yeah, I guess I could. Let's get together here again Thursday. Hopefully, we will have volunteers by then."

Chapter Thirty-Eight

Great progress

Huda knocked on the office door of Police Chief Kazim Sahm, a short, fully-bearded man decked out in formal black robe and turban. "Come in."

"Sorry to bother you, sir, but our life-protection task force has decided to ask for police-department and retired police as volunteers to pose as either nursing-home staff members or patients in order to catch the geriatric serial-killer or killers. Who do you think would be good at such a risky job?"

Mr. Sahm replied, "We have drug-enforcement personnel going undercover all the time, but none of them could pose as older nursing-home residents. Perhaps, a retired policeman would be willing to pose as a demented, older patient."

"Well, I was thinking that they could imitate patients who become completely paralyzed by accidents of some kind, but I'll take up your suggestion first."

"By the way, Huda, how is your task force working out?"

"We find that Issah is a valuable addition to the group, but the absence of Srour and Touma decreases the number of minds brainstorming cases and the people investigating them."

"I see. Perhaps, sometime in the future, we can find the money in the budget to add a policeman and a detective to help you out."

"Thank you, sir."

"Say, Huda, I really appreciate the way you've taken charge of the LPTF. How do you think your name would sound after the title 'First Detective'?"

Abasi was suddenly seized with self-doubt and said, "I'm not worthy of such a position; it would also be a lot more stressful. I honestly don't know what I would say if you offer me that position. My first impulse would be to decline the position. I also think the idea is a bit premature, since the present First Detective hasn't stood trial yet."

"I hear that the case against him is pretty solid, though."

"It does seem to be, but let's not jump over the camel's head just yet, sir."

"Okay, Huda. I guess that's wise."

"Thank you for the thought, though, sir."

During the next hour, three retired volunteers surprised Huda by jumping at the chance to play the role of patients with dementia. As seventy-nine-year-old Mujeer Musaid, said, "I'm willing to do anything to catch those serial-killers of geriatric people."

* * *

The LPTF met again at the appointed hour on Thursday, February 26, 2086. Huda announced with a big smile on his face, "We have three retired-police volunteers willing to make attempts to catch the serial killer or killers. They couldn't come to our meeting, but they will pretend to be nursing-home residents. How should we support them?"

Ghanem spoke up, "All of us need to be at one nursing home when the first one encounters the killer in order to apprehend him. After I let you know when the ruse begins, let's all camp out near the Ali Nursing Facility before 3:00 A.M. to catch a serial-killer of old folks."

* * *

On March 3, 2086, two ambulance personnel wheeled undercover, retired policeman Mujeer Musaid into Ali Nursing Facility to live as a resident in a room on the west side.

That night, the LPTF planned to do a stakeout near the home in an attempt to apprehend the perp.

* * *

A short, unshaven Mujer sat in his wheelchair in the Ali dining room that evening with a staff woman sitting alongside to feed him. He mumbled, "Careful. I don't want to get my red robe dirty." He fumbled with his brown gown.

Another resident, ninety-seven-year-old, toothless Abbas Karam, the oldest man at Ali, who ate what seemed to be baby food as he sat directly across from Mujer, said, "How are you doing—really, Mujer?"

Mujer said, "I'm doing as well as can be expected. I just don't remember where I am, how I got here, and where I came from. It's frustrating!"

That night another staff orderly helped to dress Mujer in his night robe and tuck him into his bed. He thought, *I have to stay awake.* His mind drifted back to the good times he spent with his own grandfather when they played humpless camel-cards with his family. *If anyone had killed my grandfather, I would have had a hard time keeping from killing him with my bare hands.*

The nurse on duty entered Mujer's room on Ali's west side to check on the two residents at about 2:30 A.M. and to give sleeping pills to his sleeping roommate. At 3:00 A.M., a shaft of light penetrated the semi-darkness when a shadowy figure slid into the room.

The hairs on the back of Mujer's neck bristled with adrenaline and hope for an arrest. The thin, black-shrouded ghost drifted with a scraping sound toward him. He barely saw a white handkerchief a few millimeters from his face. Mujer shook off his blanket, grabbed his nine-millimeter, and shouted with all of his lung-power, "You're under arrest for attempted murder!"

The black-clad criminal turned to slither out of the room, when Farhan and Akilah tripped him with their feet from both sides of the door. However, before they could apprehend him, he scrambled to his feet, mounted his hoverboard hidden in his robe, sailed north to the northwest entrance, and burst through it, setting off an alarm. The commotion set off a crowd of cries from the residents.

Furious Farhan flew on his own jet-propelled board after the speeding ghost and exited the building to pursue him. The black-clad figure zoomed high until three high-flying hydrogen-cars convened their convention around the perp with two above and below him. From one of the cars, Huda and Maloof shouted with guns drawn, "Hands up! Put your hands together behind your neck."

Flying Farhan came up behind the frozen-in-the-warm-air, black-dressed, humbled statue suspended above the end of the first block; ripped off his black mask; and shone his flashlight into his face to reveal the killer, Ali Nursing Facility Administrator Mustapha Kamal.

Akilah caught up with the justice group in her own fusion-car and said, "Ali Administrator Kamal, you dishonor the namesake of your nursing home!"

* * *

In the interrogation room illuminated by the early morning sun shining through the squad-room windows' blinds, Detectives Huda and Daher sat across the table from the thin administrator with a grim face and folded arms. Huda said, "Mr. Kamal, it's appropriate that we meet as the sun of justice rises on you. Let's get to the facts. We found chloroform on the handkerchief that you dropped as you fled.

"In your pocket was a syringe of a powerful muscle relaxant that killed the other nursing-home residents. We have you dead-to-rights attempting to attack our undercover police officer.

"You also attempted to evade arrest, thus demonstrating your guilt. You are on a path to a firing squad unless you implicate the other criminals in your so-called mercy-killing of residents in the three nursing facilities.

"We also confiscated your metal-plated boots that make a scraping sound that many residents reported the killer having. What do you have to say for yourself?"

"Nothing."

Daher said, "What I don't understand is why you killed your own residents, who all meant income for your facility. If you turn in other possible killers, we can ask the prosecutor to lessen your sentence from death by firing squad to, perhaps, life in prison."

Kamal thought, *if I stay quiet, maybe I could escape this setback.* He said through clenched teeth, "No comment. I want to see my lawyer."

Huda said, "That's your right, but I don't see what an attorney could possibly do for you."

Feeling duped by the man's hypocrisy, Farhan entered the room and asked, "How could you have been so cooperative with us when it turned out that we were investigating you?" Silence answered him.

Chapter Thirty-Nine

Swift justice?

The GPN wheels turned quickly in an attempt to administer justice to Mr. Kamal, who never revealed anything he knew about other killers, if there were any. At his arraignment on March 5, the judges set the trial date for a week later on the 12th.

* * *

That day brought dark clouds to New Tehran, when the three judges gaveled the proceedings to order in the Star Chamber, the first-floor criminal court.

With an audible sigh, the middle judge said to the prosecutor, "What other prominent authority figures are we going to try?"

He responded, "Well, your Honors, I don't know. However, I will prove beyond a shadow of a doubt that Mr. Mustafa Kamal, a self-appointed angel of death, murdered many older, Alzheimer's-inflicted residents of his own nursing home facility, at least three people that we know of. He also killed three other older, helpless victim-witnesses at the Muhammad Manor out of fear that they could recognize him as the murderer."

The beleaguered defense attorney declared, "Your Honors, this trial is a travesty. The whole incident at the Ali Nursing Facility is a huge misunderstanding. My client was merely checking on patients in one of his rooms when the police entrapped him."

The prosecutor—dressed in a shiny, black power-robe and turban—smirked and said, "I call Medical Examiner Dr. Kaysan Nejem to the stand."

When Dr. Nejem had settled in the witness box, the prosecutor swaggered to the front and asked, "What was your role investigating the many deaths of older people in New Tehran nursing facilities?"

"I examined the bodies once and made the mistake of declaring them dead because of natural causes due to their old age. Then, when residents in those homes said that they suspected foul play, we exhumed the bodies.

"Upon closer examination, I discovered in the victims' bodies traces of succinylcholine, a super-powerful muscle relaxant. It can kill older people with low resistance by paralyzing them and stopping their hearts. As a result, I changed their cause of death to murder by injection of a lethal drug."

"Thank you, doctor."

At the judges' nods, the defense attorney slouched to the front and asked, "Do you have any direct knowledge of the defendant's connection to those poor people's deaths?"

"Well, no."

"Thank you. I have no other questions."

The prosecutor stood straight as a hovering-camel hitching-post and said, "Next, I call New Tehran retired policeman Mujer Musaid to the stand."

Mujer marched to the front with his arms swinging freely. The prosecutor asked him, "Mr. Musaid, what was your part in the events early in the morning on March 4th?"

Mujer said with a stern scowl at the defendant, "On the 3rd, an ambulance brought me to Ali, and an orderly rolled me into that building in a wheelchair. That night at about 3:00 A.M., a black-dressed figure approached my bed within a meter of my face with a handkerchief in his hand. I threw off my blanket, pulled out my gun, and yelled, 'You're under arrest for attempted murder!'

"The figure ran out of the room and the building. I caught up with him and the other members and consultants of the police force in time to see that he was Ali's administrator, Mustapha Kamal, the defendant."

"What evidence did you find at Ali Nursing Facility and in his pockets that pointed at the defendant as the killer?"

"In my room not far from my bed, we found a white, chloroform-soaked handkerchief. Also, when we searched him, we found a syringe of the powerful muscle relaxant that the medical examiner had found in the bodies of other old victims."

"No more questions, your Honors."

The defense lawyer rose at his table and said, "How do you know that Administrator Kamal wasn't merely checking on a new resident?"

"I saw his chloroform-soaked handkerchief in his hand near my nose. That's how!"

"Weren't you there playing a ruse to try to entrap anyone who might enter your room?"

"Well, I guess I was pretending to be a patient with dementia in order to catch a multiple murderer, but the defendant showed his true colors as an angel of death."

"Do you believe in putting animals out of their misery when their quality of life is very poor?"

"Yes. Sometimes euthanasia of animals is necessary to put them down."

"How is the mercy killing of older people whose minds are already gone and whose quality of life is almost gone any different from a pet's death at the hands of a veterinarian?"

"I believe that humans are not animals. I also believe that though Allah (may he be praised) made both of them, humans have souls, not animals. Besides, the killing of older people is illegal, whereas vets who kill animals are not breaking the law."

Because the defense attorney felt as if he had made the mistake of asking a question without being certain of the witness' answer, he grimaced as he said, "No more questions, your Honors."

The prosecutor then called Farhan to the witness stand and said, "What did the security person at the Ali Nursing Facility say after you and your partner asked for the surveillance-camera recordings of the nights when the residents died suspicious deaths?"

"He said that all of those recordings had mysterious, twelve- to eighteen-minute gaps in them before and after 3:00 A.M., when the patients died."

"Who has access to the recordings?"

"All staff members can look at and erase those recordings."

"Including the defendant?"

"Yes, the defendant has full access to them."

"Dr. Issah, what was your part in the 3:00 A.M. events on March 4th?"

"My police-consultant partner and I waited in the west Ali hallway after we observed a man all dressed in black entering Mujer Musaid's room. We flanked the doorway and tripped the man as he left the undercover agent's room. However, he scrambled to his feet and fled the building on his hover-board at the northwest corner as we flew after him. However, five police hydrogen-cars surrounded him in the air within a block. We then shone a flashlight in his face. We all identified him as Ali Administrator Mustapha Kamal."

"Please point him out if he is in the courtroom."

Farhan obeyed the command abruptly because of his keen sense of justice, "He's that man."

"Please record that Dr. Issah pointed at the defendant. How do you know that he wasn't merely checking on one of his residents?"

"I searched his pockets for a weapon and found it—a syringe that the medical examiner found to contain the same muscle relaxant that he found in the older people's bodies."

"No more questions. Your Honors, the prosecution rests."

The defense attorney said, "No questions, and the defense rests its case as well."

A faint gasp went up from the gallery.

The senior judge, whose mind questioned the defense attorney's wisdom of mounting no defense, said with wide eyes and raised eyebrows, "I see. Then, we'll ask for your closing statements."

The prosecutor in his silky, black garb said, "Your Honors, we have an open-and-shut case. Mr. Kamal fooled everyone as a nursing-home administrator by day and an angel of death by night. It became obvious to the police that he was a serial killer of his own nursing facility's elderly residents whose minds no longer worked, probably to put them out of their misery.

"Someone mysteriously erased the Ali surveillance camera recordings of the dead residents at the beginning of their induced paralysis that led to their deaths. He had full access to those recordings.

"On the night of his apprehension, he was caught wearing all black, just the way previous residents described the murderer. They also said that the killer had a high-pitched voice like the defendant and walked with a scraping sound. The defendant had boots with metal on the soles. He had moved within a meter of our undercover officer with a chloroform-soaked handkerchief. Trying to avoid his arrest, he fled from the authorities, also showing his guilt.

"The police and consultants positively identified him as the defendant and found a syringe in his robe's pocket that contained the same powerful muscle relaxant that paralyzed and killed several other Ali residents. These facts alone should require him to receive the death penalty for taking many elderly people's lives."

The defense lawyer said, "Your Honors, this case contains only circumstantial events that the prosecution has strung together to claim that my client—a fine, moral, family man—did those despicable crimes. These accusations are not only false but are slanderous to the defendant's good reputation.

"The prosecution has not one shred of real evidence that my client is an 'angel of death.' The police could have planted the handkerchief in the room and the syringe on him to catch him because of their frustration that they couldn't solve this case.

"The truth is that my client was merely checking on a new Ali resident with Alzheimer's disease to see how he was doing. Police entrapment makes him appear guilty, but your Honors have to deal with facts, not just accusations. End of story. Doubts abound in the prosecution's fabricated case."

The judges' spokesman said, "We will take this case under advisement." They then exited to the conference room.

* * *

"The courtroom will now be in order. The case before us presents a dilemma. On the one hand, we need to protect our senior citizens against murderous people, no matter how good the killers' motives are. On the other hand, the questions that are on our minds are these: What were the defendant's motives, if he did the crimes? Why wasn't there any clear evidence to link him with any of the murders? Is the defense's explanation for his actions plausible? Are the police's testimonies airtight to avoid creating doubts as to his guilt?

"In the light of these considerations, will the defendant please rise?...It is our decision to give you, Mr. Mustafa Kamal, the verdict of 'not guilty.' You are free to go."

Tears greeted the verdict on both sides of the trial. Tears of joy welled up from Mr. Kamal's family and friends, while many tears of grief came from the eyes of the victims' families.

The police, consultants, and detectives threw up their hands and huddled. Farhan said to the other justice-seekers, "How could the judges have come to that decision?! I believe that God will judge the judges and Mr. Kamal. I leave them in his hands."

Chapter Forty

The big days finally arrive

On Friday, March 29, 2086, Farhan and Shirley's church held their usual Friday morning worship celebrations. However, their worship was especially fervent, since the occasion was Good Friday, the worldwide Christian church's commemoration of Jesus' painful, suffocating death on top of a hill outside of Jerusalem on two wooden crossbeams.

To mark that special day, Farhan and Shirley invited their friends with whom they celebrated Thanksgiving and Christmas to their home for an evening dinner celebration. Farhan began the meal with prayer, "We praise you, Jesus, for deciding to suffer and die for all believers' deliverance. Bless this food and our fellowship. In your amazing name, amen."

After they had moved to the living room following dinner, Akilah said, "Muslims and Christians couldn't interpret this occasion more differently. Muslims, on the basis of the Qur'an, say that God snatched Jesus from the cross before he died and provided another man to die there.

"On the other hand, even though Christians believe that Jesus was and is fully God as well as fully human, they say, on the basis of the Bible, that he died on the cross and was buried in a new tomb, as I've read in Mark's book. Incredibly, they also believe that Jesus came back to permanent life and exited that same tomb on the following Sunday, as I've also read there.

"How can you believe that those unbelievable events happened, Farhan?"

Farhan replied, "Akilah, as you say, all of the four gospel writers in the Bible—two of them direct eyewitnesses, Matthew and John—testify that Jesus died and came back to life that will never end. For example, Jesus' follower John, whom he loved—as his writing described him—wrote that he saw the same Jesus that he had followed for three years die and also saw a Roman soldier plunge his sword into Jesus' side to make sure that he was dead."

Akilah responded, "That description is very hard to believe, Farhan."

Farhan said, "Nevertheless, I believe it's true because of the many trustworthy eyewitnesses, who were all willing to die but never took back their testimony. How else do you discover true history except by depending on true eyewitnesses who all agree with each other and who never give up their stories in the face of three sources of severe opposition?" **(See the rest of the discussion on pges 247-248)**

* * *

When Tuesday, April 16, 2086, arrived, Farhan came into the kitchen for breakfast. Shirley sat at the kitchen table. Feeling a tornado of whirling thoughts, she had a far-away look on her face. Farhan remarked, "Why do you look so thoughtful, dear?"

She said, "Farhan, I have something to tell you."

He feared bad news but said, "Fire away."

"Honey, we're pregnant."

"We are?! How did it happen?...I mean, when did you find out?"

"The doctor's office just called. The test came back positive."

"Wow! We're going to have a baby! We're going to have a baby!" Farhan exclaimed, as he danced and pranced around the kitchen. "Did they say when you are due?"

"August."

He suddenly thought about her and stopped in his tracks, "How do you feel, sweetheart?"

"I'm excited but also scared. What if I'm not ready to be a mother?"

"Oh, you'll be a great mother, dear," Farhan said, as he caressed her belly.

"I hope so."

* * *

At 9:00 A.M. sharp that morning, the three criminal judges gaveled the Star Chamber courtroom to order. Their spokesman said, "Prosecutor, do we have our second corrupt-policeman murder case in a year?"

The prosecutor's confidence in his case against Srour showed in his extended chest and upright stance as he said, "Yes, your Honors, I'm afraid so. We intend to show beyond the shadow of a doubt that New Tehran First Detective Fahyim Srour is guilty of leading a double life as a police detective and a serial rapist-murderer."

Then, the defense attorney, who was equally sure about his defense of the persecuted detective, said, "This case is another police-entrapment and circumstantial trial, your Honors. My client is the victim of the police's professional envy and must be declared 'not guilty.'"

"Mr. Prosecutor, you may present your first witness."

"I call GPNU Assistant Criminology Professor Dr. Farhan Issah to the stand."

After Farhan with his usual, upward-sent prayer settled into the witness box, the fully-bearded, tall, stiff prosecutor, dressed in his shiny-black, power turban and robe, asked him, "What has been your involvement in the serial-women-murder case?"

"I have assisted my fellow criminology consultant, Dr. Akilah Jamal, as part of the life-protection task force's investigation of the disappearances, rapes, abuse, and murders of seven New Tehran women and the assaults of two more women."

"What was your relationship with the defendant, First Detective Fahyim Srour?"

"We were both on the police department's task force investigating those women's killings."

"You mean that the defendant investigated with you the murders that he is accused of committing?!"

"Yes. For a long time, his hypocrisy kept us from suspecting him as the murderer."

The defense attorney, dressed in similar lawyer's garb, almost jumped out of his sandals because of his righteous indignation, "Objection, your Honors. The witness has characterized my client with hypocrisy, which has not been demonstrated by the evidence."

The middle judge spoke for the others, "Sustained. Please stick to the facts, not opinions."

"When did you begin to suspect your leader, First Detective Srour, of being the serial kidnapper-rapist-murderer?"

Farhan said, "I first suspected him when Mr. Srour showed us through his home and workshop. Then, he described the absence of his father, his mother's abuse of him, and his abuse of animals during his childhood. Also, he admitted that he lit fires in his neighborhood and read about Jack the Ripper in high school. The majority of serial killers had all of those characteristics and did those actions when they were young.

"In addition, his fancy house just didn't seem to fit a detective's salary. As a result, I suspected that he might be a crooked cop.

"Also, when all of us attended the Colossal Camel Clash together, he implied that he sometimes bets money, an action that violates Muslim principles. That slip showed me that the defendant probably didn't always play by the rules.

"In addition, the kidnapper-murderer attacked the eighth woman and was injured when the camel bucked the woman and perpetrator off. The defendant took the following day off as a personal day. His limp when he returned to work made me suspect him more."

The prosecutor smiled and said, "That's quite a clue-list, Dr. Issah. You certainly aren't clueless," he said with a chuckle echoed by the gallery. "Your Honors, I reserve the right to recall this witness at another point in the trial." The judges nodded.

The defense attorney swaggered to the front to face Farhan and said, "Your observations are interesting, Dr. Issah. However, how could the defendant be both your leader investigating his own alleged murders and at the same time the murderer?"

"Well, I believe that he was an excellent actor who thought that his eager involvement in the investigation would keep people from suspecting him of the crimes."

"Isn't it true, however, that not one bit of direct evidence ties my client with the nine women's kidnappings and the first seven women's horrible deaths?"

"Well, possibly, but...."

"Your Honors, I have no more questions."

The prosecutor, unruffled by his opponent's questioning of Farhan, said, "I call Second Detective Abasi Huda to the stand."

After Huda settled into the witness box, the prosecutor asked him, "Detective Huda, what was your relationship with the accused?"

"We were partners on the New Tehran police force as First and Second Detectives and participants in the task force investigating the serial murders."

"Do you have any incentive to pin these crimes on the defendant in order to take his place as the First Detective?"

"No, certainly not. I am happy with my position and have no ambition to replace him. There's a lot of pressure in being a boss in any organization, especially in the police department of a large city."

The defense attorney marched to the front and said, "Aren't you now the Acting First Detective?"

Huda sat up straight, "Yes, I am, but I would readily give it up. Do you want the job?" The courtroom rustled with suppressed giggles.

"When you were the accused's partner, did you in any way see or hear anything that reflected negatively on the defendant?"

"No, I didn't."

"No more questions, your Honors."

The prosecutor said, "I call criminology consultant Dr. Akilah Jamal to the witness stand."

After Akilah, dressed in a white dress buttoned to her neck and a matching scarf, marched to the stand, the prosecutor said, "Dr. Jamal, tell us the events in which you participated on the evening of January six."

"Dr. Issah and I stood on two sides of the elementary school on the edge of New Tehran, while his wife, Mrs. Shirley Issah, an elementary teacher at that same school, began jogging on the parking lot to a path through a palm grove. I saw a dark shadow glide toward her from behind a large palm tree and speak to her. Suddenly, he grabbed her and she went limp. He then began carrying her through the grove away from the school on his hover-board. At the same time, Dr. Issah, two policemen, a fusion-powered camel with a police rider, and I raced to rescue her and capture her assailant. The speedier camel and rider intercepted the perpetrator first in spite of his attempts to swerve away from them. They knocked him out. Keeping my eyes on the assailant, I ran to shine my flashlight at the man in black. I then removed his black bandana."

"Please tell the court who the attempted kidnapper was."

Her sense of justice filled her mind as she pointed at Srour, "He was that man, Fahyim Srour!" The courtroom buzzed.

The prosecutor said, "Let the record show that the witness pointed at the defendant, Mr. Srour."

At that point, the middle, senior judge called an hour-and-a-half lunch recess.

Chapter Forty-One

The plot thickens

In a cafe on the west side of the city square, Akilah and Farhan ate camel-meat sandwiches as they talked. Akilah said, “How do you think the trial is going, Farhan?”

With hope welling up in him, he said, “So far so good, but I think the best is yet to come.”

“However, we can never know with certainty how the judges are going to rule.”

Farhan stared at his sandwich and said, “That’s true....Akilah, I’ve always wondered why the Qur’an forbids the eating of pork but not camel, which the Old Testament also forbids.”

“Pork is an unclean meat. Doesn’t your Old Testament also say the same thing?”

“Yeah, some Christians also avoid pork and other unclean foods including certain kinds of fish. However, based on the New Testament, a large majority of Christians believe that Jesus’ death did away with the outward form of the Old Testament laws. Instead, God makes us able to begin to follow the inner principles of all the laws. For example, God with his own voice commanded in the sixth commandment, ‘You shall not murder.’ Well, the inner principle of that requirement is not only avoiding murder of other humans but also the protection of his valuable gift of life. It’s that value that makes me eager to protect life as part of the LPTF because of my love for Jesus.” **(See the rest of the discussion on pages 248-251)**

* * *

A thud accompanied the bearded middle judge's booming words, "The courtroom will now come to order. Will the witness who testified this morning come forward? Defense attorney, do you have any questions for this witness?"

"Yes, your Honors, I do. Dr. Jamal, what is your relationship with Dr. Farhan Issah?"

"We are fellow criminology professors, criminology consultants for the police department, and good friends."

"I observed you talking with Mr. Issah during the lunch break. The city square 5-D cameras come in handy some times. Is that kind of conversation typical of your relationship?"

"Yes, we have had lunch together often since Farhan moved here almost two years ago."

The defense attorney felt that he had to put Akilah on the defensive as he asked, "Doesn't your relationship go beyond friendship? Aren't you lovers?"

The defense attorney's questioning offended Akilah deeply, but she responded with calm, firm assertiveness, "No, we're only friends."

"Well, what is your relationship with Dr. Issah's wife?"

"We have been best friends since our days as GPNU students. She's my best female friend, while Farhan is my best male friend."

The prosecutor jumped to his feet and bellowed, "Objection! Your Honors, this line of questioning is irrelevant to the case before us."

The middle judge said, "Where are you going with your questions, Counselor?"

The defense attorney said, "I intend to show everyone shortly."

"In that case, overruled for now. However, get on with your questioning."

"I will, your Honors....Dr. Jamal, you are a real tight-knit threesome. What is your relationship with the rest of the police force?"

"I am on an investigative task force with three detectives, Dr. Issah, and two policemen. Mr. Srour as First Detective used to lead our group, but he left us when he was arrested."

"Dr. Jamal, I heard that the members of your cozy task force have been meeting at each other's houses during the lull when the murderer took several months off. Is that information correct?"

Akilah wondered where his questioning was going but answered, "Yes, we thought that informal meetings would unify us to become more effective in capturing the criminals we were trying to catch. In fact, Farhan and I found a couple of clues in this case during one of those get-togethers."

The black-clad defense attorney got red in his face and shouted, "Then, how could you show disloyalty by turning on the head of your task force, the defendant?!"

Akilah's steady gaze and words answered his anger, "Well, we had to go where the case's clues took us."

"I have no more questions of this traitorous witness."

The prosecutor said with the judges' three simultaneous gavel thuds, "Objection, your Honors! The defense attorney's words put the witness down."

"Sustained! Please show respect to the witnesses, or you will be in contempt of this court and serve jail-time!...On that late note, court is adjourned until tomorrow morning at 9:00 A.M."

Chapter Forty-Two

Justice pursued

Farhan tossed and turned in bed that night with many persistent prayers in anticipation of his climactic testimony the next day. He had cancelled his Wednesday classes, since he knew that he had to testify again against Srour that day. He had also asked every Christian he knew to pray that God would give him steady, truthful words to speak so that justice would occur.

At daybreak, he sent a prayer to God, *Lord, I turn this day over to you, the God of justice. I pray that you will show your just nature today in Srour's trial. At some point, enable him to turn from his evil ways and to you, the 3-in-1 God of the Bible, for your forgiveness because of Jesus' death. Through him alone, I pray, amen.*

After his night wrestling with God, he awoke that morning at peace. As he approached Shirley and his unborn baby in the kitchen, he went to her, saying, "Good morning, sweetheart and little one! By the way, what are we going to name him or her?" He then patted her tummy.

His smiling bride said, "We do have a little while to think of names, dear."

"We'll probably come up with names of students we have both really liked. On the other hand, we probably won't name our baby after any rascals that we've known—especially criminals that I've taught about."

"Yes, I think you're right, Farhan."

Farhan smirked, "How does 'Fahyim' sound to you?"

Shirley returned his smirk, "I...don't...think...so!! By the way, how do you feel about your big day?"

God's serenity filled Farhan as he said, "I wrestled with God much of the night and then experienced his peace as the sun peeked over the horizon."

"Yes, I felt your wrestling match. I'm thankful that God gave you his promised peace that Paul describes in the Bible. He will make you calm in the face of the defense attorney's fiery blasts. I'll pray today that he will give you his gifts of calmness and truthful words."

* * *

"Order in the court! Mr. Prosecutor, please call your next witness."

Dressed in a brown outfit, he said, "I call CSI Ameer Muhammad to the stand."

After Ameer walked to the front with his head held high, the prosecutor said, "What evidence did you find to put First Detective Srour under suspicion?"

Ameer and Farhan had discussed their testimonies with the prosecutor, and all had agreed that the former would defer to the latter on one piece of evidence. As a result, Ameer said, "Well, Dr. Farhan Issah found white fibers at the Muslim Mall, one of the apparent crime scenes. Those fibers were the same kind as a monogramed handkerchief with chloroform that we found at Mr. Srour's house.

"In the defendant's farmhouse basement, our superviolet laser-light revealed multiple blood spatters radiating out in all directions from a table with stirrups hung above its end. They were just like the stirrups used in hospitals for pregnant women giving birth."

"How do you account for the fact that you found no fingerprints or DNA on the body bags buried at Harley's Place—except for those of the boys who found them—and in the farmhouse basement?"

"The perpetrator washed the whole basement and the body bags with bleach, almost as if he knew exactly what the police would be looking for."

The defense attorney yelled, "Objection! The witness is drawing a conclusion that puts my client in a bad light!"

After the three judges whispered with each other, the middle judge declared, "Denied. The CSI can draw his conclusions based on his expertise."

With a slight grin, the prosecutor thought, *one justice point for the home football team.* He then asked, "Mr. Muhammad, based on your experience, what conclusion would you draw about the blood spatters around the farmhouse basement table?"

"I have investigated two other similar scenes. The spatters radiating out from that table with stirrups point to violent deaths there."

"Who owns that farmhouse?"

"First Detective Fahyim Srour inherited it from his grandfather."

"Please point him out for us." When Ameer did so, the prosecutor said, "Let the record show that the witness pointed at the defendant as the farmhouse's owner. No more questions, your Honors."

The defense attorney said, "Mr. Muhammad, how can you be sure that the white fibers found in the parking lot were from my client?"

"Well, fiber matches are not exact science unlike DNA and fingerprints, but..."

"So, you can't say that those fibers definitely came from the defendant's handkerchief, can you?"

"No, not definitely."

"Furthermore, with the absence of DNA and fingerprints at the farmhouse, how can you say without any doubt that the defendant actually caused those blood spatters?"

"Well, someone violently caused them, and the defendant owns the place. We found DNA and fingerprints from no one else."

"I take your response as 'I can't say without any doubt that they came from his actions.' Is that a proper conclusion from your statement?"

"I guess so."

The defense attorney thought, *One point for the visiting team*, put out his chest, and addressed the court, "Your Honors, the court is to rule on the defendant's involvement without a shadow of a doubt. Here, you have such a shadow."

The middle judge reprimanded him, "You are not making a final argument, Counselor. Please stick to your questioning without any comments to us."

"Yes, your Honors. I have no other questions for this witness."

The judges' spokesman said, "Mr. Prosecutor, call your next witness."

The brown attorney said, "I call Medical Examiner Dr. Kaysan Nejem to the stand."

Dr. Nejem limped forward to settle in the "hot box."

The prosecutor said, "Dr. Nejem, what are your findings from your examination of the seven women's bodies?"

"The perpetrator beat them repeatedly, since they had many black and blue contusions. He used a sharp object to perforate the tops of their uteruses. He carved them up with a large, very-sharp knife. Thus, he abused them physically, sexually, savagely, and brutally over a period of at least a month while they were in captivity."

"Doctor, what kind of a person would act this way?"

"Well, I'm not a psychiatrist, but he more than likely hated his mother enough to take out his rage on women in that manner."

The prosecutor's disdain for the defendant was obvious as he leered at the defendant. He then looked at the judges and said, "No further questions, your Honors."

The black-dressed defense attorney with a smug smile strutted straight to the witness and said, "Did you find any direct evidence that the defendant perpetrated any of the abuse done to those poor women?"

"No."

"No further questions."

The middle judge said, "Since it is about noon, we will have a lunch break until 1:30 P.M."

A few minutes later, Farhan and Akilah entered a city-square restaurant and took a booth at the back. She asked him, "Farhan, are you ready for your testimony?"

Farhan smiled inwardly as he said, "God has made me ready. I tossed and turned much of the night in prayer with him. At sunrise, he gave me his peace that he has promised believers in the Bible. I'm much calmer about the trial now."

Akilah's perplexity showed on her face, "I don't understand that peace. How can you have it before your testimony?"

Farhan sent up his joyful thanks to God as he responded, "Well, through Prophet Paul, God gave us his letters to the churches. In Philippians chapter four, he led Paul, who was in prison awaiting possible death, to call us to rejoice in the Lord always and pray to God with requests and thanksgiving. The result, after persistent prayer, would be what he called God's 'peace that transcends understanding,' a permanent calmness and acceptance of our situations, even suffering, as parts of God's will and plan for our lives."

"I still don't understand it."

Farhan leaned forward and grinned, "That's why it 'transcends understanding,' Akilah. My stressful circumstance hasn't changed, but God has changed me to relieve me of my fear.

"After my wife died, expressing my anger at God, I asked him repeatedly over several months why he allowed her to be taken away from me at such a young age. He, of course, didn't bring her back. However, through Jesus' victory, he did enable me to accept her death as part of his plan with that same peace. He stopped my anger and grief.

"He also enabled me to be much more prayerful and dependent on him as a result of her death. The reason is that I, for the first time, faced the reality of death and found hope in Jesus' return, his resurrection of our bodies, and his forever-gift of a new, future world."

"Farhan, you never cease to amaze me."

Chapter Forty-Three

Farhan's justice

The brown attorney said, "The prosecution calls psychiatrist Dr. Jabir Bashir to the stand....Dr. Bashir, you've read Dr. Issah's testimony earlier in this trial that the defendant admitted to having an abusive mother and an absent father. He also admitted that in his youth he read a lot about Jack the Ripper, lit fires, and tortured small animals in his neighborhood. Do these admissions fit the characteristics of a serial-killer?"

"Yes, they all do. Serial-killers find small ways to vent their anger at their childhood, dysfunctional family. When they are older, they express their rage at their mothers by terrorizing and brutalizing women as mother-substitutes. As a result, many of them also find a thrill in abusing women."

"Are such murderers always loners separate from society?"

"Some of them are, but a large number appear to be productive members of their cultures. Some of them blend in well with the people around them like normal people."

"Are they all mentally-sick psychopaths?"

"No, a majority are legally sane."

The prosecutor thought as he glanced at the defense attorney, *Ah-ha! Take that counter-punch, Counselor!* "No more questions, your Honors."

The defense attorney jumped to his feet and bellowed, "Do you have any reason to relate your analysis to my client, doctor?"

"No, but...."

"No more questions, your Honors."

The prosecutor then said, "I now recall Dr. Farhan Issah to the witness stand."

Farhan walked forward to take his place as he arrow-prayed, *Dear God, fill me with the Spirit and give me your calm, truthful words to speak.* The prosecutor, moving stiffly with tight muscles as he expected a knockout punch, said, "Dr. Issah, you testified earlier that your suspicion of the defendant increased while you attended a New Tehran Symphony Orchestra concert. Please explain how a symphony concert could have possibly helped you solve this case."

"Well, when our task force brainstormed over our lack of evidence for catching the serial-killer, First Detective Srour gave us a tour of his house. On the back wall of his den was his collection of British-police Bobby's equipment for fighting crime. I noticed that the mannequin wore a telescoping British policeman's Bobby stick along with many other items on its belt and wondered aloud how the Bobby could run down suspects with all of those tools attached to him.

"After the medical examiner pointed out that the women's wombs had numerous punctures from a sharp object, my wife and I attended the concert. As a result of seeing the conductor's baton waving in the air, I connected the defendant's telescoping Bobby stick with the many inflicted womb-wounds to arrive at the conclusion that the defendant was guilty of those horrendous killings."

"How did you confirm your conclusion?"

"Members of the task force gathered at the elementary school where my wife teaches and caught Mr. Srour trying to abduct my wife, Mrs. Shirley Issah, as she jogged there."

"No more questions, your Honors."

Feeling very confident, the defense attorney marched to the rail at the front of the witness box and asked in a voice barely above a whisper and with his nose nine centimeters from Farhan's nose, "You cannot say, can you, that my client's Bobby stick was in any way involved in those seven deaths?"

Farhan leaned forward as he thought, *God, help me deliver your justice's victorious, final score against horrible evil.* He then said in measured tones, "Yes, I can! After the CSIs confiscated the defendant's British Bobby display, they looked for any DNA and fingerprints on them. They failed to find either evidence on the surfaces, since he had wiped them clean with bleach. However, hidden under the Bobby stick's ridge between the telescoping sections of the baton were three congealed drops of blood, which were a 99.8% match with the blood of two of the dead women!"

A collective gasp went up in the courtroom, while the defense attorney's eyes widened and his mouth dropped. He thought with dismay, *Game over.* He turned to the judges and exclaimed, "Objection, your Honors! This evidence is new. I have not seen it. I move for a mistrial, since the prosecutor should have given this evidence to me before this trial started."

With glances at the other judges, the middle one said, "This is the GPN, not the USA, Counselor. You should know that we don't have to advise suspects of their rights when they are arrested or submit all of our evidence to the other side in our trials. Your objection and motion are both denied."

The defense lawyer, wearing a deeply-creased brow, paced back and forth. He then said, "What do you say, Dr. Issah, to the fact that the DNA match is two-tenths of a percent not a match?"

"After all these years, DNA is still the best tool we criminologists have to catch and convict criminals. The DNA results point conclusively at your client as the perpetrator of those horrible crimes, no matter how much you and he protest."

The defense attorney turned and slumped toward his seat as he said with a low voice, "No...more...questions."

The courtroom erupted with a muffled buzz until the judges gaveled the gallery quiet.

With a slight grin, the prosecutor said, "The prosecution rests."

The middle judge said, "Due to the late hour, the court is adjourned until Saturday morning."

* * *

When the court convened, the stoic defense attorney went through the motions presenting his side of his greatly-weakened case that showed many people's high opinions of First Detective Srour's moral character.

He gave an impassioned plea for the defendant's life.

Then, the prosecutor merely listed the many witnesses and mountain of evidence that implicated "upstanding" Srour, including the women's blood droplets on his Bobby stick.

Inevitably, without the judges' usual conference in the adjacent room, their gavels fell with the verdict of "guilty" on all counts. Then, the senior judge said to the convicted assailant, "Due to your many despicable crimes, we unanimously find you guilty. We sentence you to be shot by a firing squad at sunrise tomorrow morning. May Allah (praise him) have mercy on your life."

The families of the murdered women thronged to the prosecution and the task force with handshakes all around.

In the meantime, Srour fainted and fell like a sack of camel manure to the floor. The sergeant-at-arms revived him with smelling salts and returned him to his cell for his last night and meal.

At sunrise on Sunday, April 21, 2086, seven black-masked, armed, army soldiers lined up to face a hooded Srour. A voice asked him, "Do you have any last words?"

He secretly felt a tiny bit of remorse for his destructive deeds but shouted, "I denounce this killing because I, a police detective, am innocent of those kidnappings and murders!"

Seven point-blank shots rang out ending Srour's life because he had ended seven women's lives and attempted to end two more lives.

Chapter Forty-Four

Protecting precious lives

Time seemed to fly by, as Farhan and Shirley finished their school years and experienced the heat and humidity of the GPN summer. One morning when Farhan entered their kitchen, he saw Shirley sobbing at the kitchen table. He rushed to hug her, "What's the matter, sweetheart?"

"I'm crying about the timing of our baby's birth. I'm already very uncomfortable, but I also have to endure most of a hot-and-humid summer in New Tehran."

Farhan paused a moment with his hand on his cheek and then said, "Well, why don't we go to Indiana and Tennessee on the air-conditioned zip-train to visit our families and escape some of the oppressive summer weather here by the Atlantic?"

Shirley's face actually showed Farhan a little smile, "Yes, why don't we? After all, we have this time off. People often say that teachers and professors have it easy with their summers off. However, we definitely make up for it the rest of the year."

"Yeah, we sure do. That's my girl." Feeling relieved, Farhan hugged her with both of his lanky arms.

* * *

The Issahs' passenger zip-train floated above tracks from the New Tehran train station at 1:00 P.M. on Saturday, July 11, 2086. When Farhan and Shirley settled in two theater-style seats, he noticed a purple-turbaned and robed man sitting two seats ahead of them. The fully-bearded man slouched in his seat. Shirley left to find a bathroom, as she often did those days.

Farhan's natural curiosity kicked in as he said to the man, "Where are you going? We're going to see our families in the USA." Silence greeted his attempt to be friendly. In fact, the man remained stationary.

As a result, Farhan buried himself in a murder mystery.

Shirley returned and began reading a baby book. She said to Farhan, "We really haven't discussed baby names. We intentionally didn't want the doctor to tell what gender she or he is so that it would be a surprise. Therefore, we need to decide on a girl's name and a boy's name."

Farhan looked up, "Yeah. First, though, should the names be Muslim or American?"

"I guess you have a point, honey. Another related question is whether we are eventually going back to live in the States. Isn't that future decision related to the present one too?"

"Yeah, I hadn't thought about that eventual decision either."

"Farhan, our children's names should fit in with other children's names in their schools."

"Yeah, this decision is a lot more complicated than I thought. Let's pray about this whole situation for a while—first, to seek the kind of name God wants for our child and, second, where he wants us to live in the future."

"Yes, you're right, honey. Prayer should come first."

Suddenly, the purple man came to life as the train zipped north toward the USA border and as the conductor came through the car asking for the passengers' holo-tickets. Farhan and Shirley each gave him their tickets with their 3-D images' projections, which identified them.

Then the conductor took the purple passenger's ticket and walked two steps beyond him. The bearded man lunged at him from behind, drew a knife out of his robe-pocket, grabbed the conductor around his middle with his left arm, and put the knife to his throat.

He then yelled, "No one move or say anything, or you will get hurt! I'm taking this train-car hostage. My partners have entered the train by hydrogen-packing down from that road we just passed, and now we are in charge of this train."

The conductor plumped down in the nearest seat, as the purple perpetrator produced duct-tape to restrain him.

Farhan and Shirley sat there, stunned by this turn of events. The urgent need for justice, life-protection thoughts, and prayers were churning in Farhan's head about what he could do to stop this terrorist train-hijacking. He whispered to Shirley with a tight face, "Let's pray for God's guidance in this more-immediate situation, sweetheart." She nodded as they bowed their heads.

The purple hijacker yelled in their direction, "No talking, you two!"

The train soon came to a stop. Half an hour later, three other hijackers—wearing red, white, and blue robes—entered the passenger car, all brandishing guns. The purple hijacker commanded the dozen passengers to put all of their valuables in his gunnysack. All obeyed. They then duct-taped all of the passengers to their seats and moved on to the other passenger cars toward the front of the train.

Farhan whispered to Shirley, "Sweetheart, can your right hand reach my left pants pocket and get out my Swiss Army knife? I'll try to move up toward your taped hand to make it easier."

Farhan raised his pocket as high as he could, while Shirley extended her arm to get her fingertips into it. She pulled his knife out onto his left thigh. Then, he moved his left arm as far as he could to grasp it with his fingertips. He then cut the duct-tape on both of them and on the other passengers.

They all huddled to decide what to do and how to do it. Farhan asked, "How are we going to combat these hijackers and protect all of the passengers' lives and their property?"

A clean-shaven, middle-aged, green-robed man spoke up, "I'm Harun Mahmood, a New Tehran lawyer. We would be completely within the law to retake the train by force, but how can we do it?"

Farhan scratched his head, prayed for a moment, and then said, "I have a hunch that these thieving terrorists are going to collect all they can find in valuables. They will then blow up this train to kill all of the witnesses to their crime and to send fear throughout the GPN. Let's find out what weapons we have."

Harun said, "I have a Derringer gun for protection."

Shirley said, "You have that Swiss Army knife, honey."

A young blue-robed woman said, "My husband and I both have guns. I'm happy that the thieves didn't search us. It may have been an oversight that brings about their downfall." She and her brown-robed husband produced their laser-guns.

With hope building in him, Farhan said, "Well, we have some weapons to use. Now, how will we proceed?"

A creative light bulb went on in Harun's brain as he spoke again, "Maybe, two of us can get on the roof of the train and tiptoe to the front. Then, we can wait for our opportunity to regain control of the locomotive. Perhaps, we can take those criminals' weapons and work our way back through the rest of the cars. We do have the element of surprise on our side."

Farhan exclaimed, "Harun, you're a genius! I'll go with you to recapture the locomotive, hopefully retake the rest of the train, and incapacitate the hijackers."

After Farhan kissed his very-pregnant bride, the two intrepid life-protectors took the two laser-guns, walked to the end of their car, climbed up to the roof, and crept camel-like toward the front of the train ready to "sit on" the terrorists. The remaining passengers re-taped each other to make the terrorist-thieves think that their situation was unchanged. In a few minutes, two of the criminals returned but suspected nothing. They didn't miss the two missing passengers.

Chapter Forty-Five

Lives protected and arriving

As Farhan and Harun approached the locomotive tiptoeing centimeter by centimeter, they saw two terrorist-thieves-turned-engineers guarding the train's engine. They spied two hooded and duct-tape-tied engineers sprawled on the floor of the engine.

Farhan motioned to Harun with his arm to go around the right side, while he would climb down the left side. Then, after Harun's fingers counted 1-2-3, they jumped down at the same time into the cab, brandished their guns at the two terrorized terrorists, and untied the engineers. Farhan said to them, "We can't start the locomotive again until we've secured all of the cars. How many thieves took you by surprise?" One of the engineers held up three fingers, as he shook the life-protectors' hands several times with unashamed tears of joy running down his cheeks.

Then, Farhan and Harun worked their way through each car, untying dozens of passengers and cautioning them in whispers against making any noises that would attract the criminals' attention.

When they came to the last passenger car, they spied the three terrorist-thieves with the purple one at the back of the car and train. Farhan motioned for Harun to walk silently with him on the roof and to jump down behind them.

As they did, Harun said, "Hands up, you mangy maniacs! We're making a citizens' arrest. We will hold you for the GPN authorities."

The terrorist-thieves raised their hands, submitted to their own duct-tape, and lay down on the train-car floor like camel feed in a long, air-cushioned manger.

* * *

"How was your trip from the GPN, son?"

Farhan thought that he would have a little fun with his parents and said, "Oh, we had a little problem with terrorist-thieves trying to commandeer our train, but otherwise it was uneventful."

"You what!?"

Farhan downplayed the event, "The main facts are that we're here with you in Indiana for a week and that all three of us are safe."

His father smiled and said, "Welcome to our home. Come into our living room and tell us all about your adventure."

Farhan told his parents all of their trip's details several times, since they had a hard time believing it. He concluded, "The bottom line is that I had to protect the lives of my beautiful bride and my unborn baby, as God guided me, Dad and Mom. He was the real Rescuer." They and Shirley nodded, as she beamed at her hero.

* * *

"How were your trips from the GPN and Indiana, daughter?"

"Well, Dad and Mom, criminal-thieves took us hostage on the train in northern GPN, but we came through okay. Nothing else really happened."

Shirley's mom exclaimed, as she ushered them into their dining room to eat dinner, "No one was hurt, were they?!"

"No, Mom. God used Farhan and a lawyer to rescue us."

As they began the meal, Shirley's father offered a prayer of thanksgiving for God's gift of the food and their daughter's, son-in-law's, and unborn grandchild's safety. He also prayed for their safety on the remaining trip of all three to the GPN.

Then, over a dinner of meatloaf, potatoes, salad, and vegetables, Farhan again shared their adventure's details. He concluded, "I had to be a faithful representative of the life-protection task force of which I'm a part and of God, our real Rescuer." After dinner, Shirley's dad, Homer Jones, slapped Farhan on the back and shook his hand until he feared that it was going to come off.

It didn't.

* * *

Two weeks after Farhan and Shirley had left for the USA, they arrived back home to enjoy air conditioning as much as possible until their first child's birth. They spent several sessions discussing names.

On one of those occasions in late July, Farhan led Shirley to their house's living room after supper and said, "We only have two weeks left until the doctor's predicted time. We have to decide on a boy's and a girl's first and middle names."

"Are you thinking that we should have English or Muslim boy and girl names?"

"Since we both grew up in the United States, I'm thinking English names. What do you think?"

"I think that you're sweet and that we should give them USA names. Also, our trip to our parents' homes made me a little homesick."

Farhan grinned, "Yeah, I felt a little nostalgia too. Why don't we choose names from the Bible? How about Methuselah?"

Shirley shared his grin, "However, would his nickname be 'Meth'? I...don't...think...so!"

"Okay. Did you ever teach a boy named David?"

"Yeah, in my USA class—he was a real rascal."

"Well, then, that name's out."

"How about Matthew—Matt, for short?"

Farhan asked, "That name sounds good. What middle name would go with it?"

Shirley deadpanned, "Hezekiah?"

"Ya mean, 'Matt Hezzie'?"

She frowned, "Well, let's go with Matthew John Issah."

Farhan said, "Yeah, that combo sounds good. What about a girl's name? How about 'Shirley'?"

"No way! I don't want to saddle her with my unusual name."

"How about Deborah?"

"Yes. Then, she could be Deb or Debbie. Okay, what female middle name can we give her?"

"How about Mary? Deborah Mary Issah?"

Farhan's eyes and mouth opened wide, "Good. Hey, our last name means 'Jesus' in Arabic. All of those biblical names go really well with our last name too."

* * *

Early on a hot August morning as Farhan entered their kitchen, Shirley's brow was creased. She cried, "My water just broke, and my labor pains just started."

Farhan in full panic-mode jumped around the room and blurted, "What should I do next?"

Shirley thought, *It's ironic that I'm the calm one this time.* She leaned forward and said with a grimace and a steady gaze, "Please get my suitcase out of our bedroom closet, call the doctor, and get me in the car to zip to the hospital." She then felt the sharpest pain of her life, contorted her face, and grunted, "Ouch!"

"Oh, yeah!" Then, he retrieved the suitcase as he thought, *I wish I had a hydrogen-car!*

Farhan and Shirley flew through New Tehran, as he smashed the speed limit to smithereens. No police cars were in sight.

When they arrived at the hospital emergency room, Farhan and a nurse ushered Shirley into a room. Then,

Farhan remembered his Lamaze training and "coached" her in slow, steady breathing until the hospital crew rolled her bed into the operating room.

* * *

The doctor said, "Stop pushing!" with Farhan's obedient echo. Shirley contorted her face, squirmed, and yelled, "You try to stop pushing!!"

Farhan caressed her hand and said, "Dear, it's okay."

When the baby finally arrived with a wail, Farhan held him high in both hands, looked up, and declared over his son's howling, "I praise you, Creator God, for your precious gift of our son, Matthew John Issah! Give us grace, Jesus, to protect and nurture his valuable life! Amen." Then, the security cameras turned toward him.

He then delivered Matt into his relieved mom's arms.

THE END

Important Note for discussion groups: Discussion-group leaders may get a free leader's discussion guide for all forty-four chapters plus the twenty-one whole-novel discussion questions by emailing ***dividedtogether7@gmail.com***.

The guide gives leaders tips for guiding discussion and reviews the whole novel. The author would love to try to answer any of your group's questions at the same email address. May God bless all readers of this novel. Bruce Leiter (leiterthewriter.com).

The rest of the story—Farhan and Akilah's in-depth discussions:

From chapter five—Farhan and Akilah's different Gods:

Akilah frowned and said, "That idea [that God is three Persons in one God doesn't make any sense, Farhan. However, Muslims also believe that Allah (may he receive all praise) is mysterious as the Creator of the universe. Alevis differ from the idea of the vast majority of Muslims, who believe that he is not a person, by believing along with Sufi Muslims that he is one person. In addition, Alevi Muslims also honor a threesome: Allah (praise to him), Muhammad (may he have peace), and Ali (peace to him)—one God and two humans.

"However, most Muslims believe that Allah (may he be praised) is completely different from humans; therefore, they say that he can't be a person. I now agree with them."

Farhan gestured with his hands out both sides of the booth and said, "Then, we agree that the Christian and Alevi Muslim Gods are both personal, not merely powerful forces."

Akilah was relieved that she and Farhan had found some common ground, at least with her Alevi past, but replied with her own curiosity, "But the Jews and the early church changed your Scriptures, didn't they? Like other Muslims, I accept the original writings of the prophets Moses, Elijah, David, and Jesus.

"However, we all say that the Bible you have today is very different from the original documents. That's the reason we say that our Qur'an and your Bible agreed with each other in the Bible's original manuscripts, not in their present form. Of course, we believe that Muhammad (may he have full peace) is the final prophet."

Farhan's eyes narrowed as he said, "I understand your faith. Followers of Jesus have many good reasons to trust that God preserved his Word, the Bible, over the centuries, just as Muslims believe that your God preserved the Qur'an, but...," as Farhan glanced at his old solar watch, "we'd better get to our homes. We have to teach classes tomorrow."

From chapter seven—Farhan's testimony about how he became a Christian:

[Farhan:] "Furthermore, in Revelation 2:8, the same prophet received a vision from Jesus with a dictated letter to one of seven churches of that time in far-western Turkey in the town of Smyrna.

"However, I discovered that in Jesus' dictation of his letter to that church, he introduced himself this way, 'These are the words of the First and the Last, who died and came to life again.' Therefore, Jesus claimed in his vision to be the eternal God, to have died a physical death, and to have risen from that death to permanent life.

"...Akilah, what point was I making? Oh, yeah. I also found out that Jesus' death devastated his followers, who had high hopes that he would be the nation's earthly political leader and that they would be his famous advisors. They thought that he was the political Messiah for whom the Jews were looking. However, he died a criminal's death instead. Thus, that horrible event dashed their hopes.

"Three days later, an event changed his followers' lives from discouragement about their leader's death to courage. They testified that they had seen Jesus alive. Over the next forty days, he appeared to them many times and even ate with them more than once. More than five hundred people saw him alive from the dead on one occasion.

"Therefore, those eyewitnesses, who were willing to die in the face of severe persecution and never recanted their stories, convinced me of the Bible's historical truth and of Jesus' full deity and humanity. As a result, I found a church of Jesus' followers in our small town to attend and join."

From chapter seven—Farhan's four other reasons why the Bible has not changed:

Encouraged, Farhan continued, "My second reason is that the events and teachings of the Bible are far beyond human thought. For example, Matthew's list of the people in the line from Abraham to Jesus includes three women. Two were prostitutes and the other, an adulteress, Bathsheba. What humans would include women with immoral behavior in their ancestor lists, especially since men were the heads of families at that time? No one. Thus, that description must have come from God.

"Akilah, my third reason is that the Bible makes many observations and descriptions showing that the Jews and early church could not have changed the original manuscripts. Let me mention several: For example, Noah, one of Muslims' recognized prophets, got drunk one night after the flood. Also, ten of Israel's tribal leaders, who were brothers of Joseph, another prophet accepted by Muslims, showed their hatred for their favored sibling by selling him into slavery. In addition, Judah, one of the twelve tribal ancestors in Israel, committed adultery with his daughter-in-law, Tamar.

"Moreover, Moses, another Muslim-recognized prophet, resisted God's call to lead Israel out of Egyptian slavery by making excuses and stalling for time, even though God appeared to him in an unburnable, burning bush on Mount Sinai, an event the Qur'an describes too. Furthermore, David, also recognized as a Muslim prophet, committed adultery and murder—both actions that God obviously forbids—to fulfill his lust for Bathsheba, the mother of King Solomon and an ancestor of Jesus."

Akilah rocked back in the booth as if shot, gasped, and raised her eyebrows, "I never knew that those events were in the Bible."

Farhan grinned as he said, "In the New Testament, you can read the fact that Peter, one of Jesus' twelve closest followers, one of the inner three, and a 'pillar' of the early church, rebuked Jesus when he predicted his death and resurrection and denied three times that he even knew Jesus during his trial before the kangaroo court Sanhedrin.

"What's more, Prophet Paul, when he was known as Saul of Tarsus, put Jesus' followers in prison and agreed to their deaths. However, he later testified before kings who could put him to death for his ideas that he had met the risen Jesus in a blinding light. Because of his experience with Jesus, he became a preacher and church planter for him throughout the north Mediterranean Sea against three kinds of severe opposition.

"The church certainly would have removed all of those actions that put their heroes in a negative light, if they later changed the Bible."

Akilah's eyes bugged out as she interjected, "Jesus predicted his death and his life from the dead?"

"Yeah, several times. However, his followers ignored his prophecies because they had no idea what kind of a leader he was—a spiritual leader of his later world-wide church, not the political leader that they expected would rule Palestine.

"Also, when you think about Jesus' life, if the early church changed the Bible, why would they leave in it Jesus' death as their religious leader? After all, he claimed to be fully God and fully human. How could he die? However, the four gospels by four different writers—two of them direct eyewitnesses—testify to the facts of Jesus' death and subsequent resurrection.

"I could go on and on to describe all of the Bible's contents that Jews and Christians would never have kept in the Bible if they had changed the original manuscripts."

Akilah felt exhausted, sighed, and said, "That's quite a list. I might consider reading the Bible."

Farhan felt as if Akilah was perhaps becoming more favorable to his faith and responded with raised eyebrows, "I invite you to read it through, as I have done many times, Akilah. You might start with Prophet Mark's book as the first one written of the four accounts of Jesus' life. You could then read the other gospels—Matthew, Luke, and John.

"Now, what are my remaining two reasons for the preservation of the Bible?... Oh, yeah. I remember now. My fourth evidence is that the commands of the New Testament are much harder to follow than those of the Old Testament. Who besides God would possibly extend his condemnation of adultery to lust in Jesus' teaching? He also made anger, the desire to attack others, as bad as murder. In the light of Jesus' teaching about self-centered anger, where do you think terrorists belonging to any religion stand before God?"

"I see your point, Farhan."

"On top of those amazing teachings, Jesus called his followers to love their enemies, unlike all of the teachers of that day. The early church would've taken that command out of the Bible, as most humans would, as being too hard to follow."

"Farhan, your ideas are mind-boggling and very thought-provoking."

"Akilah, in addition to those amazing statements in Jesus' Sermon on the Mount in Matthew's account, he called us to be perfect as God is perfect, not just good enough.

"Furthermore, Prophet Paul called us to 'rejoice in the Lord always' and to have constant joy, prayer, and thanks—all very difficult verses that the church certainly would have changed to make them easier to follow."

Farhan's reasons left Akilah feeling tired as she said, "I'll have to think about your evidence, Farhan."

"My fifth support for the New Testament's preservation is that over 25,000 manuscripts of that document exist at four different sites: Alexandria in Egypt, a Mount Sinai monastery, the Vatican in Rome, and Syria.

"Suppose that two hundred years after Christ, a bishop in Syria decided to change John's gospel in many verses to say that God is three persons in one God, the way the book says today. The trouble with that supposed attempt would have been that the other three manuscript traditions, which we know go back to the third and fourth centuries A.D., would disagree with such changes.

"The reason is that the church was not one unified group then, the way the Roman Catholic Church under one Pope was later. Furthermore, two of the complete New Testament manuscripts date back to a century before the church unified under a pope and only two or three centuries after Jesus lived in Palestine.

"Yet, all of the four manuscript traditions agree with each other on the Bible's history and teachings and disagree only on minor matters. In addition, the copiers of the Bible considered it sacred literature that no one should change, just the way Muslims believe about the Qur'an.

"Moreover, all Christian scholars of various schools of thought and Bible interpretations agree that the New Testament's manuscripts are intact and are just like the original writings. The so-called 'corruptions' that some Muslim scholars talk about are minor differences that in no way change the teachings and history of the Bible, which is by far the best-perserved ancient document. We welcome more manuscripts like the Dead Sea scrolls so that we can compare them. The more, the merrier."

From chapter ten—Farhan and Akilah's discussion about whether we can become God's children:

[Farhan:] "I believe that even though humans lost their perfection when Adam and Eve ate the forbidden fruit in Genesis chapter three, they still retained some of God's likeness in positive human qualities. Therefore, because humans are like God, he can make Jesus his unique Son and us as adopted sons and daughters through our personal trust in him."

Akilah frowned as she thought, *Christian ideas from the Bible are beyond belief and far from reason! However, Farhan shares them in such an agreeable way.* She said, "Farhan, because that teaching seems so unbelievable, I can't accept your reasoning."

"Akilah, you don't have to. He thought, *I'm thankful that God enabled me to research all of these questions when I talked with other Muslims while at the University of Purdue.*

He continued with his handsome grin, "Well, it seems to me that Jesus was divine even while living on earth. The reason is that he claimed to be God and then confirmed that claim by rising from death to life. In Prophet John's book about Jesus, he quoted Jesus as making some seemingly-outlandish claims that all began with the words 'I am.'

"For example, in the sixth chapter, he quoted Jesus as declaring, 'I am the bread of life,' soon after he fed more than 5,000 people with a few loaves and fish. Only God ultimately feeds people physically and gives them the new life to believe in him. Therefore, since Jesus used the same words, 'I am,' that the God of the burning bush used to give his name to Prophet Moses on Mount Sinai in Exodus chapters three and four, Jesus' words were his outright claim to be that same God.

"Also, in John chapter six, Jesus said that he was the divine-human Successor to Moses, since he claimed to be the divine Manna that was somewhat similar to the heavenly bread with which God fed Israel during their desert wanderings, as the Qur'an also says. Then, he said, 'I am the bread of life,' a claim that could only come from the God who is the Source of our food.

"In addition, Jesus said in John chapter ten, 'I am the good shepherd.' Prophet David had written in Psalm 23, 'The LORD [Yahweh, meaning "I am" or the eternal, faithful God] is my Shepherd.' Jesus also claimed, "I am the gate to the sheep's pen, implying that he was the genuine, divine way to God's loving care as the same good Shepherd of David's psalm.

"Finally, when the miracle of Mary's virgin birth without a man took place, the Bible says that the Holy Spirit, the third Person of God, hovered over Mary the way he did over creation at the beginning. He united the second divine Person with Mary's egg to produce Jesus, who was fully God and fully human. Of course, God could do that amazing action. After all, he's the God who made the universe and also created us to be like him in certain ways."

Akilah's eyes opened wide in astonishment, "That teaching seems like fanciful fiction to me."

"Well, Akilah, you can believe or disbelieve what you wish, but I know that God used those amazing truths and that awesome Jesus to transform my life and to keep changing me, even though I'm far from perfect."

Akilah frowned as her shoulders slumped, "I don't believe that human nature ever really changes. We can only try hard to live up to the will of Allah (all praise to him) and to hope for his favorable judgment at the last day."

From chapter fourteen—Farhan and Akilah's discussion of children's innocence or guilt:

"Also [in addition to Farhan's summary of David's teaching in Psalm 51 about his being born guilty before God], Jesus passed through Jericho on his way to his death at Jerusalem. Chief tax collector Zacchaeus, a short man who was hated by the crowds who gathered to see Jesus and who apparently wouldn't let him see Jesus, climbed into a sycamore-fig tree to get a good look at him. The Lord Jesus walked up to the tree, called Zacchaeus down, and invited himself to his home for dinner.

"After the meal, Zacchaeus said that he would give half of all his wealth to the poor. Jesus replied that salvation from sin had come to that house and that his mission was to seek and save the lost.

"Akilah, I believe that we're all born lost enemies of the true God of the Bible like Zacchaeus, as Prophet Paul says in the second chapter of his letter to the Ephesian church. All other belief systems that I know about think that we can reach up to God. Instead, biblical faith says that he reaches down to us through Jesus because we're all born lost, blind, deaf, and dead to God and far from being capable to measure up to his perfect standards.

Akilah said, "You have such interesting ideas, Farhan, but I still think children are born innocent. How could they know right and wrong?"

"I think that we are born with the poisonous venom of evil that will eventually kill us unless God rescues us through Jesus' antidote to make our souls live forever. Akilah, is that belief in children's innocence the reason that some Muslims wait to circumcise them until boys are old enough to discern right from wrong, as we saw in the video at Abasi Huda's house?"

"Farhan, my research has shown me that the practice of circumcision began with Abraham. The Qur'an says that

God called Abraham to circumcise himself and his thirteen-year-old son, Ishmael."

"The Old Testament also clearly shows in Genesis seventeen that God commanded Abraham to circumcise himself at the age of ninety-nine and Ishmael at the same time when he was thirteen.

"However, the Christian approach to circumcision is that Prophet Paul equated the meaning of circumcision with baptism in his letter to the Colossae Christians, both pointing to our need for God's cleansing from our imperfections through Jesus' death. As a result, in the New Testament, Christians no longer need to follow the outward form of the Old Testament laws, which point to the need for circumcision.

"Christian churches, instead, baptize infants along with their parents' profession of their beliefs or youths who profess their faith in Jesus. In either case, we see baptism as God's initiation into his family. Our conversations have shown that Muslims put a great emphasis on our need to be cleansed. Don't Muslims also believe that our imperfections started with Adam and Eve? In addition, doesn't that belief point to the seriousness of our rebellion against God?"

Akilah wrinkled her nose, "We don't take Adam and Eve's choice to eat the forbidden fruit as seriously as the Bible does."

"It seems to me that people certainly wouldn't have changed the Bible to make Adam and Eve's sin and our resulting sins much more serious than we humans generally think they are."

"Well, we believe that Allah (praise to him) made humans capable of making mistakes."

"How can you believe that his creation of humans was imperfect? How could your perfect God make mistake-prone people?"

"Well, in the Bible, didn't Adam and Eve make a bad choice?"

"Yes, but the first two chapters of Genesis show that God made everything and everyone 'very good.' It's a mystery how Satan's and our first parents' rebellions could have entered God's perfect creation.'"

"Christians often say that events and teachings that they can't understand are mysteries."

"Well, many mysteries exist—for example, how perfect-angel Satan could have rebelled, how our two perfect ancestors could rebel against God, how God can be one God in three Persons, how Jesus could be both all-God and all-man, and many other teachings and events in the Bible that we can't figure out completely.

"I believe that people's human pride makes them want to figure God and humans out. Instead, I believe that our intellects can't come at all close to God's reasoning and logic. Our reasoning powers are tiny, dim reflections of his amazing mind.

"Instead, followers of Jesus have to learn humility in accepting what God said in Isaiah 54 that his ways and thoughts are far above ours. Someday we'll know a lot more when Jesus returns. However, until that time, our puny minds can't grasp very much about God because we aren't the Creator. Rather, we're his creations."

"Farhan, on that distinction between the Creator and his creation, we both agree."

* * *

From chapter eighteen—Farhan and Akilah's comparisons and contrasts about their beliefs:

"I see. I've also seen in our conversations that your Muslim beliefs and my Christian ones have a number of ideas in common, though we differ on others."

Akilah narrowed her eyebrows, "Yes, we both believe in one God, though Christians believe that he's also three Persons."

Farhan responded, "I find commendable Muhammad's attempts to overcome the many false gods of the Arabian tribes and to replace them with one God."

"We share belief in evil spirits. We call them jinn, you call them demons. However, jinn can be different shades of good and evil, whereas your evil angels are all bad."

"Also, we both believe that Satan leads the rebellious spirits against God."

"We Muslims honor the prophets Adam, Noah, Job, Abraham, Jacob, Joseph, Moses, David, and Jesus, as you Christians do. However, we also honor Ishmael as a prophet and Muhammad as the final prophet in contrast to you Christians, who honor the others, especially Jesus as the divine Prophet."

"We Christians and you Muslims believe that God is the just Judge of his creation and that Jesus will return to us to judge all people at the Final Judgment. However, the basis for his judgment is different, for Muslims, your good works; for Christians, Jesus' life and death for our not-guilty verdict and reward, all by God's grace or free acceptance of believers."

"That's true. Don't we both also believe that Allah (praise to him) or God has his plan for everything and everyone?"

Farhan said, "Yes, the Bible is clear that God rules his universe and will someday create a new one out of the old, corrupted creation when Jesus returns."

"We both agree that prayer is so important that we pray five times a day."

"Yes, God calls us Christians in the Bible to pray all day long. However, we differ with you about the nature of the God to whom we pray and the Jesus through whom we pray."

"In addition, we Muslims and you Christians believe in generous giving to help people who are in need."

Farhan said, "Yes, the Bible calls us to give willingly at least ten percent of our incomes to spiritual causes, especially our churches. The way I understand it, Muslims are required to give a smaller percentage, right?"

"You're right about our giving."

"However, the correct Christian motive for our giving is our loving thankfulness for God's free gift of Jesus to rescue us in his love."

Akilah said, "I see one other idea that Christians and Muslims have in common. We both believe that Allah (praise to him) or God revealed his will and works in holy writings—Christians, through the writers of the Bible; Muslims, through the angel Gabriel by way of Muhammad's dictation of the Qur'an. The main belief is that he shows himself in his creation and his inspired writings."

Farhan continued, "Some of the Muslims believe that boys must be circumcised as part the initiation into the community of faith, because of Ishmael's circumcision, whereas Jesus instituted baptism for that purpose by pointing to his death that cleanses us from our guiltiness in the divine Judge's sight."

Farhan concluded their exchanges with his summary, "My reference to the just Judge points to our mutual desire to seek justice for the victims of abundant evil and lack of regard for the value of the human life that the Creator made."

"Those similarities and differences are true, and we both share that motivation."

* * *

From chapter twenty-five—the rest of Farhan and Akilah's discussion about terrorism and God's justice and grace:

"Akilah, Jesus demonstrated that his kingdom did not come with political or military force by riding a donkey into Jerusalem instead of a war stallion. He showed with that action that he was also the divine Creator in control of his creation, since his trip was on an unbroken colt of a donkey. As a result, he showed that God comes into people's lives to transform them from the inside out, not with external force like the mistaken Crusades and Inquisition, either by established institutions in the middle ages or by Muslim terrorists' similar attempts to conquer people by force.

"Furthermore, in Luke's gospel, Jesus told his followers to take two swords with them to the garden where he knew that the religious authorities were going to arrest him. When Peter cut off the ear of the high priest's servant Malchus with one of those swords, Jesus said, 'Enough of this. Those who live by the sword will die by the sword.' When he then healed Malchus' ear, he thus showed his followers that his rule comes by peaceful means.

"Then, during Jesus' trial, when the Roman governor, Pontius Pilate, asked him about his kingdom, he said that his kingdom was not of this world. Otherwise, his followers would have fought the Romans and religious leaders. You see, the war of Jesus' followers is against Satan and his followers, not people. Our weapons are spiritual, not physical, for example, the truths of the Bible and prayer."

Akilah said, "You've given me a lot of ideas to chew on, Farhan."

He said with a half-grin, "I hope you don't spit them out....

"However, I want to respond to another comment that you just made about the way in which your Allah will become merciful to Muslims. I hope you can understand that Christian beliefs based squarely on the Bible as God's Word are fundamentally different from all other belief systems, including Islam. We believe in a God of grace."

It was Akilah's turn to open her eyes and mouth wide, "What do you mean, Farhan?"

A broad smile came to Farhan's rugged, handsome face as he said, "Well, the Bible—in Ephesians chapter 2, Romans chapters 1 to 3, and Galatians—says that when we are born, we are dead to God and worthy of his guilty verdict and punishment in hell, a place in which Muslims believe too. Right?"

Akilah nodded as Farhan continued, "However, God sent Jesus to live a perfect life as the God-man, to take our guilty verdict and punishment as believers' Substitute and

Representative in his death, and to rise from the dead to give us new life. He, thus, showed believers his grace."

"Farhan, I've heard that word, but no one has ever explained it to me."

"God's great grace is his free acceptance of true believers because of what Jesus did for us in his life, death, and resurrection. Those amazing actions showed us God's Riches At Christ's Expense, his GRACE. Because of Jesus' perfect actions, God loves true followers of Jesus unconditionally without their deserving or earning any of his love. The reason is that God requires us to be perfect our whole lives, but no one can. After all, nobody's perfect.

"As a result, God as our Judge transferred Jesus' perfection in his life, suffering, and death to us by declaring us 'not guilty' and right with him. You can now see why believers in Jesus are joyful, because God through Jesus set us free from our stillborn, lost lives. All other belief systems require people to try to measure up to their God's will. Instead, Jesus has already measured up for us who trust in him because we could never be perfect with our own strength."

Akilah frowned as she thought that she found a possible flaw in Farhan's ideas, "However, doesn't that belief allow you to trust in Jesus and then live your life any way you want to, because you have received grace?"

Farhan's grin widened, "No. God's grace is his unlimited power that Jesus' earthly life, death, and resurrection released to transform believers to want to follow his ways rather than our selfish wills. He continues to change us throughout our whole lives. Prophet Paul says in his letters that Christians' lives, filled with God's strength rather than our own, involve our taking off of the old clothes of dirty imperfections with which we were conceived and born and putting on the new clothes of qualities like Jesus' perfections.

"If people who say that they're Christians have no desire to seek God's improvement in their lives, they have fooled themselves into thinking that they are followers of

Jesus, when they're not. After all, followers follow," Farhan said with a smirk.

"I don't know what to say, Farhan. That idea of grace is foreign to any thinking that I have ever heard or studied."

Farhan put his hands together and closed his eyes as if he were praying. "That concept is one of the many ideas in the Bible that could not come from human, performance-oriented minds. Therefore, God must have given it and the rest of the Bible to those who wrote it."

* * *

From chapter twenty-nine—Farhan and Akilah's discussion about God's love:

Akilah's consciousness moved to a scene with an undefined figure on a throne and the whole human race assembled in front of that figure. He spoke, "All of you who did more good deeds than bad ones, come with me to Paradise....However, I can find no one in that group. Therefore, you will all have to go to eternal punishment in hell." She shrank from that imagined scene.

* * *

Farhan sighed, "About sixty to seventy percent of humans and even some Christians think the same way you do, Aliyah. The idea that it's up to us to earn Paradise isn't just in Islam, but it appears in all of the belief systems except that of Jesus' followers, who sometimes also have that human idea because they are also part of the performance-oriented world.

"For example, Hindus and Buddhists believe in good and bad karma done by their followers that determines reward or punishment—promotion or demotion—after death. Such a view is very insecure, since a person never knows for sure in this life what his destination will be after death."

Akilah leaned forward with a wrinkled forehead, "Then, explain to me the Christian concept of love some more."

"Consider my two trials and the judges' guilty verdicts and punishments. What if my defense attorney had volunteered to take my punishments in my place without charging me any fees? As a result, the judges would have had to declare me 'not guilty' and my lawyer. They would then serve my sentences in my place."

"Farhan, that kind of substitution would never happen."

A huge smile crept across Farhan's face as he said, "I believe on the firm basis of the Bible that it did when Jesus, the divine-human Messiah, freely came from heaven on a mission to live a perfect life and die as believers' Substitute Defense Attorney on the cross. Thus, he took on himself believers' guilty verdict and their punishment in separation from God like that of hell without our paying for it at all. The result is Jesus' justification of his followers. That is, he considers true believers 'not guilty' and right with God. Amazingly, he then treats me as justified, 'just as if I'd' never broken any of his laws."

"I've never heard anything like your ideas of grace, love, and justification, Farhan."

"They aren't my ideas. They're in the Bible, Akilah. For example, Jesus told a parable to illustrate this idea of God's justification as our Judge. Two men went, perhaps on camels, to the temple, the place of worship, to pray. One was a Pharisee, a strict follower of God's Old Testament laws and many regulations that the straight-laced religious leaders had developed to protect their power over the people. In his prayer, he bragged about all of his good actions compared to the other man—a corrupt, greedy tax collector, whose profession was notorious for overcharging people for taxes. The latter man sorrowfully prayed, 'God, be merciful to me, a sinner.'

"Here's the amazing part. Jesus then said that the upright Pharisee went home unjustified or unforgiven, while God declared the other man, the notorious 'sinner,' right with him or justified. God's gift of faith in Jesus brings his justification now through Jesus' victory. The results are our confession of our many imperfections and desire to live a changed life. Another result in our life with him will be God's creation of a new universe when Jesus returns.

"The real stunner is that only God can give Jesus' followers the ability to believe in him and turn our lives around. Thus, our rescue from our guilty condition is totally to God's credit, not at all ours."

Akilah said with wide-open eyes, "That teaching is beyond human thought, Farhan."

"That's right. It could only have come from God, who inspired the Bible. Another illustration in Prophet John's gospel, chapter 9, is an actual event in the Jerusalem temple on the Jewish Sabbath day (Saturday). His disciples asked him about a beggar who was born blind, 'Who sinned, this man or his parents?' Jesus said, 'None of them, but his affliction is for God's honor.'

"He then smeared mud on the blind beggar's eyes and had him wash his eyes in the Pool of Siloam. Jesus, thus, created the man's ability to see for the first time, as only God can!

"When the man came home, his neighbors took him to the religious leaders because Jesus had broken their petty rules by healing on the Sabbath the man who was born blind. When the leaders asked his parents about the beggar, they said that he was their son and that he had been blind since birth. However, they said that the authorities should ask the formerly blind man how he could now see. They were scared of the religious leaders.

"When they questioned the man about how he was healed, he declared that his healer had to be a true prophet, a belief not shared by his hearers. He then said, 'All I know is that once I was blind, but now I see.' Their response was to kick him out of the place of worship permanently.

"When the Pharisees questioned Jesus about his disregard for their man-made traditions, he accused them of spiritual blindness.

"John includes this description of Jesus' miracle in his account because we are all blind to Jesus until he opens our spiritual eyes to believe in him and turn our lives around to follow him. Jesus' punchline was, 'I am the light of the world,' thus saying that he was and is the divine 'I AM' who revealed himself to Moses in the burning bush."

Akilah was silent for a few seconds but then said, "The Bible has many unbelievable ideas and events. How can you believe it, Farhan?"

"Only because God has given me and other Christians the ability to believe that the Bible is God's Word, just as Jesus made the man who was born blind able to see. Therefore, instead of being God's enemies, we all have peace with him and security in Jesus' arms."

* * *

From chapter thirty-five—Farhan and Akilah's discussion about Mark's book:

"However, how can you possibly believe that you and other Christians are God's children, when you are imperfect and God is perfect?"

Farhan grinned his biggest smile and said, "I believe that teaching because Prophets Jesus, John, Peter, and Paul all said that every genuine follower of Jesus is a child of God. How is that change from enemy to friend possible? I don't know, but Jesus was and is God's unique Son, born of Mary without a male involved.

"Also, God is the all-powerful Creator, who can do anything, a belief that you also have about Allah. We believers are all adopted sons and daughters—spiritual siblings of our Brother Jesus—thus, we're all children of our Father in heaven. Couldn't Allah have made Muslims his children, if he wanted to?"

"Well, I guess so, theoretically. However, in Islam, we believe that we can never really become Allah's children; he is too different from us. We, instead, are his servants."

Farhan replied, "By contrast, Jesus said to his followers on the Thursday before his Good Friday death that they are no longer his servants but his friends, a new relationship that he brings to us with his death and resurrection. God's covenant began with Abraham, whom the Bible also described as God's friend. How do you describe your relationship with Allah?"

"Our relationship is more one of respect than love, Farhan."

"Well, I love Jesus because he first loved me enough to rescue me with his death and resurrection. However, we also love and respect our great Creator-God. It's a little bit like sports teams' relationship with good coaches. In that situation, players say that they both like and respect their coach or manager."

Akilah then conceded, "I must say, though, that Jesus' healing of a bleeding woman, raising of a dead girl, feeding of a large crowd with a few loaves and fish, and walking on the Galilee water—all in Mark chapters five and six—were very impressive. However, God could have done those miracles through a thoroughly-human Jesus as his prophet. In fact, the Qur'an implies that Jesus raised dead people."

"Akilah, Mark described all of Jesus' miracles as divine signs leading up to his death and resurrection from the dead to show that he was and is God. It's a claim to which Jesus testifies more in the other gospels that you will get to, especially in John's book.

"Also, the disciples' clear unbelief in response to Jesus' demonstration of his divine power is another description that the early church certainly would have removed—thus whitewashing the original pillars of the church—if they had changed the manuscripts. In addition, if Jesus' disciples and the early church had made up the account of Jesus' death and resurrection, they wouldn't have described themselves as cowards deserting him. Also, they wouldn't have had the women be the first ones to see him on Easter morning, since women weren't considered credible witnesses in first century culture, especially in court."

* * *

From chapter thirty-six—discussion about the topic of uncleanness in Mark chapter seven:

[Farhan:] "However, don't Muslims, on the basis of the Qur'an, believe that it continued through his son Ishmael to the Arabs? At any rate, we believe that God's covenant continues with all who believe in the true God of the Bible.

"That discussion aside, under God's inspiration, Mark interprets Jesus' rejection of the Pharisees' ceremonies as his declaration that all foods are clean. As a result, Jesus' coming did away with all of the Old Testament's outward regulations like the unclean foods, but he also emphasized the unclean or immoral thoughts and actions that come from our unclean hearts."

Farhan read from his New Testament, "For example, in Mark 7:21-23, Jesus listed 'evil thoughts, sexual immorality, theft, murder, adultery, greed, malice, deceit, lewdness, envy, slander, arrogance, and folly.' He then commented, 'All of these evils come from inside and make a person unclean.'"

"Farhan, as you know, most Muslims avoid pork as unclean. However, Alevis basically agree with Jesus that our most important task is to overcome those same imperfections that start in the center of our being, the heart.

"Furthermore, Alevis believe a few of them can attain the status of the 'Perfect Human' by great effort."

"Really! I never knew that some were perfectionists. We believe that only one 'Perfect Human,' Jesus Christ, had that status by resisting all temptations to commit all of those evils that are in all other humans' hearts. He could resist those influences because he was also completely God. He struggled against those impulses because he was human. As a result, everyone who believes in and follows him receives Jesus' perfect status in God's eyes as our Judge."

"Fascinating! Are you perfect, Farhan?"

"Yes and no. As my Judge, God gives me his 'not guilty' verdict because of Jesus' perfect life and death as my Substitute, who then took my rightful 'guilty' verdict on himself when he died for me.

"On the other hand, in my daily life, as my Father, he gives me his power through Jesus by the Holy Spirit within me to make progress in overcoming the evils in my heart and replacing them with his perfect qualities like patience instead of impatience and submission to replace my frustration. I believe that we never get there in this lifetime, because we still have these fallen bodies and our sinful natures. However, a minority of Christians do agree with Alevis that a few believers can become perfect."

"I can't believe how many parallels the two belief systems have."

"Yes, but the natures of the Gods for whom we gain spiritual progress and the ways we are able to gain that improvement are very different. Those differences are very great."

"True. Muslims and Christians need to understand each other more."

* * *

From chapter thirty-nine—further discussion on Good Friday about Jesus' death and resurrection:

Grabbing his New Testament, Farhan found the place in John's gospel and read from John 19, "When he had received the drink, Jesus said on the cross, 'It is finished.' With that, he bowed his head and gave up his spirit....Instead [of breaking Jesus' legs to suffocate him], one of the soldiers pierced Jesus' side with a spear, bringing a sudden flow of blood and water. The man who saw it has given testimony and his testimony is true. He knows that he tells the truth, and he testifies so that you also may believe.'

"Now, John and the other followers of Jesus were eyewitnesses of his death, either up close or from a distance. Furthermore, on the following Sunday, they said that they also talked and ate with Jesus, who was alive from the dead.

"God used those events to revolutionize Jesus' followers' lives to replace their discouragement at his death with the courage to spread that good news against the opposition and persecution of the Jews, Greeks, and Romans. All of them died holding to their testimony that Jesus actually died and rose again. You can't get better historical observers than people who are all willing to go through suffering and death while still holding on to their testimonies as eyewitnesses.

"I also believe in those events because God has given me the power of Jesus' death and resurrection to make progress overcoming my many imperfections and replacing them with God's good qualities, though I still have a long way to go."

Akilah said, "However, how could Jesus die if he was God?"

"He could die because he was fully human as well as fully divine. He received that human nature through the virgin Mary, when the third Person of God, the Holy Spirit, joined the second Person from heaven to Mary's human nature to create a perfect, divine-human baby, who grew up as a perfect human to die purposely with his focus on his past and future followers."

* * *

From chapter forty—further discussion about ceremonial and spiritual uncleanness:

Akilah said, "As I said last time, it's the same with many Muslims' ceremonial washings before meals. Alevis don't do them but do pray for Allah's (praise to him) inner cleansing from our shortcomings. However, I began them when I became a Sunni as a symbol of my inner life."

"That's an interesting practice."

"Don't you Christians believe that you are unclean too?"

"Yes, we also pray for God's cleansing of our many imperfections through Jesus' death. An interesting passage that you'll come across in Prophet John's book is chapter four. Jesus meets an unclean Samaritan with an immoral lifestyle. She had been divorced five times and at that time lived with another man without getting married—all actions that the Bible forbids. Besides, the Jews never associated with half-breed, 'unclean' Samaritans.

"At any rate, Jesus rested from his journey at Jacob's Well in Samaria north of Jerusalem. While his followers went into town to get food, the Samaritan woman came to the well to get water. In an unheard-of move, Jewish Jesus asked her for some water from the well and then offered her living water so that she would no longer thirst spiritually.

"To make an amazing, long story short, he made clear that he was the Messiah that the Jews and Samaritans were both waiting for. She then spread the word in her hometown that she had met the Messiah, the Coming One.

"The point is that Jesus offers to us the Father, himself, and the Holy Spirit as the one God who can cleanse our lives and slake our thirst for him."

"That story is very thought-provoking, Farhan."

After paying the bills, they then exited the restaurant to sit on a park bench in the city square with a view of little children swinging on the swings and sliding on the slide.

Akilah said, "Farhan, I've been reading Luke's book. Jesus returned to his hometown, Nazareth, but they rejected him."

"Yeah, they also tried to throw him off a cliff, but he escaped their grasp."

"Why would people who knew him best reject his being a healing prophet and at the same time try to kill him?"

"They knew him as he grew up. He could now preach God's Word and do miracles. They thought that they understood him, but he had become a preacher instead of a carpenter like his father, Joseph, who had probably died. (The reason people have thought that Joseph died before Jesus started his ministry was that of his parents the Bible only mentions Mary, not Joseph, from that point on.) At any rate, it's my guess that the people of Nazareth may have thought that he should stay home to carry on the family business as the oldest son to support his mother, Mary, rather than traveling around teaching people."

"It also says that he couldn't do many miracles there because of their unbelief. If he was God, why wouldn't he heal many more at Nazareth to impress them with his divine abilities?"

"He did his healings mostly when people had faith or trust in him, not to make a show but instead to point people to God. You can see that Jesus was not a showman, since he told many healed people to keep their healings quiet. The reason is that the crowds wouldn't attempt to make him the country's ruler before the Father's time for his death. As you probably noticed, Jesus as the hidden Messiah is also a theme in Mark.

"In addition, instead of showing off his special healing abilities, he wanted to train his followers for three years until it was God's time for him to die to cleanse believers from their inborn imperfections. Then, after his permanent resurrection, he called all believers to spread the good news about him.

"A little while ago, I read through Prophet Moses' third book, Leviticus, and was impressed with the need for the shedding of blood for Israel's cleansing from their uncleanness in God's sight, which avoiding unclean foods also pictures.

"The New Testament also says that a perfect person must shed his blood and die to clean our lives. It says that Jesus' death on the cruel, criminal's cross as the perfect God-man was his substitution for us who deserve eternal death separated from God."

"Farhan, I can't accept the Bible's teachings, but they are fascinating."

Switching emotional gears, Akilah with a joyful gleam in her eyes said, "On another note, Shirley called me this morning with the wonderful news that she is pregnant. What great news!"

Farhan gave her his biggest smile, "Yeah, we wanted to start a family. Now, God has blessed our desires. Maybe, we'll be here swinging our first child on those swings later. I guess that we won't have to wait twenty-five years, the way Abraham and Sarah did in the Bible for their son Isaac....I also guess that we'd better get back to the courtroom for the trial.

* * *

Divided Together 2084 questions for discussion groups (a free leader's guide at **dividedtogether7@gmail.com**):

Chapter One:

1. How do you feel about the kidnapper and his "prize"? Explain.

2. What more do you learn about Farhan in this chapter? Explain.

3. List what you know about Akilah so far from this chapter? How do you feel about her? Explain.

4. What do you suspect Farhan and Akilah's relationship will become? Why?

Chapter Two:

1. Where were Farhan and Akilah originally from? How does that fact help explain their willingness to learn about each other's religion? Explain.

2. How have your feelings changed because of this chapter? Explain.

3. What present-day United States area does the Great Peninsula nation occupy? From what present-day city's name has the author changed the capital city? Why do you suppose the author chose that area? Explain.

4. Why do you suppose a camel-hauling truck would be in New Tehran and in that area of abundant water? Explain.

Chapter Three:

1. Exactly what is the difference of opinion between Farhan and Akilah about their differing beliefs? Explain.

2. What is your response to Farhan's following statements? "As far as I'm concerned, you can believe anything you want to. I will never try to change your or anyone else's opinions." What is your opinion about his approach to the

delicate subject of differing belief systems? What lesson can Christians and Muslims learn from him? Explain.

3. What are your first impressions of the life-protection task force? Why?

4. What is your specific reaction to First-Detective Srour? Explain. How tall is his two-meter height?

Chapter Four:

1. How does Akilah's Islamic-studies lecture help you understand the geography of the author's fictional countries? How is her revisionist, fictional history different from real European and American history? Explain.

2. What surprises you about Akilah and her environment in this chapter? Why?

3. Why do you suppose the Great Peninsula Nation University has Saturday, Monday, and Wednesday classes instead of a Monday-Wednesday-Friday schedule? Explain.

4. What does the last scene of Farhan and Akilah's questioning of a GPNU student show about their abilities as criminologist consultants? Why?

Chapter Five:

1. How do you feel about the alternating scenes of the futile investigation and the perpetrator's abduction, rape, and murder of another victim? Explain.

2. What else did you discover about the LPTF? Explain.

3. What else did you find out about Farhan and Akilah? Explain.

4. What else did you discover about the serial killer? Explain.

Chapter Six:

1. What surprised you about the Muslim Alevi faith? How can they still claim to be Muslims? Explain.

2. List the differences between Alevis and other Muslims.

3. What differences are there between the GPN and DSA technologies, according to Farhan? Why do you suppose that country would lag behind the USA? Explain.

4. According to Farhan, what is the basic difference between the Muslim and Christian faiths? How do you feel about that important contrast? In what ways is the Christian faith unique among all religions? How does that uniqueness make you feel? Explain.

5. What do many Muslims say about the Old and New Testament Scriptures, according to Akilah? (Clue: Her claim is nonfiction, as are all of Farhan and Akilah's discussions.) Explain.

<u>Chapter Seven:</u>

1. What surprised you about the camel-alligator confrontation? Explain.

2. What was your response to Akilah's explanation of the presence of camels in the GPN? Why did you react that way?

3. Why do you suppose Christians meet to worship on Fridays instead of Sundays in the GPN? Explain your reaction to that surprising schedule.

4. The camel-wrestling event is like similar ones in Turkey. What is your reaction to that kind of event? Explain.

5. What political statement did the camels make in their fight? How do you respond? Why?

6. What surprised you about the serial-killer's abduction scene? Explain.

<u>Chapter Eight:</u>

1. What did you think about Farhan's explanation of his Muslim name? His conversion to the Christian faith? Explain.

2. Which ones of Farhan's reasons for the Bible's preservation are the strongest ones? The weakest ones? Overall, how convincing were they? Why?

3. How has God affected your faith through Farhan's conversion and reasons for the Scriptures' reliability? Explain.

4. How do you feel about the author's combination of Farhan's assessment of the serial-killer and his actual abuse of his victim? Explain.

5. What was surprising about the final dungeon scene? Why?

<u>Chapter Nine</u>:

1. What is your reaction to Harley's Place's full name and its setting? Explain. (It's an actual place, though not in "Florida." It has a similar name, as you can probably guess.)

2. Which characteristics of serial-killers surprised you the most? The least? Why?

3. What effect does the author's putting the serial killer lecture alongside the final scene in the chapter have on you, the reader? Explain your reaction.

4. How has this chapter affected your faith? Why?

<u>Chapter Ten:</u>

1. How is this case similar to the serial killer case? Explain.

2. What are your responses to the LPTF's discussion about this latest life-protection case? Why?

3. How do you feel about the suggestions that the DSA president could ride a camel, a motorcycle, and a bicycle during his visit? Why do you feel that way? Why do you think the author uses humor in his writing? What purpose do you think it serves in this novel? Explain.

4. During Farhan's trial, how just were the trial and final verdict? Why?

5. What did you think about the judge's "merciful" sentence for Farhan's "crime"? Explain.

6. What were your reactions to the three rescues in this chapter? Explain.

Chapter Eleven:

1. What is your response to Farhan's reasons for believing in Jesus as God's unique Son? What do you think about Christians as God's adopted children? Explain.

2. People have said that we should never discuss religion. What do you think about Farhan and Akilah's discussion without anger? How is their kind of interaction possible? How can we follow a similar pattern with fellow believers and with unbelievers? Explain.

3. How do the informal social gatherings of LPTF help you understand the members better? Why do you think the author included them? What details in those scenes stand out for you? Why?

4. What do you think is the significance of the team's departure into "cloudy, deep darkness"? Explain.

Chapter Twelve:

1. Why do you think the author introduced Shirley Jones to his book's plot? What two of Akilah's earlier references to her have prepared us for her appearance? Explain.

2. What interests do Akilah and Shirley have in common?

3. How do you feel about this chapter in comparison with the previous chapters of the book? Why?

Chapter Thirteen:

1. What did this chapter reveal about the LPTF members? About politics? In what ways?

2. What part of this chapter stood out for you as important? Why?

3. How did the author depict First Detective Srour? Explain.

Chapter Fourteen:

1. How do you feel about Farhan and Shirley's new relationship? How disappointed are you that Farhan and

Akilah remained good friends instead of dating? Why do you suppose their relationship remained that way? Explain.

2. What does this chapter show about possible consequences of Christians' living in a Muslim country? In what ways?

3. What do you think about Farhan's two times when he forgave in Jesus' name two unjust judges in spite of their guilty verdicts? Explain.

4. What do you think this chapter's events did for Shirley and Farhan's relationship? Why?

5. What events of this chapter did you enjoy most of all? Least of all? Explain.

<u>Chapter Fifteen:</u>

1. How do you feel about Akilah and Farhan's discussion concerning the innocence or guilt of babies? What do you believe about that issue? Explain your reasoning. What does the Bible say?

2. What do you think about Farhan's statement that Christians have to accept many biblical mysteries? How far can our reasoning go without being unbiblical? Explain.

3. How do this chapter's events affect Farhan and Shirley's relationship? Why?

4. What difference does it make how seriously you view Adam and Eve's rebellion against God? Why?

<u>Chapter Sixteen:</u>

1. How do you feel about the arguments for tough, restrictive laws against abortion? About the adoption option? Have a group discussion about the issue.

2. What does the Bible say about life and death issues in relation to God the Creator, for example, 1 Samuel 2:1-10 (especially verse six), and Psalm 139 (especially verses 13-16)? In the light of the Bible's teachings, how do you respond? Why?

3. What theme or focus for the LPTF's cases is emerging? Explain.

4. Remember who strongly defended the right of unborn babies to be born for your reading later in the book. In your own words, why should we let those babies live instead of taking their lives? Explain.

5. How well do you think Shirley and Farhan will get the 999,998 things done for their wedding? Explain.

6. How positive are you that Farhan and Shirley will have a lifelong marriage? What clues in their relationship show their commitment to each other and to God? What factors make a marriage fail? Make it last a long time? Explain.

Chapter Seventeen:

1. What qualities do you enjoy most in the personality of Farhan? Shirley? Akilah? Give examples for each character.

2. What does the abortionist case have in common with Farhan and Akilah's discussion about young children? Give examples.

3. What does Farhan's reference to Mary's visit with Elizabeth in Luke chapter one have to do with the case and discussion in this chapter? Why?

4. How do you feel about Farhan, Akilah, and Shirley's senses of humor? Why?

Chapter Eighteen:

1. Why do you suppose the author paralleled pregnancy, baby, and wedding subplots in this chapter? Give examples to support your thoughts.

2. What biblical quality does Farhan's personality demonstrate in his personal relationships, for example, his suggestion that Janice might be the one to help catch the abortionists? How does he show that characteristic?

3. Discuss the following statement by Farhan in this chapter: "Abortion is an illegal felony because it's considered murder except when the birth clearly threatens the mother's life." What are the pros and cons of such a law? Why?

Chapter Nineteen:

1. How do you feel about Mel and Janice Whiting's decision to be the "bait" to catch the serial-baby-killers? Why?

2. Which similarities and differences between Muslim and Christians' beliefs do you find are the most important ones? List both on paper. Which ones do you think are most crucial? Why?

3. Which Christian actions and beliefs do you think should be goals for your Christian life? In other words, from which ones does your life fall short? How will you decide to seek God's power for progress? Why?

4. Why is it important to read God's Word daily? How can we read it in order to find God's grace to change our lives for the better? Explain.

5. Which set of beliefs (Christian or Muslim?) is more persuasive to you? Why?

Chapter Twenty:

1. How surprised were you that the group's plan didn't work? Why do you suppose it didn't?

2. What do you find out about Basim's detective abilities in this chapter? Explain.

3. How protective is Jan of her unborn child? Why don't more mothers have the same instinct when it comes to theirs? Explain.

4. How is Farhan an encourager? How can we be such an encourager rather than being negative people? How can we overcome anger at God and others in our struggles? Explain.

Chapter Twenty-One:

1. What is your response to the wedding? Why?

2. What is your response to the pastor's meditation on 1 Corinthians 13? Explain.

3. How did you respond to the honeymoon beach scene? Why?

4. How did you feel about the mall scene involving two incidents of women and a man? Why?

Chapter Twenty-Two:

1. What is your overall response to this chapter's events? Explain.

2. Why does Farhan search his vehicles? Explain.

3. What surprised you about the characters' actions? Why?

4. What clues point to Touma as the inside abortionists' helper? Explain.

5. How would you characterize the attempts to punish abortionists—witch-hunts or justice accomplished? Why?

Chapter Twenty-Three:

1. How convincing to you is Basim's summary of the clues pointing to Touma? Explain.

2. What is your reaction to the visit of Akilah's spiritual leader with Farhan? Why?

3. How different are Akilah and Farhan's interpretations of Jesus' phrase "Son of man"? Which method is the better one? Why?

4. What was Farhan's explanation of Jesus' use of the title "Son of man" for himself? How does it relate to Daniel chapter seven? How surprising to you is his interpretation? Explain.

Chapter Twenty-Four:

1. What is your impression of the Thanksgiving dinner and sports event? Explain.

2. How does this chapter help develop the book's characters further? Which ones, especially? Why?

3. If you like to watch sports, why do you? If you don't, why not?

4. How thankful are you for God's blessings in your life? How can we become more thankful?

Chapter Twenty-Five:

1. If you were one of the judges, would you bring back a 'guilty' or 'not guilty' verdict? What are your reasons?

2. Was the sentence too severe, or did it fit the crime? Give your reasons.

3. How did this trial fit into the larger, life-protection theme of the book? Explain.

Chapter Twenty-Six:

1. How surprising to you was the body-bag discovery? What earlier clues and details in this book pointed to the location of the body dump? How well did you guess its location before the author revealed it? Explain.

2. What is your reaction to Farhan's apology for Western nations' Crusades and Inquisition? Explain.

3. Why does Farhan bring up the Final Judgment? What does that future event have to do with their discussion? Why?

4. Summarize Farhan's explanation of God's grace. What is your response? Why is God's grace a strong argument for the Christian faith? Explain.

5. Why isn't God's grace an excuse to continue in our old, sinful pattern of living? Explain.

Chapter Twenty-Seven:

1. What is your reaction to the interviews with the two boys and the motel employee? Why?

2. How much do you think that the woman's report of the attacker and her fingering a possible perpetrator is the big break in the perplexing case? Why?

3. What is your general reaction to this chapter's plot? Explain.

Chapter Twenty-Eight:

1. How do you think the LPTF members felt about the ex-con's confirmed alibi? How would you feel? Explain.

2. How do you think the ex-con felt about the police's taking him into custody and about their questions? Explain.

3. Who do you think is the serial-rapist-women-killer at this point? What clues lead you to that suspicion? Explain.

<u>Chapter Twenty-Nine:</u>

1. What do you think made Farhan "solve the case," when he watched the symphony conductor direct the orchestra? Why?

2. At the Christmas celebration, Farhan says, "I guess there are good and bad things about every place a person lives." From your point of view, list the possible good aspects of Muslim cultures that the author shows in this novel so far.

3. What possible bad aspects of Muslim cultures does the author show? Why?

4. What political statements do the racing camels make? Explain.

5. How surprised were you to find out that the LPTF arrested First Detective Srour, who seemed driven to investigate the criminal, as the serial killer? What clue will finally convict him? Or will the judges declare him "not guilty"? Explain.

<u>Chapter Thirty</u>:

1. What "smoking gun" do you think CSI Ameer found that might be Srour's undoing? If you have no idea, guess what clue might lead to Srour's conviction.

2. Explain in your own words the difference between the Bible's view of who will go the heaven and hell and the Muslim belief. Why is this difference crucial to their discussion?

3. What is Farhan's definition of God's love? What illustrations does Farhan give for God's love? Explain your reaction to his explanation.

4. At this point, which approach (Christian or Muslim) to belief do you favor? List your reasons.

Chapter Thirty-One:

1. How much did Farhan and Shirley's kissing at the far end of the thrift store really violate the judge's order and the law? Why or why not?

2. What is your reaction to Farhan and Shirley's "breaking of their probation" behind blue jackets? Why? To Farhan's appearance before Shirley's fourth-grade class? Why?

3. How just were the three judges' decisions to bind over Srour for trial and to keep him in jail until then? Explain your reasons.

Chapter Thirty-Two:

1. What do you think about the team's answers to Maloof's questions about killing older people with very poor quality of life? Which LPTF members do you agree with most in that discussion? Give your reasons.

2. What do you think about assisting disabled senior citizens who have lost their mental abilities to die? Give reasons for your position.

3. What is your impression of the administrator of the Ali Nursing Facility? Explain.

4. How do you respond to the conversation between the quadriplegic Fadl and our criminologist-consultants? What is your impression of Fadl? Explain.

5. Why do you suppose the author introduced this subplot while we await Srour's trial? Explain.

Chapter Thirty-Three:

1. What is Basim Daher's answer to Farhan's question about "eternal rest"? What do you think Christians' eternal rest will be like in heaven and in the new creation when Jesus returns? Why will we be able to go there—with the Muslim or the Christian way? Explain.

2. Why do you suppose the author uses so much humor in this book? What is the value of humor in stressful situations? Explain with examples from your observations about life.

3. What clues have we learned about the murders of older folks so far? About the murderer? List them.

4. What similarities so far do you see in all of the cases? The murderers? The investigators' methods? Explain.

5. How has this chapter specified the weapon and limited the number of suspects? Explain.

6. How effective is the LPTF in brainstorming the murders in all of their meetings? Why do you feel that way? Explain.

Chapter Thirty-Four:

1. If you are using these questions in a group, list together your ideas about what the theme of this murder mystery is. What is the overall idea of the author? Explain why you have chosen that theme.

2. How do the detectives' conversations with the nursing home residents advance our understanding of the murders? Give your reasons.

3. What surprised you about the resulting deaths? Explain.

Chapter Thirty-Five:

1. What value in solving mysteries or dilemmas is people's brainstorming in a group? Why can't we just solve our problems on our own as individuals? Explain your ideas.

2. What evidence of individualism do you see in the culture around you? What are the advantages and disadvantages of people depending on themselves to solve their problems? What advantages and disadvantages do you see in depending completely on the people around you or the government to solve your problems? Explain.

3. How can we depend on God more through prayer? How can our dependence on God to solve our problems also

include help from other people like teachers, preachers, lawyers, doctors, and other people? Explain.

4. Some people think that they can use prayer without medical assistance when they are sick. How do you feel about that idea? What does using medical help have to do with God? What Bible teachings might you point to for support for your opinion? Explain.

Chapter Thirty-Six:

1. Summarize the three conflicts in this chapter. How are those “disagreements” resolved? Or are they? Explain.

2. How did you feel about the alligator-camel fight? Why?

3. With whom do you agree in Farhan and Akilah’s conversation about whether we can become God’s children? Why?

4. With whom do you agree in Farhan and Shirley’s first disagreement about a credit card and spending? Why? What do you think about Shirley’s final solution?

Chapter Thirty-Seven:

1. What surprised you most about this chapter’s further investigation and discussion? Why?

2. How do you feel about Farhan and Akilah’s partnership and disagreements? Explain.

3. How is their “divided together” relationship a model for our relationships with people of other religions? What qualities does Farhan show in his discussions with Akilah? How can Christians gain God’s gifts of those qualities for relationships with people with different religions or no belief in God? Explain.

4. Explain in your own words Farhan’s statement to Akilah that “the natures of the Gods for whom we gain spiritual progress and the ways we are able to gain that improvement are very different.” How do you feel about his point? Why?

Chapter Thirty-Eight:

1. How do you feel about the undercover policeman's impersonation of a resident and his apprehension of the Ali administrator? How well do you think those events will hold up as evidence in court? Why?

2. What clues did the author plant in chapter thirty-three during Farhan and Akilah's interview with Administrator Kamal that foreshadowed his involvement in the geriatric serial-killings? Explain.

3. With what previous events in this novel is this chapter parallel? Explain.

Chapter Thirty-Nine:

1. How did you feel about Kamal's trial? Why?

2. How surprised were you at the judges' "not-guilty" verdict? Why?

3. How do you feel about Farhan's statement that God will judge the judges and the defendant? Explain.

4. Which system of justice do you think is better—the American jury or the combination Sharia and Turkish three-judge system depicted in this work? Give your reasons.

Chapter Forty:

1. How do you think Srour's trial is going so far for the prosecution? Explain.

2. Why do you suppose the prosecutor reserved Farhan as a repeat witness later in the trial?

3. What possible information from earlier in the novel do you think the prosecutor might be withholding that the author could reveal soon? Explain why you think that way.

Chapter Forty-One:

1. What is the defense attorney trying to do by asking Akilah personal questions? How much do you think such a strategy will backfire? Give your reasons.

2. What do Akilah's responses show about her character? Explain.

Chapter Forty-Two:

1. What described actions begin and end this chapter? Why do you suppose the author constructed it that way? Explain.

2. How important is prayer in many present-day Christians' lives? What did God use to make it important in Farhan's life? How can we Christians become more prayerful without having to experience a major crisis? What is the key to becoming more prayerful? Explain.

3. How did the author show the "peace that transcends understanding" in Farhan's life after his "wrestling match" with God? Explain.

4. How is the trial going now? Toward what testimony do you think the prosecutor is building his case? Why?

5. How well did you guess the clue that Farhan shared that led to Srour's conviction? Explain.

6. What do you think about the death penalty described in this book? How well does the judges' sentence fit the crimes? What advantages and disadvantages do you see with that kind of punishment? Explain.

Chapter Forty-Three, Forty-Four and Forty-Five:

1. What does Farhan's final rescue have to do with the theme of the novel? Why?

2. How do you feel about this chapter's action? Explain.

3. Describe the contrast between the strong terrorists and the weak passengers. How does the author show those differences? Explain.

4. How well does the final scene complete the novel? What is the symbolism of Farhan's prayer during his little son's crying? Explain.

Questions reflecting on the whole book:

1. State what you think is the main idea or theme of the whole book both in the main plot and the subplots. Explain your idea with supporting examples from the book.

2. What did the actions by people in the group who sought justice have in common? What qualities did the individuals who tried to destroy life have in common? Why were the constructive people effective more often than the destructive ones? Explain.

3. How does this novel affirm the value of human life from its beginning to its end? Give several examples. Is your reaction to the pro-life emphasis of this novel a negative or positive one? Give your reasons for your reaction.

4. How does the final scene fit into the author's emphasis on the great value of life? Explain.

5. How will this novel change the way you think? The way you live? Explain.

6. How has this book helped you understand Muslim and Christian beliefs? How strong are the cases for each? Why? How much did you learn from Farhan and Akilah's conversations about their beliefs, especially the rest of their discussions at the end of the novel? Why do you think the author put the largest part of them after "THE END"? Explain.

7. What is your reaction to the justice system of the GPN as depicted in this novel, in contrast to the USA's justice system, as you know it? Why do you feel as you do?

8. A dystopian, alternative-universe novel shows the good and bad aspects of life in its setting. How does this novel show both the possible positive and negative outcomes when Christians live in Muslim countries? Give several examples to support your observations.

9. How does the novel show the images of darkness and light? What do you think is their symbolism? Give specific examples to back up your opinion.

10. All of the Arabic names have meanings that the author chose to fit the characters. To help deepen your understanding of this mystery novel, look up some of the mean-

ings of its first and last names on the Web and share a few with your group.

11. In Farhan and Akilah's friendship, how does the author show for Christians a model of outreach to unbelievers? What characteristics does Farhan show for believers to use in order to reach out to other people with the gospel? Which qualities are the hardest to follow? Where and how can we get help to develop those characteristics? Explain.

12. This book is an alternate-universe novel that shows what could happen if past historical events changed. How does it show such changes in historical events of the past? What changes in the novel happen because of those past events? Explain.

13. What were the major turning points or climaxes in the main plot about the serial-killer, Srour? In other words, how did Farhan figure out who the murderer was? What evidence did Farhan present to convict Fayhim? How convincing was that plot to you? How well did it sustain your interest? How much did it surprise you? Explain your answers to each question.

14. What different roles do the camels have in *Divided Together 2084*? Give specific examples.

15. The author discovered, as he wrote his other three books and this novel, that his writer's voice is playful seriousness. How does his writer's voice come out in this novel? Give examples of the way he showed his writer's voice.

16. How does the author show his love of contrasts in this novel? Give examples.

17. What are some examples in this book of changing technology, communication, and transportation from the present to A.D. 2084? How convincing was the author's vision of the future? Explain.

18. How does the author show that human nature doesn't change except by God's grace? Which characters' lives had changed in the past? Which ones did not change from bad human nature? How does the difference between

appearance and reality play a part in the book? Explain your answer to each question.

19. How has this novel affected your spiritual life, especially your understanding of Christian and Muslim beliefs? Why?

20. We have seen four trials. What is your opinion of an imaginary Muslim land's justice system, which is patterned after the ones in Turkey and Iran? Why?

21. How well did you foresee "the final nail in Srour's coffin," the final climax in this murder mystery? What clues led up to Farhan's disclosure of the secret DNA evidence? List them from earlier in the novel.

Acknowledgments

Many thanks go to my daughter, Dr. Deb Leiter. Also, I thank the Salaam Project, sponsored by Calvin Theological Seminary and Christian Reformed World Missions, and its presenters: David Schenk, Greg Sinclair, John Cooper, Paul Brink, Barbara Hampton, and Ruth Veltkamp. Most of all, I thank the only true, 3-in-1 God of the Bible for guiding my writing.

The following websites plus God's gift of imagination provided the background and plot of my book. However, I have not made any direct quotations from them:

1. en.wikipedia.org, "Islam in Turkey"
2. Islam Wiki, "Alevi"
3. Islamreligion.com, "How to convert to Islam and become a Muslim"
4. en.wikipedia.org, "Alternate universe (fan fiction)"
5. babynamesocean.com/origin/muslim_arabic_baby_names.html
6. paralumun.com, "The profile of a rapist"
7. azurever.co.uk, "Daily life—Turkey"
8. en.wikipedia.org, "Qur'an"
9. stephenblanton.com, "Islam versus Christianity"
10. geneology.familyeducation.com/browse/origin/muslim

11. en.wikipedia.org, "Spain"

12. simple.wikipedia.org, "Sharia law"

13. bbc.co.uk, "Religions—Islam: Sunni and Shi'a"

14. en.wikipedia.org, "Umayyad Caliphate"

15. en.wikipedia.org, "Qadi"

16. en.wikipedia.org, "Islam in the United States"

17. allaboutturkey.com, "Islam in Turkey"

18. religionfacts.com, "The Christian doctrine of God"

19. religionfacts.com, "Muslim beliefs about God"

20. religionfacts.com, "The Trinity in Christian theology"

21. en.wikipedia.org, "Camel wrestling"

22. en.wikipedia.org, "Judicial system of Turkey"

23. en.wikipedia.org, "Police uniforms and equipment in the United Kingdom"

24. en.wikipedia.org, "Baton (law enforcement)"

25. nakedlaw.avvo.com, "11 common traits of mass murderers and serial killers"

26. fbi.gov, "FBI—Serial murder"

27. en.wikipedia.org, "Serial killer"

28. shaikhsiddiqui.com, "ShaikhSiddiqui Alevi"

29. equip.org, "Examining Muslim Apologetics"

30. apologeticspress.org, "A Christian Approach to Islam"

31. islam101.com, "Basic Beliefs of Christians and Muslims"

32. carm.org, "Methods Muslims Use to Attack Christianity"

33. mtio.org, "How Muslims Do Apologetics by John Warwick Montgomery"

34. en.wikipedia.org, "Judicial System of Turkey"

35. en.wikipedia.org, "Battle of Tours"

36. en.wikipedia.org, "Sharia"

37. islamicbulletin.org, "Islam Beliefs and Practices"

38. pewglobal.org, "Muslim Publics Share Concerns About Extremist Groups"

CPSIA information can be obtained
at www.ICGtesting.com
Printed in the USA
BVHW042023191221
624462BV00015B/721

9 781635 540949